"OH, MY LOVE, YOU RIDE WELL!"

Simon cried, half-whispering so that those outside the hut could not hear. Arching and swaying, descending, ascending, he seemed to reach further within Alyx than she could have thought bearable, and still he did not bend or yield. Her inner self seemed to be melting from her, and she thought she would faint, but when she tried now to rise from him, he seemed to pursue her, piercing, withdrawing, piercing deeper and deeper. She began to shiver uncontrollably, and he pulled her closer to him, holding her tighter and tighter and then, whispering "Now," he seemed to leap into her heart.

"I think I must want to die," she whispered.

Little did Alyx realize it then, but what lay ahead of both Simon and herself would at times make death seem sweet. . . .

Big Bestsellers from SIGNET

- ☐ **MACLYON** by Lolah Burford. (#J7773—$1.95)
- ☐ **FIRST, YOU CRY** by Betty Rollin. (#J7641—$1.95)
- ☐ **THE DEVIL IN CRYSTAL** by Erica Lindley. (#E7643—$1.75)
- ☐ **THE BRACKENROYD INHERITANCE** by Erica Lindley. (#W6795—$1.50)
- ☐ **LYNDON JOHNSON AND THE AMERICAN DREAM** by Doris Kearns. (#E7609—$2.50)
- ☐ **THIS IS THE HOUSE** by Deborah Hill. (#J7610—$1.95)
- ☐ **THE DEMON** by Hubert Selby, Jr. (#J7611—$1.95)
- ☐ **LORD RIVINGTON'S LADY** by Eileen Jackson. (#W7612—$1.50)
- ☐ **ROGUE'S MISTRESS** by Constance Gluyas. (#J7533—$1.95)
- ☐ **SAVAGE EDEN** by Constance Gluyas. (#J7171—$1.95)
- ☐ **LOVE SONG** by Adam Kennedy. (#E7535—$1.75)
- ☐ **THE DREAM'S ON ME** by Dotson Rader. (#E7536—$1.75)
- ☐ **BLACK WORK** by Macdowell Frederics. (#E7538—$1.75)
- ☐ **SINATRA** by Earl Wilson. (#E7487—$2.25)

ALYX

A NOVEL BY
Lolah Burford

A SIGNET BOOK
NEW AMERICAN LIBRARY
TIMES MIRROR

Library of Congress Catalog Card Number: 76-18883

This is an authorized reprint of a hardcover edition
published by Macmillan Publishing Co., Inc.

SIGNET TRADEMARK REG. U.S. PAT. OFF. AND FOREIGN COUNTRIES
REGISTERED TRADEMARK—MARCA REGISTRADA
HECHO EN CHICAGO, U.S.A.

SIGNET, SIGNET CLASSICS, MENTOR, PLUME
and MERIDIAN BOOKS
are published by The New American Library, Inc.,
1301 Avenue of the Americas, New York, New York 10019

First Signet Printing, September, 1977

1 2 3 4 5 6 7 8 9

PRINTED IN THE UNITED STATES OF AMERICA

Chapter 1

THE DOOR to the breeding hut was closed, but the men beside him pushed it open, and pushed him inside. He heard it close behind him, and the bar across it pulled to into place. The sound was not new to him. He had heard it so many times he made nothing of it, no more than of the work before him, now. He took off his breeches, a courtesy left him now, since he had proved tractable, to do for himself, dropping them by the door where they could be easily found again, the darkness all about him, thick and silent and warm. He gave no thought to what he had come for, although his body anticipated the brief comfort, moving by habit across the small room in the dark to the bed that was the only furniture or object of any kind in it. He reached down and pulled the spread aside to slip in beside the woman who would be waiting, willing as himself or quiescent, her features never known to him,

1

only the unchanging soft warmth of breast and belly, and passages made free to him, and the bittersweet smell of unwashed sweat that was no longer unpleasant to him. For a moment only his hand touched flesh. The spread was pulled away; and the stillness was broken by sudden movement, a gasping sharp intake of breath, the sound of the cloth on the dirt floor on which bare feet made no sound, and then silence again.

He did not speak, his reactions dulled to the unexpected now, and speech no longer a habit with him. He felt the bed again and found it empty entirely, and then after listening with a sudden sharpened intentness made his way without hesitation to the corner of the room where the faint sound of panting breath could be distinguished. He felt material under his fingers, and as he grasped it, with another gasping cry, the girl slid out from the cloth and was gone. Surprisingly, and to the girl terrifyingly, he still himself did not speak, or make any sound. There was very little left in him except the functions of animal habit, tired now after the day, expecting to do quickly what was expected of him and then to rest, and knowing from experience what would come to him if he did not, the woman knowing too, and both now used to it. With a certain patient purposefulness, one hand against the unseen wall, he came on, heard the girl move again, shaking the dark air with brief movement, then still again, pursuer and pursued both working in silence, eluding, the girl's panting breath louder now, panic taking her, until she ran into him direct. He caught her against him, she screamed, pulled free in his momentary shock, and was run down at last, into a corner of the room. He took the wrist he had found in the circle of his fingers, and pulled her to her feet, along with him, ignoring the frantic slapping of her free hand, until his feet discovered the spread dropped on the floor. He picked that up with his free hand, and going back to the bed sat down on the edge of it and pulled the struggling crying fighting girl towards him, catching her other wrist now with his other hand, and finding keeping what he had caught hard work. He spread his knees apart and pulled her between them, clamping them against her.

He still had not spoken, but inexplicably she grew quiet, held up by his hands, her breath coming and going in quick gasps, and when he released his grip slightly, felt her slip between his knees to the floor, and her own knees, her hands still caught between his. His hands slipped hesitantly from hers, touching her body questioningly in the dark, discovering her youth in her breasts, both his hands resting then on either side of her waist. He was full now, and mistaking her quiescence, would have made a beginning sitting, pulling her onto him, up from her knees and onto his across them, but even as he felt her stiffen at the touch of him he had discovered that for the first time in his life he held what must be a virgin untouched. She was helpless to move from him, his arms clasped behind her back in an iron band so that she could only come forward, but neither could he use his hands to help him in this strange situation. He continued to probe against the frightened unyielding flesh, unable to move himself, hard and insistent and unmistakable. The girl began to cry and plead unable to push away from him, and her flesh not parting to enclose him as he tried to bring her forward. She began to scream then in pain, but more fright than pain, and as he ceased to press her forward, she began to plead with him in a soft terrified voice not to hurt her but to let her go.

He sat, mute now with astonishment, unwilling as well as unable now to speak, while the child he had held, partly released, fell again to her knees, her head on his, pleading. He knew, as she apparently did not, that there was no way out either for her or for him, but he was helpless then to touch her or go on with the business in the face of a voice whose words and tone might have been those of a sister or a sister's friend, bringing sharply before him the world he had been taken out of and had thought himself dead to. He could not trust himself to speak, the rusted words of another time locked and rusty behind his tongue. She was sobbing now, and he patted her head awkwardly, his roughened fingers catching in her soft hair, and then he pushed her away from him and got up and went over to the door where his breeches were. He put them on awkwardly, shamed, his mouth twisting, and stood leaning against the door, staring out through the bars of it at the patch of starred sky shining beyond it, until the men returned to take him away before dawn. He did not know what the girl had done during that time while he stood motionless, half-sleeping, unwilling to think but his numbed brain stirring, the experience too painful for him too. But he did know that trouble was likely to come out of his action, or his lack of action, and the surprise was that it did not, or not immediately in the expected form.

Chapter 2

"SMITH," he heard the overseer say, "you were sent to the hut last night."

"Yes, sir," he mumbled, slurring the words under his breath, his head bowed, not lifting his eyes. The overseer's riding crop caught him under the chin, forcing his head up. He did not struggle, knowing the next step, if he did.

"You are not sent there to sleep."

"No, sir," he said, the crop digging back against his throat.

"The girl is intact," the overseer said without delicacy. "Don't speak, Smith," he said unnecessarily. "She has been examined, and there is no question of it. Surely you can deal with that?"

"I was tired," he said, his eyes blank.

The overseer allowed himself a profane comment. "You will go back tonight, Smith, and if you are again tired, I will have you flogged tomorrow and the girl too."

"Give me some oil, then," he said, his voice expressionless, "a virgin is hard."

"She will cry harder," the overseer remarked, "if I send Hodge in. I sent you in thinking the result would be a good line, but I will not wait on you twice, Smith." He got no answer and seemed to expect none, for he dropped the crop, releasing Smith's face, as he spoke. When he was out of sight, the man he called Smith carefully spat where the overseer's shadow had been, but he continued working.

Before he was taken to the hut that night, he was given time and opportunity to wash, taken then to the hut, stripped and put like a bride into the bed himself, the oil he had requested on the floor beside him. It was a real bed, not like his own bed of cane, and when his escort had closed the door and left, he fell asleep, not troubling about the rest of the night, out of weariness. He was wakened by a rough hand on his shoulder, shaken broad waking quickly, and pulled to one side while another person he supposed to be the girl of the night before was pulled and pushed in beside him. He could feel her shaking beside him, and her soft skin against his own, but remembering the night before and her voice desire tonight was absent. He refused the escort's offer to remain, or to tie the "little gel," if she was vixenish, and when the door had been closed and locked behind them, took the girl beside him in his arms quickly before she could skip away. She stiffened but she did not try to elude him until with a quick motion and without preliminary he anointed both himself and herself with the oil he had asked for. Then pressing her tightly back against the bed, and not attempting to woo her, he attempted to finish the fact. His desire was beginning to return, but at the first touch, she twisted away, and began screaming. It took all his strength to hold her, and he thought grimly that if she had like himself been threatened, she seemed unafraid of the threats, unlike himself. Her struggles, however, not helping her helped on his desire, touching off an instinct he had not known he had. The slipping oil helped him to effect what he could not before, and unable to use his hands which held hers outstretched over her head, or his legs for anything but keeping hers a distance apart, he prodded, ignoring her cries, until he found her maidenhead, pierced it roughly and inflamed by her screams that were now in earnest, pushed his way in and upwards gradually, dislodged by her struggles but returning harder and further, her screams diminishing slightly, until they became gasping moans. He had done the one thing but not the main. Her frame was shaking now with long shuddering sobs, that reached to him inside her. He shuddered himself, and released his seed as she cried again, this time pleading with him to stop and to make an end. He stayed where he was, though, gently stroking her hair as she cowered with his calloused hands, sliding away then, finally, rolling over, and leaving her.

She was no longer sobbing, her breath coming in little gasps and hiccoughs, and as he made no move to touch her further, she did not move from where he had left her. They fell asleep so, or he did, still not speaking, until the men returned to remove them, their faces still unseen.

Chapter 3

THE THIRD night he was brought to the breeding hut he found the girl tied down to the bed. He knew the screams had been heard. He had been the butt of open jokes because of them during the day, but he had had nothing to say. He had smiled slightly and let it pass. The position of studhorse was much envied, not so much for the flesh involved, but the material comforts otherwise added to the day and night. Those men held for stud were flogged less, and fed better, and though they worked during the day, the work they were given lacked the killing power of much of the work the place required, and during the heat of the day, after noon, they were given time to sleep. In return they were expected to perform without nonsense on demand, without shame or preference, and keep the stock high and steady. ("That at least is my own, and I shall put it where I choose," he had said, but he found that in this too he was mistaken. Being not only personable but young and strong, he had found quickly that this part of him was considered among his major assets and his potential to supply good seed owned along with the rest of him by his master.) Owners who could preferred to raise their own, looking to the future, and replacing dead stock in emergency only with the ready bought. The boredom of the life led, which it was for all its hardship, made the act easier than he would have thought, in another life, though in his other life he had even then found it easy enough. And when he had finally been broken to the point of working at all, he could lose no more of his pride or his honour than he had. He never saw the women he serviced. He stayed with one until it was certain she had conceived, then he was put to pasture to rest for a month, then set to another. In his experience the women where he was were glad to bear children, for they were treated better if they did and while they did, and they enjoyed the short infrequent nights in the breeding huts. Most he rather thought were black, but he had never seen his children, or known whether they lived or died. Deformity, he knew, was not tolerated, nor illness, nor frailness. A quick snapping of the neck, and the problem was gone. But he supposed, without amusement or interest, his features in some measure walked about. He had not been there all told long enough for one to come out into the fields where the men worked, and he had been at stud hardly five years. The rebelliousness of his spirit had kept him unpredictable until hope had died in him, under the pressures of time and starvation and abuse and calculated dishonour, but time principally had accomplished the change, taking from him

thought and memory and even, in the end, speech, as
an unused door rusts finally on its hinge.

The overseer's comments about the screams had been
brief, and had reflected upon his finesse. The girl had
been examined, and had been broached, but badly.

"I don't know virgins," Smith muttered, as he had
before. Untouched girls, if personable, went first
through the hands of the big house, or through the
overseer. He supposed they must be on mercury with
the pox, or away, but he found he was wrong.

"The master wants the two stocks crossed particularly. See to it, Smith, and better, or you will find
yourself back in the mill. And don't butcher the girl.
There is time, and with her kind it may take time.
You are not staying tonight, not long, the camp needs
its rest, and expect it tomorrow for any scream. You
can surely do better than that."

The man called Smith said nothing. He had been
stirred by the girl's voice as by nothing in years, but
had she disappeared that day or the next, he would
not have continued to think about her, or missed her.
He heard the door now lock behind him, but the
sounds ceased too quickly, and he did not believe the
men who had brought him had gone away. He stood
in the darkness a moment, breathing, then bent, and
took his breeches off as on the first night, and stepped
uneasily to the bed. There was no sound, no stirring.
He put out his hand, found the cover, and feeling yet
further, felt bare flesh. It jerked at his touch, but there
was no sound. He drew the covers back, and found
with his hands the outline of the girl, but though he
felt her stiffen and pull slightly away, there was still
no sound, and she did not essentially change her position. He felt down the spread leg reaching near him
and discovered a cord on the ankle, and found the

rope ran across and beneath the mattress, pulling her apart, beyond movement. He could not see in the dark, but the discovery caused his heart to pound in a powerful anticipation, as hers was pounding when his fingers explored further. Her arms had been stretched apart in the same manner, and corded, and he knew from her silence, even before his fingers touched it, that her mouth was bound. He did not release her. There were men waiting for him outside, and he did not, seeing in his mind what he had found, imagine they would see any reason to have to wait long. He stood for a moment almost sickened with the rush of desire that flooded him, and then he put himself between her outstretched legs. He had forgotten to bring oil but he moistened his dry lips and spat on his fingers, moistening himself and her; free tonight to use his fingers, he found the place he wanted. He paused, and then with his fingers, he parted the lips and in the dark placed his own different lips against them. He had never done such a thing, and the sensation he received shocked him by its intensity. He kissed them again, pressing his tongue inward, as if to soothe and heal what he had hurt, feeling with his hand her belly above him tight as iron bands against him. He removed his lips reluctantly and pressed his finger against her, and entered, exploring gently, the tense muscles about him rigid and stiff, further then and rougher, his other hand stroking the thigh beside him in the dark. He felt her move convulsively, the cords holding and keeping her, and felt merciful nature respond, despite the girl's fears, his fingers slipping now and soothing the hurt edges. She might conceive tonight, he thought, putting his hands now beneath the small of her back, pushing her up to meet him as much larger than his finger, than his fingers, he pushed his way through the lips the cord on her ankles held strained apart. He forgot then who he was or who she might be, moving back and forth steadily, each time more deeply, the rigid flesh holding him back and then more firmly encasing him. He was all the way in now, as he had not been the night before, and forgetting the girl's terror and inexperience and possible pain, he used her as he would a seasoned woman, forgetting her lack of resistance came from the tight cords, enjoying the tension of her fighting inner muscles, overriding it and riding finally home. He fell exhausted then, his work completed on her, and stayed there until the door opened a few minutes later, and hands were at him to bring him to his feet. He put his breeches back on, and went out, ashamed and exhilarated, emotions he had long been a stranger to.

The next night he took her quickly and left, then seeing he was not come for, he loosened the cord from one of her hands, and brought the two together and bound them. He returned then, hesitantly, with his lips as before and his tongue, moving up with his lips over her belly, slipping between the ring of her arms, up to the hollow between her small breasts flattened as she lay on her back, taking them gently in his teeth, and then his lips against her neck while he took her again. He felt her bound hands caress his back, holding him to her, and with his hands, took the cloth from her mouth, and put his lips against hers, and his tongue inside, against hers. Spasm after spasm shook him then, shaking her too, pulling herself down to ease the strain on her legs. He cursed the cord holding them, pulled himself out and released her, and plunged in again into the wave crashing over them both. When they were both quiet, he released her mouth and drew her against him, forgetting her bound hands encircling

him, endearments rising unthought of to his lips. Then
remembering, he worked at the cord on her wrists,
but found it too tight now to loose in the darkness.

"Oh my love," he whispered in the darkness near
her ear, forgotten words rising to his lips, "I must talk
to you. You will not scream?" he whispered.

She had begun to shake again, at the sound of his
voice, and he was suddenly afraid of the whip and put
his hand over her mouth.

"Please, love," he whispered, "do not scream. I am
so afraid of the whip. Please do not scream."

She lay very quiet then, and he took his hand away
a little, and then all the way.

"I will not scream," she whispered. "I don't want
you to be whipped. Why would you be whipped if I
scream?"

Her words were simple, but too complicated for
him to know how to answer. Instead, he shook his
head and was silent, and then he took her hands in his.
"I did not want to hurt you," he whispered. She was
silent, not believing him, and he saw she did not in her
silence. Again the complications were beyond his
power to speak. He bent and kissed her hair near her
temple gently, and as gently she returned his kiss. He
sighed and gathered her more closely against him.

"If you have a son," he said, and felt her stiffen, and
stopped and did not finish what he seemed to have
started to say. Instead, after a moment, he asked,
"How old are you?"

"Sixteen," she answered. She paused, and then she
said, "No, seventeen, I think, now. I am not sure," she
added uncertainly. "I do not know what month it is."

"You would have been six or seven when I came
here," he murmured. "A child. Where did you come
from? When you were home, child, and not here?"

"No," she said, "I cannot tell you." He felt her body stiffen, that had fitted closely to his a moment before, and he heard feet outside the door.

"Kiss me," he said under his breath, "and do not ask me why." He put his arms about her and felt her respond, with a quickness that sent a startled emotion through him he did not recognise—was it delight, or hope? His arm was grasped then, and he was pulled up to his feet, firmly but not roughly, and taken out.

Chapter 4

THE MEN who took him back had a few words to say, and there was some amusement gotten the next day over "Stud" Smith and his returned abilities.

"Tamed the vixen, by God," was the general tone. "The ones that cry hardest come round to it first." "Stud" Smith smiled his slight twisted smile, hunched his shoulders, and went about his business peaceably and silently, and let the jokes ride. God knew there was little enough to smile about, and the rough jokes did not touch him, any more now than they had before. They all did it when they could, with one another, if they were unlucky and were not used for service. There was little else to do—that, or pray. He, himself, did not pray. Even his ability to dream had left him some years before.

When it was time to go to the hut that night he walked with his escort and saw the girl approaching with the two women who brought her. They met before the door of the hut. The night was less dark than the hut, but moonless, and he could only see the white oval of her face, surprising in its whiteness. He went to her and put his hands on her shoulders on the greyish cloak that covered her, and bent and kissed her, wondering if she would have the sense to respond, and so avoid the binding. Her arms slipped about his neck, and his own about her waist, under the cloak, her skin soft against him. With a sigh he put one hand against her thighs and picked her up lightly in his arms, holding her against him, and pushed the door open. She had not said a word. Only the softness of her lips answering his and the softness of her skin not resisting him, her head ducked in against him resting against his shoulder. Behind him, he heard the door lock. He let her feet down, to stand while he unloosed his breeches, and then he picked her up again in his arms, and sat down with her on the edge of the bed. She kept her arms about his neck, her face hidden, as he put her against him as he had done the first night, moistening himself and positioning her, the head almost within, the touch warm and sending small thrills even through his wrists. He lifted her face then to his, featureless in the dark, and touched it with his fingers as the blind might, as if that way he could see her as she was. She lifted her fingers then to his face, and felt it delicately, tracing his lips, the outline of his teeth, the distance between his nose and mouth, the bridge between his eyes, the angle of his cheekbone, the texture of his hair, the shape and angle of his ear. He waited patiently until her fingers stopped, and she gave a half-sob, and then he kissed her features and her tremulous mouth, and held her close to him. They stayed that way a long time, the beating of their hearts against one another the only motion and the only sound.

"Do you know," he said then, his thoughts driving him to speak, "that when I have done what I was sent here to do, when it is clear that I have, that you will go back to wherever they keep you, and that I will not see you again, or you me, or if I do, I will not know that it is you?"

She did not speak, but her hands held him closely.

"And do you know," he went on, "that after this child you have been sent to have conceived on you is born it will be taken from you and given to another woman to take suck from and that you will be given some other woman's child to have your milk, and that you will never see the child again to know it is yours, nor will I see it either? And that if it should be born in the dark or you not be able to see it that first moment, you will never see it at all? It will live and die and you will not know, or even know whether you bore a girl child or a boy."

"I do not want to have a child at all," she said faintly, her voice a half-sob. "It is not by my choice at all."

"It should be," he said shortly. "If you do not, by me or the next man, you could be sent to work cane, unless they take a fancy to you in the house. Do you know why I do this?"

She did not answer.

"Because if I do not I go back to the mill," he snapped angrily, furious at himself and at her and at all the circumstances of his life and hers and their encounter. He had not felt this helpless anger and fury for some years now, and the emotions cut through him like a knife, hurting him.

He took relief from them in the only way open to

him, pushing her abruptly from him and taking her roughly and without care. He heard her gasp, catching her breath, but she did not scream or cry out, and when he had finished, she lay quite still.

"I am better than most," he said bitterly after a little. "As you will see. They will not send me back to you, you know. The next time it will be someone else. And after that someone yet again. But not me. There are no full brothers or sisters here, and they do not mean for there to be."

"Do you mean that after tonight I am not to see you again?" she said, her voice frightened, extracting from the many words the one fact.

"I should not think, child, you would care very much if you did not," he said gently.

"I would care," she whispered.

"Why, child?" he asked. "Why should you care?"

"Because," she whispered, "when I begged you to stop, that first night they brought me here, you did stop because I asked you, when I was afraid, even though I know now you knew they would whip you for it."

"I was not whipped," he said. "Tho'," he added, "I did think I might be."

"Why did you stop?" she whispered.

"Because of your voice," he said simply, "when you spoke."

"You did not the next night," she said, "though I cried still."

"I told you," he said impatiently. "I do not like to be flogged. Me, another, it would for you have been the same. There was no help for it, for either of us. I cannot help you, child, never think it. I cannot even help myself. It was not kindness, that first night, only surprise."

"Why did my voice surprise you?" she asked, after a few moments' silence, again taking the one fact out of his words.

"Because we are the same kind," he said roughly. "I have not met your kind for ten years. Tho' I do not know who you are or how you are here, or why. You have not been here long," he said bitterly, "that is obvious, or you would not have protested. Protesting is no use here."

"What is the kind we are?" she asked.

"You should know," he said bitterly. "Myself, I would rather forget."

"I do know," she said. "I have known since you first spoke. Your voice shocked me, too. But before you spoke, your hands spoke for you—and mine for me," she added. "I had met nothing since I left my home but cruelty or indifference. You were cruel too, and after that first night, indifferent, but in your hands you were kind and they were not indifferent."

He was silent and then he asked: "Why then would you not tell me your name, when I asked you?"

"I was ashamed," she whispered. "I am still ashamed. I did not know I was like this."

"How is like this?" he whispered.

"You should know," she said, repeating his words and as he put his arms about her, returning the embrace. She slipped down from the circle of his arms, her face against his belly, and placed one of her hands on his sex softly. He stayed perfectly still, only breathing deeply, as she closed her hand on it. When it sprang to its own life, he whispered to her to place herself on the tip, directing her with his hands, a little above him. She held to his hands with hers, his supporting her, and she heard him sigh, and then cry out.

"Have I hurt you too!" she cried, making as if to

rise and disengage, but he held her where she was, and
pulled her down a little nearer.

"No!" he gasped, crying out again, "No! Oh, my
God!" he cried in an exquisite agony, "Oh, my God!"

He felt her hands move to his lips and press them.

"Hush!" she said, a tone almost mischievous in her
voice surprising him. "Hush! if you scream they will
whip me." He bit her hand lightly, appreciatively, and
groaned again into her hand, arching his back now
and moving upwards to meet her. The motion took
her by surprise, pierced her brief self-satisfaction and
drew from her a cry matching his.

"Hush, love. Oh, love!" he cried, half-whispering.
"Oh, my love, you ride well." Arching, and swaying,
descending, ascending, he seemed to reach further
within her than she could have thought bearable, and
still he did not bend or yield. Her inner self seemed to
be melting from her, and she thought she would faint,
but when she tried now to rise from him, he seemed
to pursue her, piercing, withdrawing, piercing deeper
and deeper. She began to shiver uncontrollably, and
he pulled her closer to him holding her tighter and
tighter and then, whispering "Now," he seemed to
leap into her heart. A cry was forced from her,
despite her, and then she realised it was over and she
was lying quiet in his arms on his breast, the hard rod
now a quiet fish slipping from her.

"Oh, my love," he whispered, kissing her eyelids
and the tears running down her cheeks. "Oh, my dear
love."

"I think I must want to die," she whispered. "It is a
little like dying, I think, this. That must be why I do
not hate for you to do it, for it is like a kind of dying,
here in the dark. That is surely it."

"You do not want to die at all," he said firmly, "and

dying is surely not at all like this, or we would none of us mind it. You want to live, and you must live, and somehow, someway, I will help you."

"You cannot help me," she said piteously, a little wildly. "And you know you cannot. You above all people. And if you could, even if you would, it is too late. I thought, if I had to live like this, it did not matter. But it does," she whispered, "it does. I am so ashamed. I think for a moment I must have been mad. Why, I do not even know you!"

He took her fingers, resisting, then limp, and kissed them in his mouth, then put them again to his sex and held them there. "You mean, I think," he said, "that you do not even know my name," and she could feel him smiling, even through the darkness. "Fustian, my dear, what better thing for you and I to do, lost as we are, in this land and in this darkness where I cannot even see my fingers or your face, or know where I am or you are except to touch. It is because this is the only real thing anywhere for either of us that you do not mind what anywhere else you would faint to contemplate, and I would never dare to execute, you being you and I being I, in any other life. If it should ever chance we do escape into our own selves again, which I do not see how we shall ever do, but should it come about, let us never forget this. I know I shall not. I hope you will not." He pulled her up to him, and pressed his mouth hard against her sex, breathing in and out until she quivered and was faint again, and then she did faint. She woke almost at once to find she was in his arms, the taste of her sex on his lips and mixed with hers. She sat up, breaking from him, and took his sex gently in her own mouth, and then returning her stained lips to his, they lay still, breathing quietly in and out until they seemed somewhere quite far away and outside themselves and their bodies, in the rhythm and the scent of their entwined breaths, half asleep now, but their lips loath to part. Their escorts found them joined so, and pulled them roughly apart.

Chapter 5

HE CAME late the next night, without explaining his lateness. He let himself in the door that was locked again behind him, and went over to the bed at once still in his breeches. The room was quite still. He put out a hand, the bed seemed empty like the room. With a quick motion he put himself on the bed, and discovered the girl sitting in the very middle, her cloak still about her shoulders, her knees drawn up, the cloak entirely covering her. Her head was bent, and she did not look up or speak. He put out a hand and would have laid it on her knee, but she moved just a little over, out of reach.

"I thought you were not coming," she said in a low voice to her knees.

"Silly child," he said, his voice amused. "Why then would you be here."

"I did not know. I have been here for hours. I thought you were dead."

"That is always possible," he agreed.

"I thought I had given you a disgust of me."

"Silliest child," he said, his voice very gentle. "As if it mattered what you or I thought or felt, or had any effect on my coming or not coming, my staying or going, or on yours. No, indeed you have not given me a disgust of you, as you say."

"I thought you were dead and they would send another man. I have been extremely afraid."

"And mix the seed? Hardly," he said, his hand again on her knee.

"You did not tell me you would come again, when I asked you last night, and for hours you have not come. I have been so very afraid."

"Poor child," he said again, the amusement rippling over into his voice. "What a turnabout is this?" His hand slipped a little between her knees, but she jerked them away.

"I do not myself have the mood tonight at all. I am tired of this. Have we not done this enough now, for anyone?"

"This is indeed a progress," he said, his voice flat and no longer amused. "It will not serve, my dear. I am not your flirt, and any amusement you or I may take from this in passing has nothing to do with why I am here. If you believe I have given you reason to be demanding, you mistake. You will lie down, now please, and I will make an end quickly then to this passage tonight."

"Truly, I would rather you did not," she said, her voice a little scared by the sudden coldness in his. "I am not at all well tonight, and I do not feel like having this at all. Perhaps," she added, as the thought struck her, "perhaps it has already happened and that is why I feel so ill, then you need not do it after all."

"It is too soon," he said, his voice gently cold, "That will not fash. My dear, will you lie down now?"

"I am sure you will take the influenza," she said, but she did lie back under the pressure of his hands.

"I think not," he said curtly. He stood up a moment to release himself, then came over her on his knees. She was silent now, except for the rapid catching of her breath. He did not speak again. The cloak was in his way and he pushed it aside, but he made no efforts otherwise, but took her harshly and quickly. She lay quite still and limp for the minutes he was on and in her, but as soon as he had ejaculated and withdrawn, she sat up and slapped him with the open palm of her hand. Without a word he slapped her back, twice, and twice as hard, then pushed her down and crossed her legs and held them. He pulled the spread into a heap, and folded it under her legs and hips.

"Stay that way," he said briefly. "We will see what this can do. I will leave now, if I can make anyone hear me." He stood up to put on his breeches. She sat up at once and caught at his hand, but he pushed her off and down again roughly.

"Stay as you are, as I put you," he said curtly. "And do not waste my seed. Perhaps I am tired of this too." He stood up, his breeches on, and walked over to the door. There was a moment's silence, and then a small voice from the bed whispered, "Please, do not go. I did not mean it."

He did not answer, but stood against the door, looking out of the bars at the dark moonless world. There was a quick movement and the girl stood beside him.

"I told you to stay as I put you," he said angrily. "I meant what I said!"

"It is all gone," the small voice said beside him in the dark. "You can feel for yourself. I have wasted your seed. You will have to put it there again." A meek hand found his, as if inviting him to prove what she said. His fingers, for a moment unresponsive, closed on hers, and she brought his hand between her thighs. "See?" the meekly triumphant voice said, questioningly.

The laughter began to well up in him, from far down inside him. He took his wet hand and rubbed it across her mouth and her cheeks, as she stood meekly before him. "Rascal!" he said appreciatively. "You must have been a hellion where you lived before."

"I was," she said simply. "That was my trouble. What are you going to do about the seed?"

"Take it back," he said, bending down to kiss her lips.

"Please do not go," she whispered. "It is true what I said, that I was not feeling well. But I am sorry for all the things I said."

"All of them?" he asked, the amusement creeping back into his voice.

"I forget exactly what they were," she said honestly, reaching up on tiptoe, the cloak gone from her shoulders. He put his hands behind her, in the small of her back, further down then, causing her to jump to elude his pinching fingers, and catching her under the buttocks, he swung her up about his waist, catching her ankles behind him with his hands, and carried her that way to the bed and dumped her down without ceremony.

"What are you going to do?" she asked, a little scared.

"Put the seed back, of course."

"Can you?" she asked, her voice awed. "I mean, won't it hurt?"

"In you, not in me. Or would you rather I did not?"

"You will do as you like."

"Then do this button for me. You can do so much."

"Oh! it is gone."

"Clumsy," he said. "A penalty there, I think. All the way, now. I did the work once, you may valet me now yourself."

She crouched between his legs, rolling them down slowly, and suddenly put her face against his thigh.

"Ready?" he asked.

"I feel so ill," she whispered.

"It is the real thing then," he whispered back. "One always does. Women, I mean."

"Oh, no!" she whispered.

"Afraid?"

"Yes. I don't want a child."

"It is too late, I imagine," he whispered. "I was teasing about the seed, surely you knew."

"Knew that you were teasing? You did not seem to be to me."

"Knew about the seed. Don't be afraid, little one. Fear doesn't help."

"I think," she said, her voice trembling, "there is entirely too much being made about making a baby in me. Myself, really I do. I do not see all this fuss. Frightening me, and putting me to embarrassment, and making me do all manner of things I do not wish to do, and all for something another woman who is older than me and who wants one could do much better."

"I cannot take it back now, if it has happened. And even if I could, I would not."

"Why? What is it to you?"

He was silent, at that.

"I mean, you have told me how it will be, your not knowing, my not knowing, why then should you care?"

"But I do," he said, his voice quiet now and very serious. "I do care very much, if it should be a boy. I have never cared before, because with the women whom I gave the children to, they could be nothing but bastards to me, whatever else they might be. But then I came into this room, as I had to come, and you were here, to conceive a child, and when you spoke, I knew I would care about this child. And I was very much afraid."

"Afraid for me?"

"No, my dear. Afraid for the child. If it should be a boy, it will be to me no small thing."

"But you cannot know until the child is born," she said, "and you have told me you will not know even then."

"I know, my dear," he said. "I do know. It is important to me. Let that be enough for now."

He took her hand in his and held it, turning it idly in his. She could feel the pulse beating in his wrist.

"If you are afraid," she whispered, "must we do it again?"

"No," he said, still turning her hand in his, smoothing out the fingers. "No, not unless you wish it too."

"Strange for you to say."

"No," he said, "I have done the part required. Would you like to bear my child?"

She laughed slightly, an edge of bitterness. "Strange

words for you to say, now," she said again. "I have told you I don't want a baby at all."

"Forget it," he said, lightly. "It was just a whim. You will bear your master's child, and it will serve him, even as you and I do."

She heard to her surprise an intense sadness under his words that she did not understand. But she put her arms around him then and held him tightly.

"I would like to bear your child," she whispered, "if you would like me to."

"I would like it above all things," he said soberly, "that is, all things possible to me now. If you bear my child, I will protect you and somehow I will bring you and the child out of this place. I swear it," he added under his breath.

"But I thought you told me I must, whether I liked to or not," she could not help saying.

"I have told you," he answered patiently. "I have put seed in many women by order, and I have given no thought to them or it after my part was done, less than the studhorse they call me would have given. And I have done this to you. But with you I feel differently. And I have told you why."

"Is it because I am your dear love?" she whispered.

"No," he said. "I have never seen you, I do not even know your name."

"Then how," she said almost hysterically, "can you ask me such ridiculous questions about wanting to have done to me what you have already done without my consent! Do what you like and think what you like! It is nothing to me!" She began to weep, but he did not comfort her. Instead he lay down on one side of the bed, and put his arms over his head, and after a moment, disarranged himself to reach for the cover, and pulled it partly over him.

He did not speak again, and she had the curious sensation, hardly a thought, that speech had left him and that he would not and could not speak again. She crept very near, and kissed his lips, but they did not respond. She put her arms about him under the sheet, and then she pulled it back, and put her head against his limp sex. He made no move, towards her or from her, and after a moment she took his sex in her fingers, and held it, caressing it with her fingers and then her lips. He did not speak or move, but as it swelled and stiffened in her hand, she reached down and put her mouth to the tip and bending further, let it enter her mouth, caressing it slightly until it moved and filled her mouth and sent a warm liquid into her mouth and throat. She held it, not breathing, until it seemed finished, and then she placed her mouth next to his, and shared it with him.

"Oh my god, my god!" he whispered.

"You told me to return it," she said.

"And so do I then," he said, and slipping down, he lifted her legs, into his lap, holding her like a goat skin he was to fill, and putting his mouth and tongue then to the opening, pressed his tongue with the seed on it inside. He sat there then, holding her so, almost absently.

"It is strange," she said then after a little, "but I feel I know how you look, I see you as clearly in my mind as though I could really see you."

"What do I look like?" he asked absently.

"You have dark hair," she said, "almost black. It is not curly, not straight, but falls in a special way, so that you look always just a little as if you had come off a ship. Your eyebrows are dark, but not bushy, and there is a scar inside one of them, as if you had fallen off a horse when you were little, and someone had sewn it clumsily. Why were you late tonight?"

"I will tell you another time," he said. "You are not so far off. Tell me more how I look."

"Your nose is prominent, it is the Vienna nose, rather thin and very well shaped, with flared nostrils. Your cheekbones are quite high, and it is those bones and the width of your cheek to the ear and the line rounding from your chin which is firm that makes your face look as it does."

"Surprising," he said. "What colour are my eyes?"

"Grey, I think. They look almost dark, because of the irises and the lashes. You have lashes that should be on a girl, they sweep much too long."

"How do you know that?"

"I have felt them," she said simply. "You have excellent teeth, very white, not prominent, you are the despair of your dentist because you do not need him."

"I think you are a witch," he said slowly, "and I must warn you that they burn witches here."

"I have been inside your mouth enough to know," she said, "that does not need witchcraft, I think."

"Of a sort," he murmured. "What of the rest?"

"You are a medium height, slightly built but quite strong, your hands and feet are slender, the bones arched, the fingers straight. It is odd, but I do not know your age at all."

"You surprise me," he said. "Have you left anything out?"

"Your skin is very white," she said, "but not freckled. I cannot describe your mouth. It is your most beautiful feature," she said—

"I am almost embarrassed," he said.

"Among other features also beautiful. You have a wide smile. The lips are well formed, but not bowed, generous but not full. When you laugh your whole face laughs. But you do not laugh much now, I think." She felt suddenly his silence.

"You have seen me," he said slowly, "at some time, I think, but not here. The picture is more apt taken ten years ago. You will find me much changed, I think."

"I don't think I can have," she said. "I was describing the face of a young man I saw once, when I was a little girl. If I should see you, I would find why you think so, but I do not imagine your faces are really very much the same. They could hardly be. That was a real face, you see, of a real person, in a very different place. I saw it once in a picture in a house I was visiting on a ticket. I was just a little girl, but I fell quite in love with the face of the boy in the picture, as they do in fairy tales, you know, and so I did not forget it, as otherwise I might have done. It was in the house of someone important, a Duke, or an Earl. I forget now. I do not even know where it was, tho' perhaps I might remember. I had not remembered the picture, until now, but when I wanted to imagine you, I must have made that picture into you."

"I cannot imagine why," he remarked.

"Cannot you? For a man who has put so many seeds, as you keep telling me though I do not want to know, into women, you seem to know very little about them. When one has once truly loved, even at seven or eight or nine, one does not ever forget the face."

"And you truly loved?" he asked, half-unbelieving, yet curiously moved by the little story.

"I truly loved. But nothing came of it. I did not see the picture again, or the subject of the picture, life not being a romance, and my visit ended to those friends, and I went home. For months I made dreams about the face I had seen, and then, after a time, I thought more about other things."

"Other faces?"

"Perhaps," she said.

"Strange," he said, "for you with those dreams and those fancies, to end up here, in a breeding hut to a plantation in some God-forsaken colony. What were your dreams? Of marriage, I suppose?"

"Oh, no," she said, and her voice dimpled, even in the dark. "Nothing so poor-spirited as that. Adventures, rescues, the faithful page perhaps. But the adventures were his, not mine."

"How did you come here? he asked curiously. "Will you at least tell me that?"

"I took a horse that was not mine to ride. A silly thing to do. A bet with the daughter of a family neighbouring. The owner proved very stiff and called the law on me and there was nothing then very much that could be done. We had no prodigious influence, and the owner did. I was seventh of eleven children: my family was sorry, but my father is somewhat stern and my mother is not—well; the law said I must be transported, and I was." She paused, and caught her breath. "I was fifteen then. I did not really understand. I still do not. I did not hurt the silly horse. Please let us talk of something else. Tell me about you, or tell me what you think I look like."

"I do not know at all what you look like," he said ruefully. "I have no picture at all in my head. I think your hair is dark like mine, but only because I would like it to be. I do not know how it is arranged. Part of it seems somewhat to curl."

She had been close to tears, but she laughed a little at this.

He gave up then, tracing her features idly with his fingers.

"The fact is," he said, and paused.

"Yes?" she said.

"The fact is, I have no idea at all what you look like," he finished ruefully. "And I find I would like to know."

"Have you no woman's face you can put on my shoulders?"

"No," he said, "none at all."

"That," she said, "I cannot believe."

"I was seventeen when I was brought here," he said, "I am twenty-seven now. Does that answer you?"

"No," she said and her voice twinkled even in the dark. "There are seventeen years unaccounted for."

"I was a callow sort," he replied, "much given to being concerned with myself, much spoiled. Young men such as that, such as I was, are not likely at that age to have faces haunt their dreams, or make dreams about a face."

"Well," she said, "I am a little sorry for you now. That does seem a pity."

He wondered at the humour under her speech, and took her hands in his, the tips of her fingers lying closed together, resting on the edge of his. He leaned forward and touched her lips with his, drew back, and leaned forward again. Hers met his, clung in light contact, released, withdrew, and as she bent forward now, met again.

"You have surely loved since," he said, his lips a little way from hers.

"But of course," she said. "But one's first love one never forgets."

He bent forward and kissed her lips again, briefly, lightly, the quick reciprocated touch setting his own tingling.

"If you do not tell me how you look, how shall I know you again."

"I would as soon you did not," she murmured, lying back now at the slight pressure of his hands. His lips followed hers, and then she felt him fumble at her waist. She drew her knees up slightly at his touch, and then, with a quick twist, turned over from him, and away. He was not disconcerted, proceeding as if she had not moved, this time entering from the back, his fingers for just a moment exploring the creases. If he was not disconcerted, she was, but his hand found her mouth and muffled her protests. She tried to move, but his knees and thighs held her fast, and her hands were caught beneath her where she had hidden them from him. She bit at his hand, heard him laugh, and demand at her ear, "Tell me the colour of your eyes and I will stop."

"No," she said, "I think I like it, go ahead."

"Peste!" he said, raising her up with his hands and slipping in more easily. "Then I will come out."

"No," she whispered. "My eyes are green."

"I don't believe you," he said, pulling a little out. He heard her pant.

"Blue then."

"What tint of blue? Azure, sky, sea?" He hovered, poised, waiting, and felt her breath quickening.

"I'm tired," she said, "you may leave if you like. My eyes are not blue after all."

"Vixen," he said, with a slight grin, and the darkness transmitting it in his voice. "I do not wonder you wish to remain unknown, being so wholly shameless."

"I am not shameless," she cried.

"Entirely," he said relentlessly. "Or two creatures, one of the dark and one of the light."

"Perhaps so," she said. "By day I am blue-eyed, by night brown."

"Eyes are all the same colour in the dark, anyway," he murmured, giving up that struggle, and returning to the first, kissing the back of her neck, his hands moving under her, finding her breasts, cupping them, lifting her up against him and with him, so that she was kneeling below him, moving now with him. One hand left her breast, into the hair, cupping and caressing it as he thrust behind it. He was coming now, he thought, coming hard, and she was too. She tried to pull from him to shorten it, but he held her to him, feeling her quake inside with him, her muscles catching and caressing him inside her involuntarily, pulling him further inward, until he thought even he could bear no more of it and finished, but stayed in her, covering her, resting on her now heavily. She reached out and caught his hand and brought it to her mouth.

"My eyes are grey," she whispered. "And your eyes have colour for me, even though I cannot see them."

"What colour is your hair?" he whispered.

"White now, I suppose," she murmured. "Oh, my heart," she added, "it is brown-black, much like that I gave you, and you know how tall I am if you will just think."

"We will measure you," he said, and stretching out his feet, covered hers with his, and found then where her head nested.

"I cannot breathe," she whispered urgently. He turned over and took her in his arms.

"Stretched so, I can just touch the soft place in your throat, so," she said, nestling there. Lying so, their feet exchanged measurements, and then their hands and fingers, point for point, arms, knees.

"But what we know best we will not see," he murmured, his hands resting there, hers covering his.

"Is that not much the same, always?" she asked.

He did not answer. His hands had moved now to measure her ears, and feel her teeth, to measure the size of her small breasts, the length of her hair.

She began to laugh. "There is no help for it," she said, "when you come to find me, you must come in the dark. In the day my hair will be up and covered, and I daresay thousands look as I do."

"There are not thousands here," he said. "Is there no way I may know you certainly?"

She shook her head. "I cannot think. Perhaps you are not meant to, after all."

He was silent, holding her.

"Why were you late?" she asked. "You never told me."

"And I am not going to tell you now," he said. "I come when I am brought," and then hearing a noise near the door, "and go when I am come for." He rose reluctantly, her hands clinging to his.

"Do you think you will come tomorrow?"

He kissed her hands, the finger tips, holding them.

"But you do not want a baby."

"I want you, any way that is, to see you," she said, a little catch in her breath.

"But you do not see me," he said. "Have you not had enough?"

"My grandfather," she whispered, "was a sad rake, and I fear I am like him."

"A sad case," he whispered, trying to loose her hands.

"But do you come?"

"If the pattern holds," he whispered, and turned to the opening door.

Chapter 6

HE WAS late again the following night, and found her asleep. He did not wake her, but slipped in beside her, and fell asleep himself. He did not wake until he felt hands at his shoulders, waking him roughly.

"But I have not done it," he said. "You cannot take me yet." He was in a sudden sweat of fear, that left him powerless, at his fate, if the girl did not conceive by him, and hers.

"Give me the rods," he said in sudden decision, "and wait outside the door for me. I will not be long."

The girl had wakened now, and he thrust the rods into her hand and said, "Quick. Whip me with these, here, and here, as hard as you have strength for. Hurry, my dear. I have no time, and they will bring me up."

"Whip you?" she cried.

"Hurry," he said, "it has been done before. As hard as you can, until I tell you to stop. I am ruined, else."

"I had rather you whipped me," she said.

"It would not be the same. Hurry, girl. Even your scores. Think I am a horse that won't go. Anything. I am ruined, else."

She took the bunch of rods hesitantly, still hardly awake, and lifted them and let them fall.

"Too soft," he said, his teeth clenched. "Harder, my dear, or I must bring these men in to do it."

"Why *were* you late?" she said.

"I was at the house," he said, grimacing in the dark, "servicing its mistress." He jumped at the sudden stroke. "Vixen!" he said, between his teeth, but with satisfaction.

"Last night, too?" she asked.

"Yes," he said, "last night too. It was not my choice."

"I wonder you have any strength at all," she said.

"It is a step up," he said, "and an honour one does not refuse. Word of my success with you would seem to have spread. Does she know you by sight?"

"Perhaps," the girl said, following his bidding now as well as he could have wished. "Does she have to thrash you, too?"

"You would," he said, "I imagine, like to know. Women are after all, all alike." He groaned under the stinging rods, his forehead sweating, and began to swear softly and coherently. He heard her gasp, and the rods falter in her hand, but he had the effect he wanted now, and he turned to her, and left the seed, and left her. When he neared the door, he discovered the men had never left, and one took him now and expertly twisted his arm behind him, forcing him to his knees, and he knew the thing of things to be avoided had happened, and they were inflamed.

"Dare to mix your seed with mine," he said softly, "I will find a way to kill you. If I do not, the master will." He felt his neck bent forward as though it would snap, under the heel of the heavy boot placed on it.

"We will not mix it," the man said. "There is another place."

Held that way, swearing softly through the handkerchief stuffed in his mouth, he was made the plaything of one man, the other holding him, and then his hands bound, while he heard the man attack the girl and her muffled scream. He twisted furiously, from the hands holding him, and pulled the man from the bed, his fists crashing at random in the dark. It took them both several minutes to subdue him, and by that time it was late and they hurried him from the room, as the girl's escort came up. In the thicket beyond the hut, in the still dark air, dawn hardly breaking, they bound his hands and bent him over a fallen log, and in turn violated him again by all means known to him and some not known. He had fainted before they had done with him, the mark of the rough wood pushed into his skin.

Nevertheless, he did not himself speak of the matter, or complain. He was himself flogged for striking a guard, but he still did not complain, or attempt explanation. His skin was toughened in his years there, and pain and humiliation were not strangers to him, his spirit or his body. He had learned to take them. He took them now. He had his reward. His bruised condition disinclined the lady of the house towards him, and he was dismissed on his arrival. He went straight from there to the hut, under different escort this time, and the overseer himself walking with them.

"This is not like you, Smith," the overseer said.

He said nothing.

"You look as if you had learned better manners, Smith. Have you?"

"Yes," said Smith.

"Yes, what?"

"Yes, sir," said Smith, his head bent, his eyes on his feet, as he shuffled along in the chains put on him.

"Absurd," said the overseer. "I cannot imagine what came over you."

The man he called Smith was silent.

"I do not have to," he added, "Smith. The girl has said enough, and I have had the two men hanged. If it happens again, I will hang *you*. Is that clear?"

"Yes," said Smith.

"Yes, what?" said the overseer.

"Yes, sir," Smith said, his head bent again, after the quick startled lift in the dark.

"I will have no rogues," the overseer said. "Remember it."

The darkness covered his bruises inside the hut, and the marks the chains had scraped on his wrists and ankles, but the girl, sitting wide-eyed in the bed, there before him, had heard the noise of the chains outside the door being removed.

She felt his wrists gently with her fingers and cradled his head against her. "Oh, but you are desperate," she whispered, the tears falling down her cheeks, onto his face. He took her face in his hands, and kissed the tears falling down it, salt on his tongue.

"I saw a man hanged today," she whispered. "It was a long way away, from where I was, and I thought it was you."

"What did you do?" he asked.

"I fell down in a faint," she said, "and they all came running, and were very kind to me, and said it was my condition. When I could sit up, I saw there were then two men that had by that time been put up, and I knew then it could not be you."

They held one another closely, aware of the precariousness of their lives in the quick unrelenting harshness all around them, and her fingers touched the cuts on his back.

"Oh my love," she whispered, "but you are hurt."

"A little," he said. "It is not much."

Her fingers touched cut after cut, as he winced a little.

"But it is a great deal," she said.

"I have known worse," he said briefly. "Do not think about it."

"What did those men do to you?" she whispered.

"Do not ask me," he said, "Do not think about that either. Am I not here? And early, too, love. I am too bloody for my lady who is nice in that respect."

"Perhaps you are for me too," she whispered, "but I cannot see. Did you not wash?"

"No, love," he said. "I am just as I left you. I could not, during the day, and after they whipped me, I had not the courage." He did not mention that he had hung by his wrists the greater part of that day. "I have come to you still in my dirt. Will you, like my lady, mind?"

"I may not mind," she said. "You have shown me that very clearly. I daresay you have come unwashed before."

"I daresay I have. Lord," he swore softly, "but I am sore. In an hour I shall be too stiff to move. Make room for me, love, while I yet can." He put his hands on her waist. "You seem thicker, love," he said softly, "or does the dark deceive me? This comedy, I think, will be played out soon, this part of it, at least. But I may be mistaken. Help me, love, with your gentle fingers. I have had a hard day. When this is done, you will perhaps comfort me."

He took her so simply then that caressing his bent head with her fingers, that had a moment before under his direction helped him effect it, she was hardly aware that he had begun before he had finished.

"Don't spill this," he said, sitting up and taking her legs gently across his lap and holding them, "I am sure it is all there is."

"You take your work so seriously," she said. "A gentleman would be ashamed to."

"I daresay," he said, "but then I am not a gentleman, am I?"

"No," she said, "a gentleman would not enter a room without his shirt."

"No," he agreed, "and certainly not in front of a young lady he was not even affianced to."

"Who are you?" she whispered, her tone suddenly serious. "And why are you here?"

"Strange questions," he said lightly, putting her feet down and letting her sit up. "I am the prime stud horse of this plantation, tho' not the only one, and you know why I am here."

"I did not mean that," she said.

"I know you did not," he agreed pleasantly.

"You mean you will not tell me."

"I have not said that," he answered. "There may be nothing to tell. I was conceived as the child you are to have was conceived, born as it will be, raised as it will be, and stand now proof to the success of these methods."

"You were not born here," she said. "You have told me you have been here ten years only."

"I said only I had been on this plantation ten years only. I said nothing else." He lay down on his side, and was silent, his silence heavy in the room.

"Why would my child be important to you?"

He did not answer, and she thought he had fallen asleep, the silence all about her deep and heavy as sleep, though there was no sound of sleep's heavy breathing. After a moment she became frightened, as though she were alone in the bed and in the room. She reached out her hand and touched his shoulder, which proved to be near her. He did not move, or respond, or speak; but after what seemed a long time to her, he reached out his hand behind him and found hers.

"You said you would comfort me," he said, "and instead you ask me questions." She moved near him, and let his head pillow in her lap against the sheet she spread.

"I never said I would," she said, stroking her fingers through his hair, "but I will not ask you questions." She stroked the hair at his temples gently, and then ran her fingers lightly, almost absently, over his features again, as though they were a puzzle to be pieced together.

"Will you know me?" he asked after a moment, his voice amused yet a little sad. She did not answer directly. After a moment, she said,

"My name is Alyx de Vere. My father was Charles de Vere, third son of Charles Standish de Vere known as Beau Standish or Rake Vere."

"I knew your grandfather," the man whose head

she held remarked quietly. "I found him an enjoyable old man."

"My father did not," Alyx answered. "It was my grandfather who had given me my name. I think he paid my father to do it. My father said the money was cursed, and with such a cursed name I was bound to end badly. But he took the money all the same. It was the name, I think, of one of my grandfather's particular favourites, but no one ever told me the exact story. But it would seem my father was at least in this right," she added ruefully.

"It has not ended yet," he reminded her.

She did not answer that directly. "My father seemed to think so." She paused. "If you knew my grandfather, tho' I did not think you *that* old, perhaps you know why he wanted me to have the name, and who the other Alyx people would not tell me about was who."

"Yes," he said, "I can. You must have been a strikingly beautiful infant for your grandfather to have wanted you to have that name."

"I don't think so," she said. "My grandfather was rather eccentric, and his judgement not reliable by ordinary standards. Was that Alyx so very beautiful?"

"Yes," he said.

"Was she my grandfather's mistress?"

"I never asked. I would suppose so. She was an actress on the Paris stage, and had all Paris at her feet. She was very lovely indeed, but she was far more than that."

"I wonder then she would take my grandfather."

"Your grandfather, I understand, was in his prime also a man of considerable charm, and not unhandsome. When I knew him, he retained much of that charm still, and Alyx must have felt it. He was also, as you surely know, quite rich, and Alyx was not above money."

"Did you ever see this Alyx herself?"

"Yes," he said, "I did. She knew your grandfather, my dear, while she was still young and he was not so young. They held salon together in Paris and everyone came, everyone from everywhere who was anyone."

"Except my father."

"Yes," he agreed soberly, "except your father, but then, he was a third son."

"Did you come?" she asked, struck by a sudden thought.

"Yes, my dear. But I was very young then. Very foolish and very young."

"And you knew Alyx yourself?"

"Yes, I knew her, my dear. Alyx, whatever she may have been to your grandfather was my first mistress, most briefly, and less briefly, my first love, if one may call what a boy so young feels then love."

Her hand faltered where it had been idly stroking his head. He reached out his own and took hers in it, above his head and held it, almost questioningly. She took it between her two and held it briefly to her face.

"How strange," she whispered. "How very strange. What happened to you then? Did my grandfather know?"

"I called your grandfather out, and he laughed in my face, and said that if he was willing, discreetly, to share Alyx with me, I should surely be agreeable to doing the same with him, whose wants were no doubt simpler than mine. But I did not see it in the light that he did."

"How old were you?"

"I forget. Fifteen perhaps, perhaps not so much. I was precocious. 1 went back to England, nursing my wounded pride and my wounded heart, and played the fool. We were talking about Alyx and your grandfather, and your father, not about me. Tell me about your father."

She did not answer, sitting quietly thoughtful, her fingers among the locks of his hair, and he asked her what she was thinking.

"I was thinking that if everyone who was anyone came to their salon, and if you came—and you were fifteen—"

He put his finger to her lips. "It is all a very long time ago. Tell me about your father, the good Charles, who did not want his fourth daughter named Alyx, but all the same for a price agreed. Who was your mother, Alyx herself?"

"Oh, I hardly think so. Neither my father nor my mother were the kind to have, or even take, a love child, and they talked so freely to me of my being a throwback and a disaster to them, I am sure I was their own. There were, you see, three boys, and then three girls, that lived, and then myself, and I think by that time they were not exactly tired of having children, for they kept right on, but I did not entirely surprise them with delight and with so very large a family, and my father a third son, it was important we behave with propriety and not any of us make ourselves conspicuous. I have had time, you see, on the ship, and here, to think, and I can see that I must have many times bothered them considerably."

"Did your grandfather, I wonder, settle any large amount of money on this little girl he wanted called Alyx, enough to pay for it?"

"I don't think so," she said bewildered, "If he did, I

never knew of it, and I would surely have been told. In two years, at the most, I would have come out, and it would have been an important advantage. Some daughters even at fifteen are out, but there were three before me, and it is rather expensive."

He was silent, and did not press his question. "Tell me about your mother," he said instead, "who married a third son, and is not very well."

"You remembered?" she said in surprise.

"Yes," he said, "I remembered."

"I do not want to talk about my mother, after all," she said, her voice catching. After a moment, she said, "You must not think I was badly treated on the ship. I was not. The Captain was very kind to me, because I think he was sorry for me, and perhaps because my family had paid him money so he would be kind, I do not know. He said he would put back into port and set me down, except he would lose his licence. Anyway, he was kind, but he made me come, and I very much did not want to. At first I cried every day in my cabin, until I realised it would do me no good to cry, and also he said if I did not stop, I might as well be with the other transports. After we had been at sea a good many weeks, I think now, though I did not know at the time exactly what he meant, that he would have liked to do to me what you did do, but what with one thing and another, he did not."

The man lying in her lap turned his head a little. "I am almost tempted to ask you to explain, but I am afraid of what I might hear."

"There is not much to tell. The weather was not very good, and my clothes were voluminous and not easy of access, and it was hard for him then to remember how very defenceless actually I was. And I truly did not imagine what he would be about, and that I suppose put him off most of all. A number of times we played backgammon, and then we sailed, very clumsily I think, right into a kind of hurricane that blew us miles and miles hopelessly off our course, and the charts were wet. Fortunately, he could steer, and knew his ship very well when he paid attention to it, and he brought us into this harbour. I was meant to go somewhere else, but the man who owns this place came on board ship to see the Captain. I think he bought some of the transports who were well enough to stand, and when he learned I was also transported, he offered to buy me outright. I had been sent, I think, only for an indenture, but this man offered such a vast sum the Captain was quite tempted. And when he offered to have the ship repaired, and refitted, and fresh food and water brought on, and a new chart made, it was too much for the Captain, who after all was somewhat in his power and dependent on his good will, and though he should not have, he agreed."

"I wish I might have seen you then," he said thoughtfully, "namesake of Alyx."

"Well, he did see me," she said, "and it was horrid, the worst thing that ever had happened to me, worse even than the trial, and having to leave my home. The Captain made me take my clothes off, every one of them, and stand before the two of them, while the man who was buying me made certain he really did wish to buy me. It was something like buying a horse, only much less polite even than that. And if you are wondering why I did what they said—"

"I am, Alyx," he said, his voice faintly smiling, "I am."

"—I thought I would rather do what they asked myself than have it done to me. But it could really not have been worse. And then they would not give me back my clothes, but instead made me put on the clothes the cabin boy that died in the storm had worn, whom I also used to play backgammon with and he never tried to pinch me, and the new man took a pair of scissors out of the Captain's desk the Captain gave him, and cut off my hair. Then I was put with three other transports in a boat, and sent off, without my clothes or anything at all of mine, with the man who was paying so much money for me. But before I was put with the other transports, the three that he had bought that could still stand, he took me aside and told me I would be wise to not speak of myself or how I had come there or where I had come from. And I believed him, for he looked at me in a very ugly, meaningful way, and I was quite afraid of him."

"I am quite afraid of him myself," Smith said. "I do not wonder at it."

"And there was after all no reason for me to speak of it, for everyone here quite belongs to this man. I can see that. But I would not tell *you* because I was ashamed."

"And are you ashamed still?"

"Yes," she said, "but you were sad, and they had hurt you, and you had said you wanted to know. It was all I could think of to do to cheer you. Did it cheer you?"

"The event will tell,—Alyx," he said, saying her name softly and slowly. "But I wonder you should wish to cheer me. I should think you would rather wish me sad."

"But you see I do not," she said.

There was nothing more he could say, for the bolts were drawn back, and the door unlocked and opened. It had not occurred to either of them to notice that he had used, when he spoke to her, her first name.

Chapter 7

"ALYX," he said, when he came the next night, "who was your mother?"

"She was a second cousin," Alyx said, "to the Countess of Rousillon. They are an over-bred family but my mother's mother had married out of her order, and I think it was a good thing, for my mother was only half mad. My mother was lovely, I think, and my father must have thought so too. Or perhaps he married her because he thought he was marrying as a third son into a good thing. But nothing came of it that way for him. But he did marry her, and either they were very bored or very conscientious about their vows or they did love one another, though I never saw them give any sign of it, for I know now what I suppose they had to do and keep on doing to produce all of us, which they did, even after they had the answer to the heir thoroughly assured, and there was not very much even to inherit."

She stopped because he had put his finger gently against her lips. "Alyx," he said, his voice amused, "did you have a governess?"

"Why, yes," she said. "We all did. Though we did not like her very much, and I was a great trial to her."

"She should have been turned off," he said firmly.

"She did try," she said, her voice meek. "I was very difficult material to cut. You see, about my mother, the difficulty was that you never knew which person you were speaking to, or what she was really thinking, or whether she was really listening to you and hearing what you were saying, or hearing something else entirely different. She was simply not always the same person, or so it seemed to me. Very patient and loving and understanding, so that one was quite happy, and then the next day or hour or afternoon, even the next moment, as cold and aloof as though she hardly knew who one was, and sometimes she would be so angry, almost for no cause at all, and question us so severely sometimes the little ones cried. And one never knew which kind of person to expect, for her disposition did not seem to bear any relationship to what was happening. She was not really mad, just very difficult particularly for anyone wanting to love her or be loved very steadily. Do you see what I mean?"

"Yes," he said, "I think I do."

"I was the flightiest of all her children, at least of those old enough to show what they were like. I was also, I think now, surprisingly spoiled and indulged, but I did not think so then. I would get very angry when I was little, they tell me, and lash out with my tongue, and my feet too, at anyone who crossed me. I think now they must have thought I was changeable like my mother, and gave me my way because they were afraid my fits were like hers. But myself, I don't think they were. I just wanted my way. We all do, and perhaps I did more than most. And so, as I grew up, I was accustomed to doing very much what I pleased, and nothing happening to me for it. Until the horse. I could not understand why they were so serious, but when I lost my temper, the judges looked at me in so alarmed a way, I think they were relieved the law wanted to send me away. Perhaps my family was too. But I did not know I was so very wilful. I had so many thoughts and so many things I wanted to do, and everyway I was curbed and slowed and I could not see why I should be."

"I am sorry," he said, "your grandfather could not have lived."

"Do you think he would have liked me?"

"I think he must have liked you very much." He was silent, and then he asked irrelevantly if she or her family knew Phillip Handley.

"The Earl of Halford, Lord Dalton?" she said. "Oh, no, quite above our touch. His property was not far from ours, but we never rode there in the Park, for he did not want it."

He was silent for a while sitting on the bed beside her, and then he asked, his voice a little hesitant, "Would it have been in his house, Alyx, that you saw the picture you had the thought I looked like?"

"Oh, no," she said, "I don't think so. I do not remember going to visit his house, for he never threw it open to casual visitors that I can remember, and the Earl did not look at all like that picture, I can assure you."

"But you were very young, Alyx," he murmured.

"Yes, but I should have remembered that. No, it was a house in London, with a garden, and on a little park, where my mother took me once to visit, and two of my three older sisters. There were no other children, and I and my sisters went about at will, probably into some rooms we should not have. I saw the picture then. My older sisters teased me about it then, and when my mother heard through my governess, she called them in and told them the boy in the picture had died recently and very tragically, and they must not make jokes about him, for his mother was very sad being widowed and now with no one. They were not to tell me, but one day they did, and perhaps that is when I stopped thinking about the face in the picture. If he was dead, somehow it did not seem right."

"The dead do not care what fancies we weave about them, I think, Alyx," he said after a moment, gently, his voice quiet, "it is the living who very much care."

"But it was all so long ago," she said. "You see, I have not thought about that visit or any part of it for many years. I had other things to do, and I was very busy. I do not know why I should have thought of it again," she said rather slowly, "except I have been so very frightened, for the first time really ever, and thought so many times I must be close to dying, when they took me from my family—whom I did love, even tho' perhaps I did not show it very well, and would not let me go back, and in the prison, and then on board the ship, in the hurricane when they tied me to my bed and everything was black, and the rain beating in my face and the wind trying to take me, and then my being here and you frightening me so and hurting me, going into places I did not know I

had, and my being tied down again so there was nothing I could do any more—all this was like a kind of
dying over and over again, and I hoped to die. You
were like death in the dark taking me without any
word or any face, and so I held tight to you that you
might take me sooner and when I did that, the way it
was when I was drowning in the water on the ship,
and had given up, it was painful and yet there was
comfort in it too, and like the water choking me, it
began even somehow to be pleasant, and perhaps that
was why I saw the boy's face for your face, for he
had died too and knew what death was, and pain, and
terror, tho' he had laughed easily once, and I thought
he had come to help me. And then, of course, I knew
I was not dying, and not going to die easily, and that
I was merely ruined for any life I had once thought
to lead, and so it did not seem to matter any more
what I did."

"Come now, Alyx," he said, his voice beside her
amused, as he took her in his arms, if she had moved
him, not showing it, "you do not mean to tell me you
did not know *anything*, living on an estate, and your
mother having all those children."

"But I never thought about it," she said frankly
(the matter-of-factness of his voice dispelling the ter-
rors that for a moment had swept round her again)—
"oh," she said suddenly, "I did not expect you—not
in relation to me, or to my parents. I still cannot
imagine them doing *this*—or anyone I know."

"But we all do, Alyx," he said, "all of us. There was
something I meant to say, before you enflamed me,"
he murmured in her ear. "But no matter. Did your
mother never never tell you not to enflame men?"

She put her hands against him as if to hold him
away. Not going from her but pausing, he rested his

weight against her hands, until, with a tiny sigh that was almost a sob, she let her arms slip around him, drawing him fiercely to her, pressing her mouth hard against him, as though she would bury herself there in him as he was burying himself in her, and so meet, fighting with him and against him, to her fearful joy and his surprised delight, until she fell back against the bed exhausted, still holding him to her breast. Then he gently pushed himself a little way from her, until his elbows supported him, holding him just above her face. He stayed so for a moment as though studying her face, as though he could see it. Then his hands cupped her narrow breasts, slid over the cage of her ribs, his lips following his hands, his hands moving down her narrow flanks, passing between her thighs, resting there, moving again to her belly. She shivered in the warm night, and he bent near her face, and found she was crying silently.

"Oh, love," he whispered, "love."

"Do not call me that," she whispered in return. "I cannot bear to hear you call me that."

"Why?" he whispered. "What else is this? Is it death?"

"Yes," she said.

"I do not believe you."

"No," she whispered, clinging to him. "I do not know what it is."

"Do you not know I love you?"

"No," she uttered, her breath caught. "You loved another Alyx, and you like to make love to anyone."

"No," he said. "You know it is not so."

"I do not know it," she whispered. "You cannot see me. You do not know me except as a room I cannot keep you out from. You like that, that I cannot keep you out, and to walk up and down my passages, and make me feel things I do not think I should that frighten me after they are past because I have not been myself at all. But all your women have rooms like this inside them, and you walk up and down inside them at will, and I am no different than any of them, to you, or to myself now. If I want you whom I do not know to come inside me and stay there always, will I not want any man. Will not any man do as well? Any other of your master's studhorses? Do they not all have rods like yours? When they make me feel I am dying, and yet love to die, and want the death to stop and never to stop, will it not be just the same? I wish I had not been sorry for you," she sobbed, "I wish I had not told you my name. For then I could have kept a part of me away, and I need never put my name in my thoughts to these things I have done with you. You have not told me your name, you have kept that part to yourself. You have given me nothing of yourself, except what you were sent to force on me. And it amused you to show your skill and make me willing. And it amuses you now to think I am like your mistress whom you say you loved."

She felt him entering her again, and she gasped at the ferocity with which he came. Her words broke off, and she threw her head back, panting, as he drove hard against her, and deep inside her.

"Little fool," he said, gasping himself. "Do you think I tell whores or slaves I love them? You fool! Do you not know why you love me? And you do. A man does not mistake. You do not know why you love me, and God knows you have cause not to, but I know you do."

"Yes," she said, gasping and sobbing, "yes, I do. But not for this."

"For what then," he said urgently, pricking hard and deep as his anger at her words.

"For your voice," she whispered, gasping. "And because of your voice, I know you cannot love me."

"Fool!" he said. "It is for this, and only this you love me. Admit it!"

"Yes," she gasped, "yes, it is. If you say so, it is whatever you say it is. Oh, my God," she gasped, "oh, my God!"

"No," he said gently, releasing her, having released them both, quiet now. "Not your God. Only your true lover. Can you not see, my dear, you love me for both, and I you for both? You cannot have been more surprised than I that it should have happened, and that it should be possible in this place. But it has happened, has it not, my dear love?"

"Yes," she whispered, resting her head against his breast, and letting his arms encircle her, resting on her folded ones.

"Why do you think I cannot love you because of my voice?" he asked then. "I think I meant to ask."

She was silent, pressing her face into his chest.

"Why, my dear love?"

But she would not answer, only reaching up again to find his lips, and kissing them in a sudden complete surrender, her tears falling and mingling with them. What she might have yet said, she did not say, for his escort was at the door. When he had gone, she lay in a heap on the bed, sobbing, until her sobbing turned to retching, and she sat up in alarm, remembering from her mother's case what it might mean.

"Oh, God," she thought, when the retching and nausea left her, weak and quite spent, "has it happened? Oh what shall I do, what shall I do?" She began to sob again, and again her exhausted stomach turned upon her, stopping her sobs. "If they know," she thought, "they will not bring me again. They must not know." Terrified, she rolled the sheet up small, and hid it under the bed. Then she put on her cloak, and went to stand at the door to wait, so they should not have to come inside, pressing her fingers against her aching head.

Chapter 8

"WHERE IS the sheet?" he asked, when he came the next night. She was sitting in the middle of the big bed, her unseen eyes apprehensive in the dark. But he did not wait for an answer, but slipped his breeches off, coming to her quickly, reaching for her under her cloak, and taking her to him.

"Oh, my love," he whispered, "my dear room."

"Oh, my love," she whispered, "my dear rod."

"I am entirely yours," he whispered.

"You are not entirely mine," she whispered, "but I am entirely yours."

"I am entirely yours. May I come into my only home," he whispered.

"Oh, my dear love," she whispered, "my dear love, come in." And he entered into the room of his home and found comfort and ease. She lay very still with him then, afraid to speak, afraid it might prove their last night, the fear rising in her and overflowing until she broke from him and went by the wall and was sick. He was by her in a moment, supporting her.

"Alyx," he whispered, "you are not ill?"

"No," she said, uncertainly. "I don't think so. My mother was often this way. The sheet is under the bed. It happened again last night, after you had gone. I hid the sheet so no one would know."

He put his hand on her belly and one hand against her back, pressing slightly, lightly with his hands together.

"It is too soon," he murmured, "I thought for this, but perhaps not. Are you afraid?"

"Yes," she whispered.

"I am afraid too," he said.

"Why should you be afraid?"

He did not at once answer, but led her to the bed, and sat down on it and took her in his arms and put her cloak about them both. She lay in his arms quite spent. He ran the fingers of one hand through her cropped hair, the other he kept over her belly, almost protectively. "I meant to tell you," he murmured, "—before you enflamed me—something. It was last night, wasn't it? And then it did not seem the time. I meant to tell you—" He paused, and then when she did not say anything still or help him, he said bluntly, "What I am trying to tell you, and telling so very badly, is that I think the picture you spoke of may have been of me."

"No," she said wearily, turning her face in against him and pressing it against him. Her voice was dull and flat, but not surprised. He did not argue, but his hand that had been stroking her hair stopped and pressed her head closer still to him, and the other hand tightened slightly against her belly, both protectively and possessively.

"If you conceive a child by me, Alyx," he said expressionlessly, "and bear it, and if it is a son—" he paused and then he went on steadily, "and if somehow before that happens, I can someway contrive to have you married to me with lines to prove it—"

"Married," she whispered, moving her head so she could speak, and repeating the word as though she did not understand it "—to you?"

"To me," he said, "with lines to prove it—" his gentle hands turned her face in against him again, against her surprised start, and her protesting questions "—if and if and if, this child when he grows up and I am dead should be the Seventh Earl of Halford."

She was completely still against him, but her lips against his skin moved and said "No," his hand still pressing her hair, holding her to him.

"You have asked me my name," he added quietly, "and now I have told it you. It is a strange place, I admit, to find me, but it is my name and who I am." He paused, and released her, but laid a finger on her lips. "And that, my dear, is why your child, this child you have been sent to have conceived on you, is a matter of importance to me, for you are the first woman whose child by me I could wish to claim or whose fate I care about."

"Is this true?" she asked, when he took his warning finger off her lips.

"Yes, my dear, it is true."

"You are joking me," she said uncertainly. "It is true you have the voice of a gentleman, and even sometimes the ways of one, but I *know* the Earl of Halford. I mean, I know who he is. You even asked me about him, and I saw him not six months ago. In fact, I did not tell you, but it was his horse, and he who pressed charges."

"That does not surprise me," the man beside her said, "considering what he had done to me, and I was his nephew. Ten years ago, Alyx, I was heir to my father, the Fifth Earl of Halford, whom you were too young then to know, and my uncle, my father's brother, was next in succession. When my father took a sudden fall off one of his hunters and lay in a coma, my uncle conceived and executed the plan of removing me. I take it, from your description of your visit to your mother's house, that my father did indeed die and that my uncle wears now my robes. Is he married, Alyx?"

"Who?" she asked, her voice strange, but he did not then notice.

"My uncle?"

"The Earl of Halford? Yes, he is married."

"Has he children?"

"Yes," she said, her voice expressionless. "He married nine years ago. They have, I think, five children, perhaps six now. Four girls, and the fifth a boy."

"He lost no time," the man in the dark said, "to insure his succession. But through your child I may someday prove him an upset he does not now look for. Your child, Alyx, is my hope. Who did my uncle find to marry?"

"My eldest sister," the girl said, her voice low and unreadable. "Maria."

The man in the dark beside her began to laugh softly. "Oh, my God, here is a complication that should surprise him."

"I think not," the girl beside him remarked. "I doubt

he ever knows it. I doubt your being who you say you are, and I doubt his ever knowing of it."

"Only bear me a son," he whispered, "and he will know it, and you will know it."

"I wonder you should wish to claim it, though I do," she said her voice level.

"Your blood is good enough," he remarked. "It will do."

"But not what you would have chosen."

"My God," he said, "I do not know what I would have chosen. I was a callow boy with a head full of nonsense when my uncle had me abducted. I would then have married a common Paris whore, had your grandfather not had more sense than I."

"My namesake," she said bitterly.

"Your namesake," he agreed. "An uncommon Paris whore, I should rather say. But I think I would take even her child, to have a son, if I had papers. I am the Earl of Halford, altho' my uncle enjoys my title and my position and my lands and my house—and does not imagine I or a legal heir of my body can ever return to overthrow him. But this child could, though I never do—"

"And what if I say I will not marry you?" she said quietly. "Where are you then?"

She could almost see his look of surprise. "Whyever not? You surely cannot love my uncle!"

"No," she said, "but nevertheless I do not wish to marry you."

"You are out of your mind," he said simply. "Believe me, if I can find a way to marry you, I think you will agree to it, but how it is to be done," he added, "I know not. And nine months hardly to do it in. My uncle may win yet."

"Is it so hard?" she asked.

"Hard! God, girl! Impossible. We are properties, both of us, belonging to the Honourable August and properties may not wed. Did you not know that? And you tell me you *will* not?" He laughed, his voice low and bitter. "Girl, your lot is to live and die here a whore, and mine to father bastards. Forgive me if I did not ask you properly. I had not thought the life appealed to you. I assumed that marriage, even to me, was preferable, even in your eyes. What are you holding out for? A belted earl, and not a dispossessed, browbeaten one? Believe me, girl, after being here, in this place, should you ever leave it, you will find no one to marry you you would care to marry."

"I know that," she said, her voice very low.

"Then who are you waiting for? The Prince of your pictures? Good God, girl, the picture was of me! You have said so yourself. But I do not look like that now, if I ever did, so put that notion out of your head."

What more he might have said was cut off by the drawing of the bolts of the door.

"Alyx," he said urgently, his hands on her flinching shoulders. "I have spoken roughly to you. Please forgive me. I have told no one what I have told you. Please do not tell it."

"You need not worry," she said, her voice low. "Believe me, I would not."

Her tone puzzled him, but he could not stay to question it.

Chapter 9

He came in the next night, and stood by the door that closed and locked behind him.

"*Your* secret is yet safe," he remarked from the door. "You see I am yet here. Is mine?"

"Yes," she said dully, "I suppose so."

"Do you suppose for both?" he said, "Or do you know?"

She did not answer, and he crossed over to her, where she was crouching against the wall at the head of the bed, discovering her, and took her hands in his. She tried to withdraw them, but he held them firmly and kept possession of them in his. Her breath caught, at the steady pulse in his fingers holding hers.

"Please," she whispered, her eyes dilating wider yet in the dark, "please do not."

"But you only suppose," he said, almost gaily, his mood not hers, "It is my duty to be sure. Alyx," he whispered then, "Alyx my love, it is also my wish. Do not be out with me."

"I am not out with you," she said, her breath a half-sob. She slid a little way to meet him, and opened her thighs quietly to him, like a sigh. When she felt him, she did sigh, and took the face she could not see so near her between her hands, holding it that way, turning her own face a little away.

"Alyx," he whispered again, "do not be out with me. I cannot help who I am." With his hands, he took her hands and held them together in his, and with his lips he found hers, until she turned to him.

"Is it true?" she whispered then.

"Is what true?" he murmured, moving upward.

"What you told me."

"When?" he murmured, pausing. "Just now, that I wish you? Have I not proved that already?"

"No," she said. "The things you told me. Are they true?"

"I have said so," he murmured, his hand moving to find her belly that was tensed against him. "Do you mind so much?"

"Yes," she whispered.

"I thought you would be pleased," he murmured, his hand sliding lower.

"No," she whispered. He withdrew then partly, having found nothing, drawing a surprised gasp from her, slipped his hands under her, raising her slightly, separating, and bent his head as he had done before, his mouth and tongue delicate and questioning. She began to shiver, held in his hands, the prickling languor stealing over her, warmth spreading through her, despite her. Her hands sought him, and he slid back inside her, himself now, her hands and lips reaching for him frantically, as he held off the moment, her muscles tightening about his, pulling him in, and in, and in.

"I cannot bear it, I cannot," she cried, begging for release, but he kept her with him, until unable to bear the moment any longer himself, he let his seed spill into the heart of her womb. He felt it turn over against him, and cried aloud as she did, and for a few moments lost possession of his senses, or of time. He came back to them with a start and discovered where he was, caught in the heart of love itself. He thought the girl must have fainted too, for she lay beneath him motionless now, but her hands were locked about him still rigidly. Gently he eased himself away, and as he moved, the girl gasped and moved too, her hands relaxed, then tightened again about him. He slipped out of the passage then, resting near the entrance. He kissed her lips lightly, and her cheeks, and found them wet with tears, and her eyelids, and her lashes, which were damp. She moved under his weight, and he turned to one side to ease, and put one hand against the side of her face, against her hair damp with sweat. She answered him, her hand placed like his, against his face. Numbed by love, too exhausted to speak, they fell asleep in one another's arms in perfect charity with one another. The sound of the door bolts opening did not pierce to waken them. Hands groped, found the male, pulled him out, and took him.

Chapter 10

"You have never told me what I am to call you," she said to him, when he had come to the bed the next night. She was sitting on the foot of it, her feet over the edge, and he did not at once find her. "Have you a name, or just a title?"

Her tone was provocative, and should have warned him. She had had a bad day of it, and though he could not see them, her eyes were smudged in her white face with brown shadows. He had had a bad day himself, and the accord from the night before might not have happened. He did not answer her, but came around to the end of the bed looking for her. When he found her, he put his hand between her knees, without a word, to separate them, his sex heavy, wanting to find the place it had found before to rest in.

"Can you never just talk to me!" she cried, irritably, pushing him away. "Must you always be coming at me, when you have just walked in the door! I do not like this all the time. It is not what I wish for!"

Without answering her, and without any word at all, he slipped his arm under her drawn-up, tight-closed knees, and picked her up effortlessly, and carried her in his arms to the head of the bed, where he let her down.

Her own heart that had lain briefly against his on the brief walk was beating furiously now, in both fright and anticipation, and her resistance was now token.

"You were kinder to me before you told me your cock-and-bull story," she whispered. "It gives you no right to walk in and out of me at will, without a word. *You* do not own me, tho' you act as tho' you do. Would you treat your true wife so, or do you treat me so only because you know you can have me? You will have me now, because you are stronger than I am, but I will not like it, and afterwards *I* will not talk to *you*. You will not tell me your name, I think, because you are no one at all and you cannot even think one up. It was all a foolish story you made up because you wished to make me sorry for you."

While she chattered on nervously, his hands had been on her wildly beating heart, pushing her flat. He drew her knees apart now, and held them apart, with his hands and then his thighs. When his hands released them, they snapped back, but against his thighs which were against hers now, their muscles hard and rigid. She gave a convulsive start as he stabbed his way in, but his hands held her waist, and his mouth was on hers, drowning her protesting cries. He did not wait for her responses then either, but holding her to him, pounded his way in quickly and heavily, a short way only, and released his aching sex of its load, careless of where it fell, or how. He would have left her then and rolled over, still without a word, but she put her arms around his neck and held him to her, searching out his mouth, letting her own tongue enter into his. Her hands slid down to his bare thighs, and clung to them, her fingers digging into their flesh, pressing them against her.

"My name is Simon," a soft voice said near her ear, unexpectedly, in a gentle drawl, "and I know I have made love to you clumsily, Alyx, and left you in a state, but I have been whipped today and I really cannot do any more. Not at least right now."

"Oh, Simon," she whispered, in relief, releasing him, the nightmare leaving her.

"Yes," he said, "I have come back, Alyx—from wherever it is cruelty sends me. Your sweet self brought me."

"Why were you whipped?" she asked, not trying to understand him.

"I hardly know," he said.

"Was it very bad?"

"Yes," he said. "I never get used to it, tho' I wonder I do not. All I can do is go away."

"Where did they hurt you?" she whispered, "on your back?"

"No, love," he said, laughter suddenly brimming under his voice, "where you were grabbing me just now, in part. And it is not bad now. You have eased the worst part."

She gasped, slightly, amazed and appalled at him.

"You must not say such things to me."

He laughed lazily. "Why must I not?"

"It makes me feel like—like—it is not respectful."

"No," he agreed solemnly, "it is not—dear Alyx." The slight inflection he put on her name set her off.

"If you were—if you were who you say you are—you would not treat me so!"

"No," he said thoughtfully, "I suppose I would not. I see some fortune in our situations after all."

"You surely do not mean to go on with this masquerade!" she exclaimed, driven.

"Pardon?" the man beside her said, puzzled, the naturalness of the inflection giving her pause, even in her heated indignation.

"Tell me the truth," she whispered, doubt assailing her, "tell me you were joking me last night, as I thought, in what you said."

"About what?" he asked, genuinely puzzled.

"About—about who you said you were. Not your name—the other."

"But I cannot," he said in surprise. "Did I misunderstand you? What I told you was the truth. Did you not believe me? I had thought you did."

His tone, though surprised, was gentle. Her reaction, surprisingly, was fury.

"I do not believe you," she cried, though without conviction. "I don't want to believe!"

"I can see you mind," the soft voice beside her remarked, unmoved, "but I do not see why you should."

"Can you not?" she exclaimed passionately.

"Frankly, no," the quiet man said. "It is a point of view I have never met before. Why, Alyx?"

"Why I should mind your being a gentleman?"

"Yes, Alyx. You surely knew by my voice, as I did by yours, something of the nature of things. Do not tell me you did not. And why should you mind?"

"But I didn't," she cried. "I did not at all. I was not thinking about you at all."

"But you were, and you did," he interposed. "You asked me again and again who I was."

"Did I?" she asked doubtfully. "Then I must have known something. Oh, why, if you were going to tell me at all, did you not tell me sooner. How *could* you not? Oh, if it is true, I wish you had never told me at all!"

"I can believe you might not believe me, tho' somehow, Alyx, somehow, unreasonable tho' it is, I think all the same you do, but why should you mind? Why should you not want to believe me?"

"Because I was bred to be a lady," she flashed, "and I have not acted like one!"

Her reply seemed to stun him. Then he grinned. "No," he said grinning, she could feel he was, even in the dark, "you haven't—shade of Alyx!"

"Do not call me that!" she whispered in a fury of passion. Her hand went back to slap him, but he caught her wrist in his.

"What does it matter?" he whispered then, "for God's sake, Alyx, what does it matter?"

"Why then did you not tell me your name before, if it does not matter," she countered, "when I asked you?"

"I think because I could not remember myself," the quiet voice said.

"Oh, Simon," she whispered, her passion of anger checked, "it was not because I had disgusted you?"

He stirred. "*You?* Disgust me?"

"You cannot love me," she whispered uncertainly.

"Miss de Vere, Miss de Vere," he whispered, "do not try me. You show you know I love you or you would not bait me so on my own ground."

"It is only wallowing you care about," she said, fascinated, half afraid as always of what she sensed near her.

"Hell!" he said hard-tried. "If I stand by the door, what will it prove?"

"Restraint!" she snapped. It was too much for him. He whooped with laughter, rocking with it, still holding her wrist, and then was on her.

"You are no gentleman," she cried, her voice muffled.

"You have said it," he agreed. For a moment she pummelled him with her fists in earnest, until frightened by what she had aroused, she grew quiet. Then her hands clung to him as he grew gentler, but she was crying bitterly though softly all the time. When he had quite finished with her, he took her in his arms like a child and kissed the tears from her face.

"Is it true?" she whispered then.

"Is what true?"

"What you told me?"

"I have said so."

"But he is dead."

"So am I thought to be, I am afraid, by my dear mother. You did not mention the house in the background of the picture, columned by Nash. Or the hawk and jesses on my wrist, the artist's fancy, not mine. My gold signet ring is on my third finger of the hand holding the hawk, but I do not have it. My uncle does, having pulled it from my finger himself. The picture is doubtless now in the Dower House where you must have seen it and where my mother must now live, and no longer in the Gallery of the Hall."

He fell again into the heavy silence that frightened

her. She sat up beside him, when he continued not to speak or to move, and with her fingers, hesitantly, questioningly, traced again the outline of his features as if she were trying to see them. He did not move, or speak, and after a time she stopped.

"Do you find any trace of them remaining?" he said then, his voice remote, and speaking with an effort.

"Of what?" she whispered.

"Those features you once loved."

"You should not have let me tell you," she whispered.

He did not seem to hear her, and in fact he did not.

"I am sorry," he said, after a moment. "Did you speak? I did not hear you. I was remembering."

"Remembering what?"

"I was remembering—my uncle," he said, and was silent. There were footsteps approaching now. He roused himself, bent over her, and taking her face gently between his hands, holding it for a moment so, bent and kissed it. "I love you, Alyx," he said, and got up from the bed to meet his guards before they came in for him.

Chapter 11

WHEN HE came the next night he slipped into the bed beside her and took her in his arms and kissed her, as though he had not left. He made no move to take her, but lay down with her, her head cradled against him, and his arms around her. They lay that way a long time without speaking, either of them, and then he turned to her naturally, and she to him, and they made love to one another as they might have in another time and another place, kissing with loving hesitancy, progressing and responding, the commitment made and the pledges given, until the last seal, signed in her ring. "I, Simon, take thee, Alyx," he whispered. "I, Alyx, take thee, Simon," she whispered, taking him, giving herself. The other words they left unsaid, being unable to honour and cherish, and being afraid of death. Then returning to quiet kisses, they rested in one another's arms.

"Do you want this child, Simon?" she whispered.

"Yes, I do," he whispered back.

"Then I do because you do." She lay quiet, feeling in her imagination the seed racing through her, wondering if it were happening then, if it had happened already. She drew her legs up a little as though to help the seed. He put his hand over her belly, at her movement, and caressed it gently, lightly massaging it for a moment with his fingers, then his hand lying quiet.

"Do you think it has happened yet, Simon?" she whispered.

"Yes," he said, "I think it has."

"Why?" she asked.

"It is just a feeling," he said. He put his other hand under her back and held her clasped between the two, and then laid his cheek against her where his first hand had rested.

"I think you love the thought of it, not me," she whispered.

"No," he whispered back, "it is because I love you that I care for it. I have told you that." He sat up, and she could not see him in the dark but she could feel his shape beside her.

"Simon," she said after a moment, "are you there?"

"Yes," he said. "I am there." She put out a hand and touched him, and he felt for hers with his and took it in his, spreading the fingers lightly. He sighed suddenly and turned quietly to her and they made love again and then lay back again quietly, enclosed still in each other's arms.

"Simon," she said then, "did your uncle really have you sent here?"

"Yes," he said.

"How?" she asked. "What did you do?"

"Nothing," he said. "I existed. It was enough."

"But no one thinks he did such a thing," she said. "I know they do not. At least I think I know they do not."

"You were a child at the time," he said briefly. "You would not have known."

He lay back remembering. He had been fair game, he thought now, with surprise. It had been after the scene in Paris with the grandfather of the child lying now in his arms who had that Alyx's name. "I was not a creditable young man," he said slowly, "and my uncle, my father's brother, must have resented the waste of my father's estates on a wastrel. I do not think my character an excuse for having me kidnapped. After all, had my father wanted it done, he could have attended to it himself, and he did not himself seem excessively to mind. I was seventeen, when it happened. I had been sent down from Eton soon after term began, and I am not going to tell you why. My father arranged to have a tutor for me, and sent me for that term to Paris. He said, if I remember him correctly, that if I was going to do it, I might as well learn to do it right. He came over himself before Christmas to shop for my mother and to go the rounds. He introduced me to the salons, though his own taste was more for hunting, and there, as I told you, I met your grandfather's Alyx. After my father went home, I continued to meet her, drawing rather heavily on the accounts my father had established for me. But I have told you that story. I was not quite seventeen then, and I took it hard. I went back to London, without informing my father, resolving to go to the devil in the accepted way. I was fair in the way of doing it, when my father learned of my presence in the city through my mounting bills, and came posting up. He was pardonably shocked, but he did not lecture me. He settled the more pressing bills, and my vowels, suggested mildly that I leave deep play until I had independent means sufficient to cover such losses, and requested that I visit him at Enderly when my engagements would permit. I did not go home. I had made already the acquaintance of the younger Barrymores, and their ways suited my mood exactly. I visited at the several meeting places of their set, was introduced to Cripplegate himself, allowed myself to be initiated into their rites—and I am not going to tell you what that involved—" ("flat on the altar," he thought, "God forgive me") "—and was by this time in a very fair way of accomplishing my aim. I was drinking heavily, not because I particularly enjoyed it, tho' I carried my liquor better than most, without being made sick or belligerent, but because it was expected of me, and looking back, I daresay had my uncle left me to it, I would have myself accomplished for him what he put himself to so much trouble to bring about. It is not, as you may be thinking, easy to put away the heir to an Earldom one stands oneself then to inherit, but I laid myself open to him. My habits were by this time notorious, my taste for low friends, my uncertain hours, my wanderings without escort into the dangerous parts of London with Cripplegate and his companions. Still, how to do it without suspicion must have given him pause. Or perhaps it was my own recklessness that made him begin to think how likely he was again, if I continued, to inherit, and to consider how much better suited he was to manage the estate he grew up with, than his brother's wild son. My father was vigorous, however, and I was years still even from my majority. My uncle did come several times in London to remonstrate with me with pursed lips, but I would swear that he bore me no active ill-will then, and that his concern was then for his brother. He spoke of the grief I was causing my father, which I denied, and my father's hopes for my return to school in the Spring term. I said, I believe, that it was not his affair, and told him he might go to the devil too. Then, unexpectedly, my father was thrown from a new hunter, against a stone wall, hitting his head."

He paused, unable to go on, the memories rushing in on him, through the gap his words had made in his defences. He had never spoken to anyone of those days; he had never had the chance. His mother had written him his father was in a coma, and that he should come at once. She had sent it to him by post, and he had received it in his room and gone icy-cold with shock. It had come the day before but he had been out late, and it was midday before he woke and afternoon before he read the note. By that time his uncle had come, announced and entering as he sat there, his fingers shaking with the paper in them. He had looked up, his eyes blind.

"Your mother has sent me to bring you home with me," his uncle had said, he remembered. "You will get your clothes at once."

His grief and shock had transmuted itself to sudden anger. He laid the paper down, onto the table, out of his shaking hands.

"Sent *you?* I do not need you or anyone to bring me. I will bring myself, I thank you," he had said, or words like those, noting the red spots that crept over the cheek bones of his uncle's face. "I believe I know the way to my father's house, Uncle, and when will be the time convenient for me to leave." He did not ask whether his uncle had come from his mother. "I am out of leading strings, Uncle," he had added, his young voice shaking like his fingers, "nor do I need you or anyone else to point to me my duties."

"I only thought," his uncle had said, "that having forgot so many of them, you might also have forgot this, and I would not have you cause your mother pain at this time."

"My father is not dying!" he had said, not realising he was shouting. "He has taken a fall! Go hotfoot to my mother, if you like. I will come in my time!"

"Shall I tell her so?" his uncle had asked.

"Tell her just what you like," he had shouted. "You will do it anyway, you meddling old prose!" His uncle had turned to go, his face very grave, and he had sprung to his feet, ashamed. "Wait, Uncle," he had cried, "I did not mean it," but his uncle had reached the door, and did not hear him, or did not choose to hear him, for he had not turned. He had sat down again, grief and defiance mingling in his hung-over brain. He put his aching head in his hands and groaned, and remembered he was engaged for dinner. He would have his man pack for him when he returned, he thought, and go down in the morning. His uncle was mad to expect him to start an hour before dark. It seemed important, somehow, to keep the engagement now, which had slipped his mind at the shock of the letter. He did not stay long. "M'father's dying, I think," he had said simply. His friends had toasted the new Earl, and he had looked at them blankly, and gotten up from the table and left. His head was aching again, and he thought he would stop by the Cocoa Tree on his way home for coffee to help his head and steady his thoughts. He took a chair part way to the Cocoa Tree, the swaying motion making him feel slightly sick, and paid the bearers, and walked the rest of the way, his head aching until he could not think. The coffee soothed it somewhat, and the room about him took a defined shape, and he saw his uncle standing a little away, watching him.

"I am sorry, Uncle Phillip," he had said. "I should not have said what I did. I have a terrible head tonight, my fault, of course. But I am not thinking very well."

"I will get you another dish of coffee," his uncle's voice had said, his shape coming in and out of his nephew's bemused wavering stare. He had brushed his hand before his eyes, to try to clear them, and had accepted the dish gratefully, not thinking it strange his uncle should serve him. He had drunk the bitter liquid thankfully, hoping it would restore his wits. "My mother did not say you were coming," he had said. "Have you seen my father?"

"Not yet," his uncle had said. "I came to you, Simon, as soon as I heard myself."

"Good of you," Simon had answered. "Can't think with this head. Doesn't seem to be getting better. Out much too late. Dinner engagement this evening. Should have cancelled," he had said.

"Have you packed yet, Simon?" his uncle had asked, his face swimming again into view with his words.

"No," he had managed to say, noting his uncle seemed satisfied.

"You must do that, Simon," he heard his uncle say. "I will look in on you in the morning, and perhaps we can start together." His uncle was rising, bowing to two of Simon's friends who had come up, repeating to them what he had said to Simon. Everyone was suddenly solicitous, to no point, with his head bursting, and his vision obscured. His throat felt stuffed with cotton, and he felt he must have air, outside the stuffy smoke-filled coffeehouse. He wondered he could ever have found it pleasant. He rose, carrying his head with care, and bowed.

"Servant, Uncle. Servant, Charles," he said vacuously to the friend standing by his uncle. He smiled pleasantly, he thought, on the assembly, and walked, swaying slightly, towards the vanishing door, aware of eyes on him. "Not drunk," he confided to the table by the door. "Just a little knocked up, that's all." He found, after several tries, the handle to the door, resisted the doorman's attempts to open it for him, yielded gracefully, and made his way carefully outside with his head that now instead of aching intolerably seemed very light and on the point of floating away. The cold air exercised a brief steadying influence on him. "Must pack," he thought, "tell George to do it for me. Must go home." He did not see a chair, and he struck off in the direction that seemed to him most likely. It was hard, however, to find his way with all the lights unaccountedly out, and a sudden fog rising, and not unnaturally, he stumbled, hit his head against something, and fell. It was not a hard blow, but he seemed to lack the strength to rise, and his arms and legs would not answer him. Someone seemed to be bending over him, but he could not tell who it was. Hands were assisting him to rise, and a voice he thought he knew seemed to be calling a chair.

"That's right," he murmured approvingly. "Have to pack. My father's sick." He was sick too, then, over his benefactor, and over the chair bearer, and sick again, with the swaying motion of the chair. "S'odd," he murmured, "never knew coffee t'do this before."

"Drink this," the voice beside him said reassuringly,

pressing a flask to his lips, between his teeth, and tilting his head back helpfully. "It should do the trick." He really could not help drinking it, even when he knew it was not quite the thing, for the hand kept the bottle tilted into his throat when he faintly protested. A sharp pain stabbed through his brain and receded. "Too strong," he muttered, "not the thing," and leaned his head against his benefactor, and went to sleep.

When he woke, his throat was dry and aching and seemed stuffed with cotton. He gasped for breath, and could not find it, tried to sit up and could not, and struggling, lost consciousness again. He woke again, and this time when he opened his eyes, he found he could see, but the light hurt his eyes and his pounding head so he shut them again. He was cramped but he did not want to move, thinking if he lay very quietly his head might ease, and as he lay there, his brain clearing slightly and recognising the distressed signals being sent to it, he discovered that someone had played a silly trick on him and had bound his hands and feet while he slept. They were in fact quite numb, and there was no feeling in his fingers or his feet, and his indignation giving way to panic, he realised the cotton in his throat was not his imagination, and that he had been gagged as well, and gagged efficiently. He lay very still, trying to breathe, trying not to be afraid, and after a while he opened his eyes again, the light this time not seeming so bright, and saw his uncle standing beside him. He knew then what had happened to him, and why, and why the coffee had made him so sick. His uncle bent down and removed the gag, and while he was gulping in the breaths of air, produced the flask again and had poured a quantity of its contents into him before he knew what his uncle was about. He choked and gasped, and turned his head away, but he was weak and dizzy and the fumes of the drugged rum were again rising up to his brain, with the sharp pains and the clouding effect as before.

"Please, Uncle, no," he whispered, as his uncle's fingers pulled his jaw back and forced the head of the bottle again past his teeth and into his mouth. He choked, and fought the liquid, but with one hand his uncle held the silver flask against his tongue, ignoring the marks his teeth were indenting in it, and with the other, pinched his nostrils shut, so that he was forced to swallow, to breathe. Languor stealing over him, he was all the same aware of his uncle's hands searching his pockets, taking his watch and his seals, and his uncle's fingers gripping his ring with his signet and pulling it from his finger. He looked at his uncle, helpless anger in his dazed eyes, and saw his uncle smile, his eyes meeting that look. He shut his eyes against that smile, and stopped fighting and let the darkness sweep over him.

He had been brought to his own room, he had recognised that. It was after all, he supposed, somewhat difficult to kidnap and dispose of a vigorous young man without outcry and without suspicion. But the chairman, questioned, would have said he brought the young lord home, in much his usual condition. He had a good head for drink, and he supposed his uncle had found him difficult to put out with drugs, but he had in the end managed to do it. He supposed when it was broad light his uncle, having unbound him, had summoned his valet, indicated his condition, moralized over it, his father dying and his son, drunk and uncaring, ordered his valet to pack for him, and had then had him put in his own chaise which he must have sent round for. He supposed it must have been done in some such way, later, when he wondered about it. He did not of course know. He awoke to find himself propped against the squabs of his own chaise, the joltings even of that well-sprung coach intolerable to his head, the ache now like a broad band of iron clamped about his forehead and eyes like a vise which twisted tighter with each jolt. He had no idea of the time, or how long he had been in the chaise. He was not bound, and he sat up too abruptly, taking off, it seemed, a piece of his head. He was made so sick with the pain that he lay back limply, pressing his fingers against his forehead, nauseated and faint. His condition seemed to suit his uncle, who smiled at him faintly and lowered the small pistol he was holding in his hand.

"Oh, my God," Simon murmured, shutting his eyes against the sight. "It wanted only this. Where are we going, Uncle?"

"Towards your father's," his uncle said.

"To my *father's*?"

"*Towards* your father's," his uncle had said, a distinction Simon had not grasped then. He looked out and saw with his blurred eyes that what his uncle said was true.

"I was coming anyway," Simon had said, "it did not need this to bring me! What were you *thinking* of?" He was bewildered and, his fright passed, his terrible suspicions allayed, suddenly aggrieved, but too sick to be angry, or to talk. He lapsed into silence, trying to cushion and protect his head, and he did not see the riders approaching, their faces masked and hats well down on their heads. But he heard the call to halt, the horses pulled up with a sudden jerk that brought the pain raging again in his temples, heard shots, and shouts, a scream, and saw his uncle raise his gun to fire out the window, and the gun explode from his fingers and drop, blood on his hand, and spreading on the sleeve of his coat. He saw his uncle looking with astonishment at his hand, holding his forearm with his other hand. The riders then had reached inside and forced the door of the coach open. He had not even had a sword. He had reached across and drawn his uncle's, but it had been beaten from his hands, with no great effort, and he had found himself and his uncle pushed back, the points of the bandits' swords pressing into their throats. He had supposed it was money the thieves wanted, but he found they were after bigger game. They had demanded to know which was the Earl's son, and his uncle like a fool, he had thought then, had cried out, "Oh, don't take *him*." He had been pulled roughly from the coach, his arm twisted painfully behind his back and held there, and had seen to his dismayed eyes his groom and his coachman dead on the ground, one of the footmen leaning against the coach, his head bleeding, and his arm, like his uncle's, shattered, the other footman unhurt, but held in the arms of one of the ruffians who was even then securing his hands.

"Oh, Master Simon, Master Simon," the fellow had cried out pitifully, in dismay. "They ha' killed us all, and be they taking you wi' them?" He was weeping in his fright and in his alarm.

Simon did not answer. He heard his uncle cry out when the thieves took his injured arm to bind it behind him, but they ignored his outcry.

"Tell my lord's father," the man who seemed the leader said, "he will hear from us for the ransom." They had put Simon on a horse then, taking one out of the traces, and tying his feet with a rope lashed under the beast's belly. His hands were looped to the pommel, which he grasped with nerveless fingers, and a leading rope tied onto the bridle, and the horse whipped up to a trot. He heard the shouts of his uncle and his footman, but he was past answering, and the pain increasing intolerably in his head, he was soon past anything. He slipped in and out of consciousness, discovering once another man had been brought up behind him to hold him up, the pain stabbing him into unconsciousness again.

He awoke to find himself in a low bed of sorts, miserably sick, his own clothes gone and others on him, his hands and feet bound again. His throat was dry, and he moaned slightly in his misery and felt a large hand over his forehead. It was cool and strangely kind, and Simon felt the tears pricking behind his eyelids, at the touch, and the sound of the rough voice trying to comfort him.

"Ee, lad, thouart in a bad way, right enow. But do tha drink this and it will put thee someat to rights."

He pressed a glass on Simon that looked and smelled nauseous, but Simon felt so badly he drank it without protest. He could not feel worse, and whatever the drink was, it did ease the nausea racking him and the sickness from the pain in his head.

"Thank you," he murmured gratefully. "It does help," and lay back, feeling relief from the throbbing pain wash up him, as the pain began to withdraw.

He gave the thieves no trouble. They fed him and cared for him in their way, and did not abuse him, except to keep his hands and feet bound. They kept him in a small room in a hut from which he could not have escaped even had they left him free, having no visible window, only a small hole. After a passage of unmarked time, a week perhaps, they came in and put a gag in his mouth and blindfolded him and then carried him out into the air and into a vehicle of some sort, on the floor, and put a rug over him. The voices about him were muffled, but he recognised among them the voice of his uncle, and his head clear now, knew the extent then of his uncle's treachery against him and the limits to which his uncle was willing to go. Someone was mounting now into the vehicle, their feet on him, huddled on the floor. For one wild moment of hope, he believed his uncle would speak to him, that his uncle had come for his father to pay the ransom and that the nightmare was over. He had heard money changing hands. But no one spoke, and then he knew. "Do these men think," he wondered dully, "that they will be allowed to keep their money and live, knowing what my uncle has done? Do they think if he will do this to me, and my poor groom and my coachman, he will scruple about them?" He was not surprised when the carriage stopped, and after a moment, he heard a series of shots. He wondered how many pistols his uncle had had to bring, to be certain of none missing or firing in the pan. Poor thieves, he thought—they had been kind to him, after their fashion. He heard his uncle dismount, a final shot, silence, then, for a considerable time, and then the smell of fire. His uncle came back, and he felt his feet on him again, and the small sound of the reins, and the horses moved off.

"Where am I going now?" he wondered. "Why did he scruple to shoot me too and leave me in the fire? He could not," he thought. "He wanted them off guard. But now he could, and he does not." He lay under his uncle's feet, and thought of what had passed, and began to see a possible pattern. His uncle had wanted his ring and his watch, and had taken them, to be sent as proof the thieves had him and wished ransom. Or were they to be returned, as proof that he was dead and beyond ransom. He did not know. He wondered if his uncle knew he had heard his voice and knew him. Perhaps not. If his uncle could pretend, he could pretend too. He found himself wondering about his father, and his heart ached and swelled with grief and anxiety. Is he even now dead, he wondered, or dying, and I, his son, do not know it? The thought caused him to struggle in his bonds, fruitlessly, and his uncle's boots pressed harder on him and he stopped struggling. "I wonder if my mother thinks my uncle is out looking for me," he thought, his heart swelling with grief and rage, and then sudden fear as the carriage stopped. His uncle dismounted, and removed the rug, tightened the blindfold, checked the ropes on his wrists and ankles, and then after a moment slipped the handkerchief down that was around his mouth and removed the gag stuffed in it. His lips open, the air filling his mouth, Simon felt a quantity of bitter soft powder poured in his mouth, and the gag quickly reapplied on top of it. He was choking now, and frightened, his head filled and ringing with strange sensations, and then the unpleasant powdery choking sensation was succeeded by a new entirely novel one, exquisitely pleasant, that sent his blood tingling in his veins and brought a grimace of a smile to his lips behind the gag. He was still smiling, his eyes vacant behind the blindfold, his body limp and relaxed, when the carriage stopped again. He knew vaguely his bonds were being removed, but he did not care. He sighed with pleasure, the gag removed, his eyes rolled up in his head, a heavy sweetness weighing down every limb. The air before his eyes was full of dancing lights, and bright colours. People came and looked at him, but he paid them no mind. His uncle's voice receded in the distance. Nothing had power to touch him, not even the weights someone was applying to his wrists and ankles in a vain effort to hold him down. He smiled at them, from the airy heights where he was flying, removed and floating in his own world. He drifted into a deep sleep, unaware, rocking as though on his mother's lap.

He awoke, cold and wet. It was the cold he was aware of first, and then the wetness, though his mouth was dry, and his throat and his head seemed to be on fire. He tried to put his hand to his forehead, and discovered he was chained, thick bands about his wrists and ankles, surprisingly heavy, surprisingly uncomfortable. He tried again to lift his hand to his forehead, but he was too weak and the weight too heavy, and instead he sat up and put his head down on his knees. Either it was night or he was in the dark, and which it was he could not judge, for he had no idea how long he had been lying where he found himself. There was a continuous murmuring and moaning around him, that he had not at first been aware he was aware of. Now he listened to it, and knew that he was not alone, and however bad his case he was not alone in it. He shivered not only with cold, chilled at the sound of it. He had been swaying slightly, without noticing it, with the rocking motion of his dream world that still continued, though he was now completely awake. The rocking motion suddenly increased, and threw him over to one side, against what seemed to be dirt and stones. He lay where he had fallen, ill and miserable and afraid, weak with the drugs he had been given and thirsty, a cold emptiness in his stomach that was cramped with hunger. Then slowly he picked himself up again, only to be thrown over again by the rocking motion. He could feel somewhere not far from him a dull heavy rhythmic thumping and slapping sound. He shivered, remembering it, and remembering the despair with which he had awakened to the full and irremediable evil of his situation, and the full evil of his uncle's intentions towards him, and the girl beside him in the bed of the breeding hut put her arms about him.

"Simon?" she whispered. He left the darkness of the ship's hold and returned to the darkness of the little room, and tightened his arm about her. "Are you cold? Did you fall asleep? What happened then?"

"Yes," he said, "I am exceeding cold. Warm me, Alyx, if you can."

He lay very still, shivering slightly, and now and then a shudder running through his big frame spread beside her. She paused, and drew the sheet over them both, and carefully placed herself on top of him, fitting her sex near his, and her mouth by his. Then delicately, with exquisite care, she took his face in her hands and began to kiss him, her tongue slipping into his mouth. He tightened his arms about her, as she said, "You were telling me about your father. He had hurt his head."

"Yes," he said, "I remember. I never saw him, not then or ever again. And he must have died, then or later, for you have told me my uncle is Earl. My uncle contrived that night to get possession of my person, and I will say that with my careless habits, I did not make it very hard for him to do. He must have been very busy, going back and forth, working at his plots and allaying suspicion yet fanning the worries of my mother about my supposed kidnapping by highwaymen as he was bringing me home. I do not know much about it, except that he seems in all things to have succeeded. I lay for days trussed like a Bartholomew pig until he had made arrangements to sell me to the Captain of the Slaver. He delivered me with no qualm and no farewell into those hands and left me. It would seem he did not wish to take my life himself, that he scrupled so far, but it would have been kinder if he had. It was a terrible time, Alyx," he said shivering. "I was a careless young man, but I had been gently bred and gently cared for. I do not know how I survived, or whether my uncle meant me to survive. I was not weak, for my father had trained me to hunt and to shoot, but no one had ever hurt me, or treated me roughly. At school I lodged out, with a very good dame, and my father had never flogged me. I was still very young. The cruelty I had been put to at first quite overcame my spirits. There I was, in a rotten ship's hull, chained like a criminal with a holdful of other misfortunates, all of us meant for the plantations in the different colonies. There were Scots and Irishmen and blacks already months there brought from Africa, and transports out of Newgate, and men and women whose relatives had sent them there rather than to Bethlehem Hospital. There we were, all of us, ill, dying, dead, all of us rotting, with a captain who did not care how he had gotten us or who we had once been. We were so much flesh to him, all the same, except in degree of health or strength and the amount we would bring. I was there for months, Alyx, while he put in and out of port, trading, in calms and in hurricanes. My uncle, I think, must have stipulated I go to the Jamaicas, or even paid for it, for some places there is hope, I think, and here there is none. I was young, Alyx, and despite my excesses and my uncle's handling, and the drugs he forced down me to make me quiet, I was strong and healthy. I survived, as you see. But I did not survive well." He kissed her and pressed her tightly against him, but he did not try to take her.

"Alyx," he whispered, "I have had a terrible life here. I was as dead and lost as my uncle could ever have wished. He had nothing to fear from me. And except for your unexpected unforeseen coming, and he could not foresee it—he would never have had anything to fear. I had forgotten even how to speak. I had lost the habit. But when you spoke to me, though I could not find words at first, it was like another world, a world like the one I had once lived and moved in, suddenly here in the dark, and I remembered words and habits I had forgotten for years. I began to think again, and to feel again, and then to speak again. One does not after all really forget."

"A breath of the drawing room?" she said with an attempt at lightness, her breath catching. "It had not seemed at all like the drawing room to me."

"No," he said, his grip on her tightening, "I daresay it has not. But you must remember that whatever I may once have been, I have been taught to be simply a brute, and my safety and my comfort have been made to depend on that. Do you understand me?"

"No," she whispered.

"I have been here ten years. How long have you been here, Alyx? Two weeks? Ten years, after the months on that ship in the hold. I was taken out of that hold, Alyx, when the ship did finally come to these islands, nothing much left to me except the hatred I had for my uncle, and that had served to nourish me when there was nothing else. At night I dreamed of my home and my family, and in the lesser darkness of the day I dreamed of the revenge I would make on my uncle when I came back. But I did not come back. His plans were well laid. I was put naked except for my chains on the block like any other slave, and sold for what my bones and my wasted skin would bring. I did not sell last, but very nearly, for I did not look like much. But the man who bought you, Alyx, came one day, to see what he could buy cheap of the leavings, and he recognised me. Oh, not myself. I think he thought I was someone's bastard that had been put out of the way. I did not undeceive him. I had no proof, and I rather thought from his eyes and the way he examined my points that it would not further my case in any way I wanted. He checked my teeth, Alyx, and noted the quality, checked my eyes, my ears, my arches, all my orifices, measured my sex and produced what you produce, my dear, in me quickly and scientifically and noted how I held it, noted how I blushed under my skin the dark had whitened, tried without success to make me speak, smiled in a way that frightened me, as well it might, haggled over the price, and bought me. I found it as humiliating and as lowering as you did, my dear, and I followed him quite meekly, shuffling in my chains at a distance, dismally dripping seed. I was no hero in those days, never think it. How many times I would have sold my useless birthright for a hot bath, or a hot dinner. Nor for a cold one, no, but for a hot one, I think so, had someone offered it at the right moment. But the only man who both knew and wanted it had it already, for nothing. I even gave over my resolve not to speak, as my new master rightly figured I would, with my first whipping. And with my second, I told him who I was. He did not believe me, but he took a good laugh from it. It took me three more to find a story that I could both hold to and he would accept. What it was I forget now. It satisfied him, and he left me alone for a while, for the stripes to heal, and the dysentery I had taken on the ship to finish its course. Then he had me brought to his bed. I was seventeen, Alyx, as you will remember, and still had the remnants even after the ship, I suppose, of what the Greeks would call *ephebus*. He had had my hair deloused, and had me scrubbed, and there I was, like a maiden, in the great room. I was no maiden, of course, I knew those ways better than I should have. I resisted him at first, but I found that amused him, and also, he had me whipped in front of him in ways that did not leave me offensive. So I stayed at his call for several months, passively, until he had occasion to make a trip that was to last some weeks. He had also by this time wearied of me, I think, somewhat, and his wife was giving him trouble over me. During those months, I regained my weight, and enough health to have some spirit again. Every nerve of my hot blood was itching to be at my uncle's throat, and rebelling at what he had done to me. I did not then see the years stretching out before me, I saw only each hour and each day, and my mind was entirely filled with memories of my home and of the ship, both equally inflaming. There was very little I could do, actively. When my master wanted me, he was as willing to have me unconscious as awake, and unlike you, Alyx, I was not shocked. Sexual abuse was not new to me, or demeaning to my class. Work was, however, and the taking of orders, and both of these I found myself unable to do. I spent five years pointing this out, and those five years, once I lost the privileged place of my master's bed simply by growing older, were five years of torture I wonder how I continued to endure. I can only say that I was young, and the sense of outrage and injustice still strong in me. I was alternately whipped and starved, but as soon as I recovered strength enough to make it known, I proved intractable as ever. I think it was one such time, when I had been strung up by my hands and left there in the sun, to the mercy of the flies who had less than the overseer, that our master passed by and recognised me. He knocked my chin up with his riding crop, and I heard him say, 'Good God, it is the Earl!' his voice surprised and mocking, and with the overtone in it from his former pleasures. I had been there all day, and I could not have spoken, had I wished to. He lifted my eyelids and looked at my eyes, laughed in my face when I tried to spit at him, and had me cut down. I was twenty then, close to twenty-one, and very aware of it, and what that day should have meant. Shocked, Miss de Vere?" he said suddenly.

"Yes," she whispered, "and no."

"You would have been more so, had you been there. I had not a stitch on, and that part of me caught his attention which has caught yours. It was ever unruly, flying up when I least wished. He looked at me keenly, seeing again I suppose those possibilities for which he had bought me and which my youth and his use of me had caused to slip his mind, but he is not a fool, our master, Alyx, and he made no attempt to speak to me, seeing I was in no humour to listen. He did, however, speak to his overseer, with the result that I was put to work with the horses, breaking them. I did not mind that work; I knew what to do, and to do it was not the intolerable affront that I found work with the shovel and the hoe. Nor did I wish to die. On the contrary, I wished very much to live. And my reason for living was still, years after my taking off, to return to throw the deed in my uncle's face. But it is a strange thing, Alyx, but the breaking of those horses proved to be the breaking of me and of my own spirit that was still then rebellious and proud. It did what pain and hunger and all manner of deprivation and indignity could not do. Perhaps I saw myself in those horses that in the end were made to bow their proud rebellious heads to the bit. I received the lash less frequently, and I was fed better. I spoke only to the horses, and worked with them, and gradually found myself slipping away from the habit of speech with people. I had the horses to speak to, and I did not want to speak to anyone, and I found the simplest way to avoid speaking much was to obey quickly and to answer simply and with outward obedience and respect. These outer habits, I think, affected my inner feelings too. I stopped dreaming at night of my home and my old ways, or if I dreamed, I did not remember my dreams. When I fell onto my bed, which I may tell you, Alex, when I am not here, is a heap of cane leaves, I was too tired to plot schemes of escape or revenge, and in the day I was too busy. I lived strenuously and slept dreamlessly and put on considerable muscle. From time to time the master came and looked at me, at work; I remember once I was sprawled across the side of a horse, spreadeagled, clinging by my toes and ankles and my fingers locked in the horse's mane. I knew he was there, but I kept on with what I was doing as though he were not, then, and whenever he came. From time to time they threw a woman in to me, and I took her in the most natural and expected way. The overseer pointed out to me one of the men kept at stud, like the stallions, and briefly painted the picture of the life he led in comparison with that of the rest of us.

Shortly after that I was put to a test, though I did not know it was one, at the time. Shall I tell you how it was done? I was brought into a room, and told to strip. I had been there four years, going five, but I refused all the same. Two men attempted to hold me, but being four years older now, almost five, and having worked a year with the horses, they could not do it. I shook them off like puppies, knocking their heads together for good measure.

" 'That will do now, Aston,' the voice of the one man I was afraid of said then—that was the name I had been sold under, Aston Smith—I stood there then, knowing from experience there was no limit to what this man who owned me could or would do, to have his wishes enforced, and let the two men strip me. He had, I suppose, been in the next room all that time. He came out now, and looked me up and down, no overtones any more in his voice or his eyes, quite impersonally, and then he nodded, and ordered me to get on my hands and knees on the floor. I felt like the fool I looked, but I did it. He gave a bundle of switches then to one of the men, and had them lay on, which he did with clear relish, about my bare buttocks, and stood there watching until the switches had produced the effect he was looking for in me. He sent me then, as I was, in the broad daylight, into the next room, and shut and locked the door on me. There was a woman lying there on the bed, that was all there was in the room, a mulatta, and naked like myself, except a cloth covered her face and her hair. I needed a woman, and she was there. I walked over to her, touched her. She did not move, towards me, or from me, and I took her, without ceremony and without a word. When I had finished, I turned over, and discovered the master was watching me. He said nothing, and I said nothing. I was given back my clothes. I put them on, and left. The rage I felt, at what had been done to me and I had been led to do, I took out on the horses that day and the next. Then I was taken from that work, and put to the simple task of letting the stallions into the mares, controlling and noting the access. Have you ever seen this, Alyx?"

She shook her head, horrified and fascinated.

"It is an inflaming sight, and provocative in the extreme. When they put me with a woman that night, I needed no urging. So by day I watched, and by night I did what I had watched, and my feelings were much the same. After a week of this, I was taken from both, and set to mending harness, a quiet work which left me with far too much time to remember what I had seen and done. A week later, on edge, I was again taken to the place I had been taken to some weeks before, and again asked to strip. This time I did the thing myself. I saw the rods, and knew what was to happen to me, and Alyx, I wanted it. I felt a wave of anticipation hit me, before the rods touched me, that sent me flying out. I heard that voice, ordering the men to show me to the door, and I went with them this time past shame and with no thoughts except desire. They were very clever, those men. They had shut the door on me, before I realised the room was empty. My disappointment and fury were extreme. I paced the floor, unbelieving, furious with frustration. When the door was opened, and a young woman pushed in, I made short shrift of it. She was less willing than the first, but in the end it was all the same. Nobody opened the door, and I fell asleep with her, exhausted by the whole affair. I woke in the night twice, and took her each time, each time finding her more willing. When I woke again she was gone, and I make no doubt reported all my doings. I would have gone back to my quarters in the stables but instead this time I was set back with the diggers and the hoers. My chagrin knew no bounds. I brought myself, however, to talk to the overseer, hesitatingly, about the change, instead of making my customary rebellion. He pointed out to me the quarters of the men at stud, and asked if I would like to look them over. He did not speak directly or offer that work to me, but I saw then a number of things clearly, I thought, and I agreed to go. He took me over them in great detail, and described again to me graphically the life those few men led and what was expected of them. He then told me that I was not to work the horses any more for a time, but to work on a canal that was being cut between two fields. To his surprise, and mine too, I own, I answered him respectfully and the next day went to work without a murmur to what I had been put. I had been there now, Alyx, five years, and I knew by this time that nothing but death, short of a revolution, which was unlikely in the extreme, kept under as we were by the whip and the iron and the rope, or a miracle, that seemed even more unlikely, would take me off the island. I was young and vigorous, and my desires very keen, and to serve as stud, I realised then, would not trouble me and would be preferable to most ways of living open to me now. I could see the wind was blowing in that direction, and I thought it was my unpredictability and known predilection for obstinacy and revolt that stood in my way. So I worked at that canal for two weeks, knee deep in mud and waist deep in water, until I was well nigh spoiled for anything, and bitten all over by leeches. I thought I had been forgotten, but I worked on doggedly, the sweat pouring down my face so that when the master did come, I did not see him. 'What is my Earl doing here?' he asked in surprise, that I knew was feigned, flicking my chin up with the familiar end of his whip. I wiped the sweat out of my eyes and pushed my hair back, with the back of one of my muddied hands and stood there waiting. The hatred I felt for him must have shown in my eyes, for he seemed pleased. 'A stallion doing the work of a drudge horse?' he murmured. 'What can my overseer be thinking of?' He ordered me out of the ditch, and to come to the house, and strode off without a glance behind him, to see what I was doing. I followed him of course. The overseer met me, and directed me to a room with a kettle of hot water, and I got the mud off me and fresh clothes on me.

" 'Quite the gentleman, Earl,' the master said to me, when I had come in. 'Turn around.' I did so, slowly, cool as he was himself. 'I like your profile, Earl,' he said then. 'I would like more of it around. I like your build, too. I am thinking of putting you in the way of seeing I get both.' He then outlined briefly to me what he was proposing, and what he would expect, and when he had done that, I accepted. I was put back then to horses and to women, riding and breaking both, Alyx. I have done both for five years, and I am held to be good at both."

"Why are you telling me this, Simon?" she whispered.

"I am warning you," he said.

"Why?" she whispered.

He shrugged noticeably in the dark. "Idylls such as this don't last."

"Is this an idyll?" she exclaimed, her voice incredulous.

"Isn't it?" he asked, not answering her.

"Yes," she whispered, "yes, it is." She felt him moving towards her, and his hands moving on her. She lay very still, arching her back under his hands into him, as he moved into her. She was tired, though, and frightened by what he had told her, and she flagged, and lay limp in his arms until he had gone through her and returned. But he was not content with that, and exerting himself, he roused her against her will, exhausted and protesting. She kissed him then, passively and a little sadly.

"Should I have said, *wasn't* it?"

"I wish you had not told me any of this," she said unhappily.

"I know," he said. "It makes the raping intolerable now, does it not?"

"Yes," she whispered.

"And your response?"

"Yes," she whispered.

"You would rather have left it the unknown force in the dark, without a face other than your childhood romanticisms gave to it, and without a history."

"Yes," she whispered.

"But you cannot, my dear," he said. "For when I go, and that force goes out of your life, with its strange amusements, you are going to be left with a child, do not forget that. You will not be allowed to forget it, for it will grow and kick within you and force its way out, and I will have been its father. You cannot forget that, or that you will have been its mother, nor can I. Is it to die here like you and like me and never know its birthright?"

"Is it to be an instrument of your hate for your revenge?" she whispered. "Did you make me love you for that?"

"No," he said. "It was because you made me love

you, that I began to think of the child. Poor child yourself, made to have a child," he said, his fingers in her short hair, "and I am so helpless to help you."

"You have not tried very hard," she whispered. "You want me to have a child. For a moment, I did too, but I do not now."

"Should I have kept silent?" he said after a moment. "Should I not have spoken?"

"I wish you had not," she whispered.

"Then I am sorry if I should not have," he said, his voice suddenly dull and indifferent. "You will forgive me." After a moment, when she did not speak, with what seemed to take great effort on his part, he said, "You mistake, child. I do not want you to have a child. But you have been sent here to have one, and I have been sent here to give it to you. If I do not, someone else will. You are not meant to think of it nor I, nor in the ordinary way would I. You are here to open your loins to me, with or without pleasure, and I am here to do the thing natural for me to do placed with a woman lying exposed and open to me, as long as they choose to let me loose with her. It is all that is expected of you or of me, but in due time, I am bound to have left you with a child, if you are capable of conceiving, and I think you are. It is all very well for you to say I want it as an instrument of revenge. I do not deny it, or that it is the thought of the child which makes me desperate to act. Otherwise, not my fate nor yours could move me sufficiently, in such hopeless odds. But I think my thoughts and my wishes are not to the point, nor yours, nor your wish not to have a child at all. It is too late for that. You are going to have one, I think, and you know it too, and if you do, from this encounter, we know who its parents are and what therefore it should have a right to expect, had we met another way. I think I cannot let it live and die here ignorantly. Can you?"

"No," she whispered.

"Then we will forget your childish dreams, and mine, if they hurt us, and think only of how best we may contrive to save it. Shall we not do that?"

"Yes," she whispered. "Forgive me."

"Forgive *me*," he said heavily. "I cannot help now that I am what I am, now. But if we meet again, and if you do not like what I am, do not flirt with me. And do not tease me. I have been out of the drawing room too long. I remember it, because you remind me of it, but I have been here too long. I am not civilized—if I ever was—any more."

"Dear beast," she said softly, thinking of a story she had been given the year before on her fifteenth birthday.

"Dear *what*?"

" 'Dear Beast.' It is from a story. I would tell you now, but I am so very tired. I will tell you tomorrow."

"I hope so," he said. "I hope so, dear-heart," and drew her against his heart and held her sleeping, himself awake, until the escort, coming, parted them. But he did not come back the next night. The lady of the house took him to her, and kept him all night. Alyx was examined by her orders the next day, and the signs pointing towards pregnancy, shortly confirmed, she was not returned to the breeding hut.

Chapter 12

"I THOUGHT I had other assignments," Simon said, that next night, when he had serviced his master's lady and she lay warmly relaxed and smiling up at him.

"I am almost jealous, I think," she said, smiling at him. "Should I be?"

"No, dear my heart," he said, perfunctorily yet warmly. "I cannot think you need be jealous of anyone."

"But I am," she said. "You were never used to talk, until you went to August's last purchase. I have seen her, you know."

"Have you?" he said indifferently, his ears pricked. "She can surely not be very much. But I have no wish to go back to the fields. I prefer yours."

"Nevertheless you need not go tonight," she said. "August is away in Martinique tonight."

"I thought he knew," Simon remarked, lying back on his back to recover for what seemed to be expected. She sat up on her elbows and leaned near him, her breasts just touching his. He put his arms about her, rubbing her back lightly. The candles were lit, and he could see her very well, her full red lips, and her glossy black hair, coiled back from her pale white face which did not appeal to him. He shut the eyes of his mind, but not his eyes, which crinkled at the corners with amusement. She liked her devils bold, he had discovered.

"Of course he knows," she whispered. "Did he not send you to me first? I have hardly seen you these past days."

"It was not by my own orders that I was whipped," he replied.

"Whip me, then," she whispered.

"I cannot," he said. "It is too soon."

"Then I will whip you," she whispered.

"As you like," he replied, and turned over.

"Aston," she said, her hands caressing his buttocks, pressing them and kneading them thoughtfully, "how do they make love?"

"Who?" he said, relaxing, trying to put aside his thoughts, wondering when she would reach for the rods.

"These women in the breeding huts?"

"Like anyone," he said, his tone flat and discouraging. "In the end, whatever the approach, there is only one way."

"I think not," she said thoughtfully.

"For the purpose they are there for, there is only one way. And they do not make love, Madonna, I do."

"I think you need not go back to this one, all the same, any more," she said. "If she can conceive, by now she surely will have done so. Will you mind, Aston?"

"Mind what, Madonna?"

"Mind not making love to her?"

"Of course not," he said indifferently. "Why should I? Is not one like another?"

"Am I?" she whispered. "Would you mind leaving me?"

"But of course, Madonna!"

She paused, not certain which question he had answered. She could not see his eyes.

"Am I like other women to you?"

"You are my master's wife, Madonna, he has no other."

"When your master my husband made love to you, Aston, what did he do?"

"God's love!" he exclaimed, starting.

"Did you like it, Aston?"

"You may ask him," he replied.

"I know what he does. May I do it too?" she said, her fingers at the place.

"You have not the equipment," he said briefly.

"With my finger, I mean."

"I am here for your pleasure," he replied. "You may do what you like that you can, madonna."

"I cannot get in," she said, after a moment.

"You will need an oil," he said, putting his hands and arms under his head and resting his chin on his hands. "But I do not see the pleasure for you. Does it amuse you, Madonna, to go into men?"

He was relaxed and gave no reaction at all to her inquiring finger. After a few moments she withdrew it, and went to wash her hands, at the basin and ewer near the bed. "There does not seem to be very much to it," she said, her back turned. "I had always wondered. I would like you to do it to me, now I see how it is done."

"I would hurt you, Madonna," he said, turning over.

"I do not mind."

"You would," he said. "I am too big for you. And I would be clumsy. I have never myself done this. It has not appealed."

"I wanted you to take me a way you do not those other women."

"If you feel this way," he said lazily, throwing out at random, "tho' believe me you need not, I wonder that you can bear to have them about you for your personal maids."

"Oh," she said indifferently, "that is very different, and I rarely do, but this one does have style. That is why, I think, I am a little jealous."

"Put her from you, then," he said lazily, his hand at her where hers had been at him. "Myself, I prefer more flesh. Is this what you want me to do?"

"Yes," she said, drawing in her breath, "I think so."

"Haven't you put others from you, when they displeased you? As will you not me, when I cease to please you?"

"Yes," she said, "but you please me very much. The girl pleases me too, and my husband gave her to me. But I think it does not please me to imagine you with her."

"I should think it would, Madonna. Like the rods. Shall I come out now?"

"Yes, Aston," she said. "I find nothing in it."

"It is, I believe, an acquired taste. Madonna, and I have myself no skill that way." He rose and washed his hands. "Jacobs, now, I think does."

"I do not want Jacobs, and you know I do not.

Stand there," she whispered, "in the light, Aston, as you are."

He obliged, looking at her with the teased smile that he knew she liked. She rose from the bed, and came over to him, and put her hands out to his flanks, against them.

"Aston," she whispered, "Aston, I must have you. Must I whip you?"

"No," he said, "I am after all not going to need that. Keep your hands so, and lead me." He held back slightly, as she pulled him forward, shutting his eyes dizzily. "You are so beautiful, Madonna, I wonder he can leave you for the French ladies."

"Fool!" she said, dealing him a ringing slap, "do not presume on me!"

"I apologise, Madonna," he said humbly, looking down on her, his eyes dancing. "My mind runs one way."

"He goes for the brandy," she whispered, leaning back halfway on the bed. "When the French ships come. He likes to choose it himself. Make me feel something, Aston, and I will find you a glass."

"Why do they not come to him, Madonna? I thought tradesmen did. Stay just as you are, Madonna, and I will come up. I want that glass."

"We are at war, Aston, surely you knew that. And the ships cannot use our harbour now, nor we theirs."

"It is a lovely harbour," he murmured, "I am glad I am not a French ship."

"Pass, seaman," she murmured.

"What of the tax?" he asked, his lips seeking hers out.

"Take it," she said into his lips, "and pass."

"If I were a smuggler," he said, "I would always find a way. Perhaps sometimes they do?"

"Perhaps," she said. "When he has seen the new stock, and made his selection."

He was given furiously to think by the possibilities her careless remarks opened up to him, but he did not dare ask the questions tumbling over one another in his mind. He felt her expectant and restless, and he made his mind blank, and earned his glass.

"I have not had brandy to drink for ten years," he said, making it last, feeling it burn its way through his unaccustomed veins.

"No?" she said surprised. "Then you must have some more now, and you may pay for it later," pouring his glass brimful again.

"Madonna!" he said, "you must not! I shall get very drunk. It is very good brandy indeed."

"Then we shall get drunk together," she said, "and I think I will enjoy that. Myself, I do not like brandy very much."

He took leave privately to doubt her words. She seemed to him also to have a strong head, stronger than his own now, and he was far more likely, he thought, to speak indiscreetly than she was. He knew very well her quixoticisms, and her sudden changes of humour. She might keep him a day, a night, a week, and then forget him for a month, a year, two years, three years even. A chance encounter, and he found himself again summoned, as now. Otherwise, he rarely saw her. Their ways did not ordinarily cross. Occasionally she had come in her carriage, with a parasol, and much lace, with a friend, to watch him work the horses. He could expect then, other things being convenient, to be called in that night. If he performed badly, she had him whipped by her blacks, in front of her, if she felt like being amused, in the yard if she did not. It would have been unjust to say he hated her. His hatred while he still had it he reserved for his uncle. These people he rather feared. The helpless anger sparking in his eyes at her claims on his flesh amused her, and she insisted on the candles being lit to better see it. In the end he had pitied her, for he thought her case in some ways worse than his own, and though he did not like her, he humoured her beyond what was forced of him. He thought her dangerous, without justice and without mercy and without much sense, and the knowledge he had gained of where Alyx was in no way comforted him.

He reclined on his elbow, sipping his brandy slowly, watching her over the edge of the glass, wondering as he smiled at her what else he could learn from her, and wondering how long he would be kept there before he was allowed to leave.

"Such brandy," he said, smiling at her, "is surely worth a trip of any length. I do not wonder now that he goes."

"It is not so far," she said. "He could have returned, had he wished."

He made no answer and no comment. He was wondering which way the French island was, East, North, West, or South, and he saw no way to ask. But there was no one else for him to ask at all.

She had her hand, he discovered, somewhat possessively, on his genitals. He carefully tipped his glass, let some of the liquid spill on it, and on himself. He was slightly drunk, he thought, with some awe at the symptoms so long absent and produced on so little, wondering how far it would carry him.

"Oh!" he said. "I have spilled the brandy. It is much too nice to waste." He put a fingertip on the spilled liquid, fast evapourating, and tasted it, and then, his eyes dancing under his long lashes still enchanting in his tired haggard face, he offered it to her. She accepted, delicately and tentatively, the fingertip faintly flavoured with brandy and semen mixed, and then put her lips to the source.

"Ambrosial," he agreed, lifting and kissing her stained lips. "I am very drunk, Madonna. Are you? I am going to make some more, this time for me. Lie down, Madonna." She obeyed the touch of his fingers, relaxed and sprawling like an overblown flower, he thought, one of the pale crocuses, perhaps, that had bloomed on his lawns. He tipped her slightly up, and poured a little of his glass into the opening where he had just been, still moist and slippery, took a drink from his glass to fortify himself, and then applied his mouth and then his tongue. "Ready, Madonna?" he whispered, withdrawing and kissing her lips. She shivered and clung to him as his seasoned tongue penetrated her mouth and the edge of her throat.

"Make some more," she whispered, clinging to him.

"In a moment," he murmured. He sat up, and carefully, thoughtfully, filled her navel with a little of the brandy still in his glass. "There," he said, surveying his handiwork, "that is the house, where we are. Don't move," he cautioned. "And that was the harbour, where I just was. In a moment, I shall make waves come in the harbour. But first," he said, "I must come to the house. Where are my quarters?" he asked, his fingers travelling lightly over her white rounded ampleness. "Don't laugh," he warned. "You will empty the house. Show me my quarters, so I may come from them." She frowned, and then she placed his fingers just below her ribs.

"So far?" he murmured. "Yet I will come. What are these?" he asked, touching her breasts with his lips, taking the nipple of one lightly between his teeth, and releasing it. "I have not seen any mountains. The cliffs behind my quarters where the sun rises?" She nodded. "Then I must leave them," he said. "I do not know the way. Here I come to the house," he said, moving with his lips downward, pausing to drink the liquid he had poured in the hollow, "and now I follow the forested path, so, down to the harbour again, which is so beautiful, and take ship." He carefully filled the entrance again with some of his brandy. "The small boat again, or the large?"

"The small," she said, "just as before."

"The waves are too high for the small," he said after a moment, withdrawing. "We must send the large."

"Kiss me, Aston," she said, her voice urgent, "just as before."

"But what harbour is this?" he exclaimed, obeying her. "Are there two? This little harbour must be for the smugglers."

"Yes," she said drowsily, "I think so, Aston."

"Where the brandy comes?" he asked, sending the large ship in. "Now we have two ships at two harbours but which has the brandy?"

"Bring the small ship into the small harbour," she whispered.

"With the brandy?" he asked, the glass poised.

"Yes," she whispered, her eyes closed.

He tilted the glass, and poured a little down her throat, opened to him, and laughed as she spluttered, and tried to sit up. "Now we make waves all over," he murmured, "all around the island, but both ships are secure, the big ship rocking at anchor and now the little ship." He buried his mouth and tongue again in her mouth as he spoke, and made waves with her as he had said. When the sea was calm again, and the ships out to sea, he said lazily, his fingers resting lightly on her belly, "I forgot to ask which ship was the Master on? When does he come back to the House?"

"Tomorrow," she said, "on the big ship."

"Not the little," he murmured.

"No," she said, "the waves in the harbour are too high."

"He is here now?" he whispered, his hand at the large harbour, moving slowly down her thighs.

"No," she said, "here," and moved his hand to her waist.

"Your other island is too near your house, Madonna," he said, lifting her hand, and placing it on his sex, lying near her. "Is not this better?"

"Much better," she said.

"And it extends," he said, moving her hand gently up towards his navel, "this way, no, towards the little harbour where the smugglers come?"

"Yes," she said. "I think so."

"Or this way?" he asked, sliding her hand down him towards his thighs.

"Up, I think," she said.

"Have you not been there?"

"Oh yes," she said drowsily, "many times, many times. But the sea is so flat, but I think," she said, her hand moving slowly, "that we went up." Her voice trailed away, and he saw she had fallen asleep, her glass in one hand, the other still on his.

He came back the next night, at her request, and she wanted to play islands again. She did not mention the girl of the breeding hut, nor other duties of his. So they played islands that night, and several nights thereafter, her husband not returning, he making many improvements on the game to her childish delight, and testing, changing, improving, learning more exactly the locations and landmarks beyond the limited area he was allowed to go in.

"You never used to talk, Aston," she said. "You are different now. I find you much more amusing."

"It is your society, Madonna," he said. "It must improve anyone." She blushed, to his surprise, and looked pleased, causing him to become thoughtful, outwardly and inwardly. He considered he played a dangerous game, that should she chance to remember their evenings with embarrassment could send him to the pits or even to the rope. They had gone far beyond the perfunctory stud service he had heretofore occasionally performed. He had had to, to mask his inquiries and her answers with nonsense and other memories more potent than his questions which he felt, were her senses less engaged, even she must surely see were not idle. That week of her husband's absence had put them on another footing altogether, of familiarity and intimacy, and he wondered still she had allowed it or that she could brook his company afterwards. But apparently she could. He wondered if he had been so blind, secure in his position, when he was young, and if he would have continued to be, had he not been uprooted and thrown into another life. Could she imagine that he loved her, he wondered, and could she conceivably want that impertinence?

"Your husband must surely return soon," he said.

"Tomorrow, I think," she answered. "He has sent word."

"I shall not, then, I think see you again," he said, his eyes briefly on hers, and then quickly lowered.

"Will you mind, Aston?" she whispered. "Will you care, too?"

"Yes," he said. It was true. He could not yet see a way out through her, but without her he could not

see any way out anywhere. His days and nights otherwise were entirely circumscribed, cut off from inter-
course with any human person except the unknown
women he would service in the hut, once she released
his nights and her husband returned, and the overseer
and the overseer's men who escorted him, to the
horses or to the women. Nor was he left alone with
the horses. There was always someone working near
him, and always the guard with the gun, who shot
down any working slave who moved from his assigned
place, and asked the reason afterwards. He had
received a bullet himself some years ago, in the fleshy
part of his leg, being valuable, but he had been
warned the next time it would be the bone. He had
believed the guard and taken care there should be no
next time.

"I shall mind very much, Aston," she whispered.
He looked down at his mistress, short, plump, her
girlish prettiness hardened and congealed, her vacuous
face vulnerable now as she looked at him, and he
thought, "God forgive me," and bent and kissed her.
He wondered he should have any qualms about using
her, since she had used him to her pleasures without
mercy and without any thought for him, and he
thought grimly, his arms tightening about her, she
would leave very little to him, if she found him out.
And he wondered if there would be tears in her eyes,
as there were now, when she had him hanged on a
pretext, as she had her other favourites over the years
when they ceased to amuse her, or sold into other
hands. Such things were well known. The danger was
not that it would be later, when he hoped he would
be gone, or not care, but sooner. He had never so
much wanted to live. He wondered, with a sudden
fear, if those tears in her eyes signified she had

resolved to have him disposed of, before her husband returned. It would be his fault, he thought grimly, for not leaving the affair casual and for having spoken to her; he had known his danger all the time. He kissed the tears from the eyelashes framing the black eyes swimming below his, and prayed silently.

"When your master returns, I cannot come here at night," he said, his eyes on hers.

"No," she said, "he would not like it. Aston," she whispered, "can you bear not to see me?"

"I must bear what I have to, Madonna," he said.

"You will go back to those women in those huts," she said, her nails digging into his back. "I cannot bear it, Aston, I cannot. I would rather see you dead first."

"I hope you will not, my lady," he said. "There will be other trips, and other brandy, and other islands," he said comfortingly. "You will see. There is no need to despair. Do not weep, Madonna, do not weep, or you slay me now." He watched her fearfully, as she raised her tearstained face to his, trying to hide his fear.

"How can you bear it, Aston," she whispered, "when I cannot?"

"Need you then?" he asked then, his heart beating at the risk, but his voice cool. "You know where I work in the day."

"Yes," she said slowly, "I do. You work with the horses. I had forgotten. You like it, Aston, working with the horses?"

"Yes, Madonna," he said. "I have some skill with them."

She looked at him studyingly, even through her tears. "Do you love me, Aston?" she said.

He took her hands in his, and held them in his two,

and bent his head over them and kissed them. "I may not aspire so high, Madonna," he whispered. "I am only at your command."

"Aston," she whispered, her hands uncurling and moving to hold his face, "look at me, Aston," she whispered, bringing his eyes up, shielded still behind her lashes. He lifted them for a moment and looked at her, and dropped them again. The ground was very delicate, and he waited for her to give him his cue.

"I think you do love me, Aston," she whispered. "Can you tell me you do not?"

"No, Madonna," he said, his voice low and humble and quite sincere. He lifted his eyes briefly, very dark in the winking candlelight, to hers, and dropped them again. She moved forward, and kissed him with unusual hesitancy, and he as hesitantly returned the pressure of her lips, and then, as she flung herself into his arms, his own arms tightened hard about her, straining her to him, as she was him to her.

"Aston," she cried then, breaking the embrace, her tears like a child's forgotten, "I think I have the very thing! You are good with horses?"

"Yes, Madonna," he said.

"Then you shall work mine," she said, with sudden decision. "You have worked my husband's long enough. He can surely spare you to me, to drive my small carriage and keep my horses. I wonder I did not think of it before. It is the very thing! I will ask my husband at once when he comes home. You will be beautiful in livery, Aston, and I shall go driving every day!"

He did not know what to say, and so he kissed her instead, his eyes grave over her head. The ice had been so very thin, and was still thin. "I hope your husband may approve, Madonna," he said simply then. "If he does, I shall try to please you."

"You shall wear red and gold, I think," she said, "with a little cape."

Chapter 13

HE WAS in the field, when the Master came to see him.

"Leave the horse, Earl," his master said, "and come over. I want to talk to you."

"You have been playing with my wife," he said, "while I was gone, poor fellow, and you have your due now. She has it in her head to take you for her coachman. So you will do that now, and keep her happy. Be discreet, Earl, that's all I ask. If you are, when she is finished, if she will leave anything of you worth having, I will see you come back here, if you like."

"I should think you would rather have me whipped, sir," he said frankly.

"You will rather I did, Earl," his master said, "before the end. I wish I had never let her catch sight of you, but I had not thought then you would prove so well. That's all, Earl," he said then, awkwardly. "You will be missed, but this crop of horses is well trained now, and you were due a spell of pasturage, though—" he added thoughtfully "—I hardly think this will be much of that." He turned and raised his hand in half-salute, and walked away, while Simon stood staring after him.

So he was set up like a monkey in livery, he thought, and he endured it, because somewhere on that vast place a child he did not know to see might be having a child that was his. That he had liked her did not weigh with him. Human kindliness and friendliness, never deep, had died in him some time during the agonies of his first years on the plantation. Neither did the sentimental memories long dead briefly rekindled by the coincidence of her name. His spirit had been touched by her voice, recalling it so suddenly into other days, and he had gone those nights after her response with the step of the bride-groom to her. She had awakened his spirit that had outwardly died in him, and proved it not dead, and nourished it, but he had known then, even at the time, that it was the child he was giving her that stirred him in any real sense, enough to move him away from her presence to action. If he could have known that she had not conceived, he would not have thumbed his nose at my lady of the house, but he would have remained uninteresting to her, unspeaking and unexerting apart from the fact, and so have been allowed to remain with his horses. He cursed inwardly, knowing that he was running headlong on death or disgrace, and he had wanted again and again to ask my lady or his master if the girl had in fact conceived. But he did not dare show even that much interest, or a curiosity that in him would not have been natural. Away from her, he was easily able to forget that he had briefly loved her, for her sex was not after all remarkable to him, and to forget the piquancy of her personality that had pierced through him in the dark with its seed it implanted in him more sharply than he had done with her veiled flesh. What moved him now was simple, and engrained in him from birth. A man of his standing did not rape Quality, or leave a girl of her breeding with his child in her unattended. Had he disliked her, his reaction towards this would have been the same, and towards the unborn child that should have had his name to wear, and have been brought up in his traditions. It was as simple as that. His desire for revenge through the child, though there, was no stronger than his attachment to the mother, for if he were able to bring the child alive out of the life it was otherwise to be put into, he was likely also to be able to bring himself out alive and capable of fathering others and of taking his own revenge adequately. It was his simple responsibility towards the child that drove him, that motive and no other. It caused him to endure caprice and to plan and to scheme, and to use powers of observation and deduction he had never adequately drawn on, ever, and that for years had lain entirely dormant. Even so, he did not know without words that could he see within the womb to know whether the child was male or female, and that it was female, the difficulties being so enormous, he would have left it to its fate. But he could not know, and the thought of its being male, and his heir, and left to die a slave, drove him.

The sexual duties attendant on his new position did not disturb or tax him. He had played the role of stud too successfully and too long to be unnerved or dismayed by any demand she could think to make. It seemed to him a small price to pay to be brought into the world of other people and into the world of the women on the place whom otherwise he met only in the dark and into the world he had learned Alyx moved in.

When he had first known how he was going to feel, and what he was going to try to do, he had not known where to start. He had hoped for a few more nights to plan his way with the girl, who had proved purposely and surprisingly elusive in her replies. But he had been cut off from her abruptly. Her reactions and her evasions still bewildered and somewhat angered him, her own anger and her unwilling tepid acquiescence in his concern for her and the child, and his resolve to give it his name. He did not think he would know her if he should meet her, and he had not known how to begin to look for her. His first thought, to put off action until the child was born, he discarded almost immediately. The record of his marriage could not be forged. Too irregular, if at all possible he must manage to accomplish it before the child was born. He had once thought, should the child be born dead or deformed or female, he need not then exert himself further, if he could have somehow arranged the marriage. But reflection had told him that it might be impossible for him or for Alyx to learn the fate of the child or its sex, once it was taken from her. Identification might prove impossible, and even if he was reasonably certain, the question would always remain in his mind, if not in the law's. He had then to find Alyx, persuade her to risk flight with him, and make his way with her to a place where the marriage could be performed and the record be preserved and accessible to him, should he ever reach his home, and the child be still alive, all this before the child was born. It seemed a formidable, if not impossible undertaking. But all other questions put aside, the escape of two adults would be less difficult than the escape of three persons, one of them a tender infant, through arduous country and possibly rough waters. If her pregnancy grew too advanced, she might not herself be able to keep with him. He could wish now, he thought bitterly, he had refused to push between her legs, and had elected instead to be whipped. He would have lost his position, and God knows what else, castration perhaps, but he was headed that way now all the same. Her child then would have been her concern, not his. But as he thought of it, his heart lifted within him, at the thought of the child. He did want it, God knew why. And he did know why. It was his blood, his seed and his father's in him, and the continuity of his name, the new always succeeding, holding the name. He did not want his uncle's line holding in his, or his uncle's children. And he had nothing else to live for. Why escape should seem possible to him now, and escape for two, he did not know, when the impossibility of it had kept him there ten years. He thought then, I cannot solve the whole. I will try for marriage first, even if the records do not hold, if I can do nothing else. If I can even do that, years from now I may be able to do something more. But if I can, I mean to do more now. For as he formulated his thoughts, he realised that he did not want the girl touched by other men, as she would surely be, after the child's birth. The thought of it filled him with helpless rage, but he did not know whether it was for herself, or for herself as his wife and mother of his child. He did know, if he was to have dealings with her, he wanted her as she was, still fresh, still tender, still herself, her honour taken only by himself, and not brutalised and coarsened as the next years must make her, if they did not kill her.

He had run through thoughts like this the day before his last night with the girl Alyx, which he had not known would be his last night, and the day before the night he had told her what place her child should hold, and the day after the last night, before he had known he was not to see her again.

He had been in a rage and a despair, kept by the side of his mistress in her bed, but he had concealed it, in the uncertain light of the candles, his voice light, his new-found wits alert, and he had learned then who kept Alyx and the way he must go. He had concealed his fear and his disappointment, when he learned he was not to meet the girl again, and that whatever was to be done he must find how to do alone, and the silly woman had told him things she should never have, besotted with a piece of him, and given him his first hope. Before that, he had been in a void, surrounded by land he knew nothing about, and water without any end that he knew of. He knew now there was an island, too far to swim to, in dangerous waters with fish that ate or mauled escaping slaves, but there, and inhabited by the French who if not friendly to him, were not friendly to the island he was held on. But his master could go to and fro, and if he could, then he, Simon, could also. It was on the smugglers that he pinned his hope, and when they came to bring the brandy he meant that he and Alyx should go with them when they left. How he was to accomplish this he did not know. But at the least he did know now what he meant to try to do.

So he let himself be dressed up, and he flattered his mistress, and bowed to her, helped her into her carriage, unobtrusively kissed her fingers, stood behind her and waited on her, drove her to neighbouring houses for visits and allowed himself to be observed, his back straight, his face wooden, drove her into the woods, without her footman, and made love to her on the ground, and in the carriage on the thick velvet squabs. He took her and her maid and two footmen and two postillions on an overnight journey to the harbour town, where they stayed at an Inn and his mistress shopped, his eyes keen and alert. He gave no cause for alarm, and conducted himself with discretion, and was not ironed at night. The putting on of irons was customary with his master, but the punishment for attempted escape or misbehaviour so instant and so severe, and the chances of success so small only fools, the master reminded him before he left, would try.

"You treat me well now," Simon had said. "But you may have the Innkeeper iron me if you think it called for."

"James was born here," the Master observed, referring to the older footman. "He will attend to what is necessary. You will see my lady is amused."

He had himself come into town without warning that night. He found Simon asleep, unironed, in his room with the other three. He walked over to Simon's bed and stood beside him with a light, observing him, and waking him by his presence. Simon opened his eyes, and looked up into the light without moving, waiting, his eyes cautious.

"I understood you were to amuse my lady," he said.

"You told me also I was to use discretion," Simon said. "There are three men servants here, one ready to iron me, and one maid servant there, and many corridors and many guests."

"You shall amuse me, then," his master said, tapping

him on his shoulder lightly, to rise. "That will not involve discretion." He took Simon to his room, and kept him there for an hour or two, and then sent him back to his room with the other sleeping servants, cautioning him not to mention his master's visit. The next morning he was gone, his last words to Simon, "Amuse yourselves well and be in no hurry," and no mention made of his visit. The next morning Simon found occasion to drive his mistress about the harbour to amuse her, he said, by seeing the ships, his eyes veiled by his lashes, but very keen and watchful underneath them. He wondered very much why his master had come into town, surely he thought not only to check on his conduct, and certainly not to have what he might have commanded at any time. He could see nothing in the harbour to connect with his master's visit, no small swift-winged sailing vessel, no ships in fact of any kind. But he continued to feel there had been implications he did not know how to read.

He stayed for two days, in the town, amusing his mistress during the day, her maid dismissed, and driving her where she wished to go. He found her most talkative after such times with him, pointing out buildings and natural objects to him from the window of her room, or from the open carriage she had hired. He was particularly interested in the churches of the town, and she did not find this interest unusual, churches being a customary object for sightseeing, especially for women. She thought his interest directed to please her. He saw quickly what he realised he should have seen at once, that the churches were involved with the plantation owners and that he could look for no help there, unless the individual priest happened to choose to help him, and he could not expect that, looking back on his own experiences in Church, he thought. Their help came from the plantation owners, and their congregations. Yet what other marriage would stand up in the courts, under pressure? He could not see his way out.

They had been at the Inn two nights when he looked up one night, as before, to find his master bending over him. At the touch on his shoulder, he rose as before, putting aside the bedclothes, reaching for his shirt and his breeches, and following his master barefoot down the hall.

"I am too old for this," he said, taking off his breeches again and kneeling on the floor obediently. "I wonder it amuses you now."

"There is no one better here," his master said unflatteringly. "And it does amuse me because of my wife."

"*I* make love to your wife," Simon said, wondering how he dared.

"Do you?" his master said. "You surprise me." He finished with Simon at leisure, and allowed him then to get up. "If you imagine I am going to let you make love to me, you are mistaken. If you anger me, Earl, one of these days I shall let myself catch you with my wife, and then I shall be obliged to kill you for it." He paused, and looked at Simon unconcernedly cleaning himself by the lamp. "You are an odd boy, Aston," he said curiously, "an odd man, I should say now. I would not think you had been listening to me. Have you no feelings?"

"No," Simon said. "Not many. Feelings are too luxurious for me." He grinned and looked at his master roguishly. "I did not understand you expected me to have feelings." He resumed his cleaning, his head a little bent, wondering where he was going and where it would take him.

"Come here, Aston," he heard his master say. "I am going to teach you how to feel then." He had raised his head at the new note in his master's voice, and then he walked over to the bed where his master had lain down, and stood beside him, and felt his hand taken, and knew the candle blown out. He let himself be pulled down onto the edge of the bed, where he sat awkwardly, feeling the man's hands upon him.

"Have you been at stud too long, Aston," he heard his master's voice say.

"Yes," he said, "I think so. I am too old. I told you so last night. Feel me," he said, "I am pure muscle."

"Not entirely," his master's voice said, chuckling slightly. "Be still now, Aston, and tell me if you find you feel anything."

He shut his eyes, as the older man touched him, and the years rolled away from him, and he was a young boy again, quivering, a little frightened, anticipating, in the hands of the first man to hold him.

"Is this wise?" he asked, as the hands moved over him.

"No," the man said, "but I am bored and you piqued me. Can you tell me now you have no feelings?"

"No," Simon said, the words wrung from him, "I have no feelings." (Barrymore, Barrymore, he thought, and the seven, using him in turn. Breeding forgotten, senses exploding.) "You will ruin me for anything, sir," he whispered, "take care, take care. God help me," he whispered, refusing to turn to the man beside him, holding himself stiff.

"Admit it," the man said, "you do feel. I am sure of it."

"No," Simon said, holding himself back with an effort, his teeth clenched, "no, I feel nothing."

"If you are a liar," the man beside him said, releasing him, "you are a damned good one. Make love to me then. It will not be hard to make me feel."

"I have not the skill," Simon said. "I can prevent nothing you choose to do to me, sir, but I have not myself any skill in this. I should only make you angry with my clumsiness."

"Get up, then, Aston," the man said, his voice tired. "You may put on your clothes, and relight the candle for me. What do you like, if you do not like this? Women?"

"I do what you ask of me," Simon said, "that I can."

"But do you like them?"

"I do not mind."

"Did you like the last one?"

"I do the work, sir," Simon replied. "But more flesh makes it easier."

He heard the man beside him laugh. "You did not know what you had," he observed. "Pearls before swine. It must be true."

"What, sir?" Simon asked innocently.

"Do you enjoy my wife?" the man asked.

"I have told you, sir. I do the work you ask me to, but to me in the dark it is all the same."

He heard the man gasp with what incomprehensibly seemed to him to be amusement. When he could speak, he asked incredulously.

"Is there nothing you enjoy, Aston?"

"Oh yes, sir," he said. "When I was in England—" he paused.

"Yes, Aston?"

"I enjoyed smuggling," he finished innocently.

There was a sharp silence that cut the air like a knife.

"Did you?" the man asked casually. "You do surprise me, Earl."

"I lived one time on the south coast," he explained. "Out of Sussex."

"I am not certain I believe you, Earl," his master observed.

"It was my grandfather," Simon ventured. "I used to visit him. I was only fourteen," he added. "I am sorry I shocked you, sir. I am sure I would not enjoy it now. It was the excitement, sir, and I was very young. I have shocked you, sir, I am very sorry. I daresay I should not like it now half so much," he offered apologetically.

"Well," said his master, after a moment. "What depths I do find in you, Aston. Go back to bed, now. I think I shall go to sleep now myself."

With that, Simon had to be content, and what impression he had made he was not sure. He was tired the next day, and he had not only to endure being summoned to his lady peremptorily in the morning, ostensibly to take a letter, but in the afternoon his master arrived unexpectedly and openly. He looked at his wife and her footman, impeccably attired and accoutred to take an afternoon's drive, with sardonic amusement, his eyes gleaming.

"Spare me your footman," he said, "and take mine instead," he asked his wife, his voice indicating no choice.

"I do not wish to spare him to you," his wife answered, her irritation not well concealed. "His livery matches my coach, and I do not wish to change. He suits me."

"I daresay he does," said her husband, undisturbed.

"Nevertheless, you will spare him this afternoon, for I wish him. And you must wish to please me, my dear."

She shrugged her shoulders pettishly and said, "If you take Aston, I shall have no one. I will just stay at home."

"You will take my footman," he answered, "as I offered you, and continue your drive, not to wound me, I beseech you, my love," more than a hint of steel beneath his voice. With a little moue, that was not charming, she obeyed him then, with a flounce to her skirts as he offered her his hand to mount into his carriage.

Simon stood silent, his face schooled, through this exchange, waiting to learn what was wanted of him. His master took him up into the carriage beside him, and signified to his coachman to drive on.

"I did not believe that whisker you told me, Earl," he said, his eyes not smiling, "Did you think I would?"

"I did not know," Simon said frankly. He had learned long ago, painfully, not to attempt directly to dissemble with this particular man.

"You told me you had no feelings for enjoyment. Do you fear nothing, either?" his master said, his lips smiling slightly, not pleasantly, his eyes unsmiling.

"I fear many things," Simon said. "I fear death, and I fear pain, and I fear your floggings and your punishments. And you know that I do, sir."

"Do I?" his master murmured. "I had thought you had perhaps forgotten such lessons."

"No, sir," Simon said.

"Did my—ah—my intimacies with you and my conversations lead you to think you might now presume with me?"

"No, sir," Simon said, his head lowered. He felt the

short riding crop his master held under his chin, forcing his eyes up, but his master saw sufficient fear in them there to satisfy him.

"It would indeed have been unwise." He continued to study Simon's face and his eyes, that he did not dare shield under his lashes. "I find no roguishness in you now. How is that?"

"I do indeed fear you," Simon said, "and your whip, and all things you do."

"But you did not, last night?"

Simon was silent, there being nothing to say.

"Do you mean my manner was such as to encourage familiarity? I will be answered, Aston," he said, no amusement in his voice as Simon continued silent.

"I do not know what to say," Simon said, his voice constricted by the crop pressing under his chin.

"You will say the truth, Aston, at all times to me. I know when you do not. Have you made carnal love to my wife this morning?"

"Yes, sir," Simon replied.

"You dare say this to my face?"

"No, sir," Simon replied, and felt his face slapped.

"How then?"

"You have required me not to lie, and you have asked me," Simon said, and felt his face slapped again.

"Impudence," his master said. "I have also required of you discretion, which should also be practised with me. Was it at your desire or at hers?"

"It was not my desire, sir," Simon answered. "I was tired, as you well know." He shut his eyes now, desperation unguarding his tongue, and waited for the blow that did not come. After a moment he opened his eyes to find his master regarding him curiously.

"You are a strange fellow," his master said, lowering the crop, his voice less harsh, but his face and his eyes still stern and watchful. "And you are quite right. I have from time to time encouraged you to be familiar, when it amused me. And I am not fair now, but I do not have to be fair. You will never forget that, Aston."

"No, sir," Simon said.

"Or I shall teach you all over again to remember it."

"Yes, sir," Simon said.

"Yes, you would like me to?"

"Yes, I will not forget, sir." He ventured a quick look upward.

"Do not, Aston," his master said, his unrelaxed gaze meeting that look. "And now, bearing all this in mind, you will tell me, Aston, why it came about that not on your own word having forgotten any lessons I have taught you you yet lied to me last night, most deliberately, not only lying, but volunteering in that lie a statement I had not even asked for. If you say you do not know what I mean, Aston, I shall have the coach stopped now and direct you to be whipped for the new lie."

"It is possible I lied many times to you last night," Simon said. "It is possible I truly do not know which lie I was caught out in." He watched helplessly as his master leaned out of the coach window and ordered the coachman to pull up.

"You may take it you were caught out in all. The one I chose to take up concerns your self-confessed smuggling activities. Have you ever smuggled, Aston?"

"You will have to whip me, sir," Simon said, his lips white. "I do not know what you want of me."

"Then I shall make it clear, Earl," his master said, "and think carefully, for the wrong answer may be your last. You have somehow learned that I am interested in the art of smuggling. I cannot see how, and I would like to know. I am not willing to believe that you made your surprising confession last night at random."

"No, sir," Simon said slowly, his eyes raised fearfully but limpidly and trustingly to his master's face, in the gaze he had used to effect years ago on his nurse, the marks on his cheeks livid.

"You did know, then, what you were about."

"No, sir," Simon said, his voice very low. He waited for the blow, and received it, wincing.

"Take care, Aston," his master said.

"I did *not* know what I was about," he said, his voice blurred. "I did not wish to displease you."

His master paused to digest this, and to Simon's surprise, accepted it.

"How did you learn of my interest?" he asked, taking another tack. "Who told you?"

"I guessed, sir," Simon said, raising his eyes. "From the brandy your wife gave me. I know French brandy, sir. I used to drink it."

"By God, Earl," his master said, his face relaxing slightly. "I think I do believe you."

"I hope so, sir," Simon said. "It is the truth."

"My wife gave you my brandy?" his master asked, slowly, incredulity and surprise mixed in his voice. "When was this, and why?"

"While you were gone, sir," Simon muttered, letting himself blush.

"As a reward?"

"No, sir, a bribe," he said, almost inaudibly, waiting for the matching blow.

"Speak up, man, so I can hear you. She gave you my choice brandy for *what?*"

"For a bribe, sir," Simon said clearly and truthfully.

"And you took it?"

"Yes, sir." His master began to laugh, strongly and unexpectedly, Simon never knowing when he would enrage or amuse his master by his frank dealings. When he could control himself, he wiped his eyes, and leaned out and directed his coachman to start the coach, giving him a new direction.

"You do amuse me, Earl," he said, bringing his head in again. "It is well you do. I am going to gratify you now, since I could not before, in return for your patience with me, and take you smuggling again."

"I lied to you in that too, sir," Simon said, his face entirely white. "I know nothing of smuggling. I have never been in Sussex, or seen it done."

"How noble," his master murmured, his eyes gleaming, "this unasked confession."

"No, sir," Simon said. "If you take me, you will find me out."

"Should you not have known earlier?"

"Yes, sir. I am sorry, sir." He raised his eyes pleadingly, looking younger than his years, truthfully pleading, his skin shrinking inside his livery at the look in his master's face. "I only wanted to go."

"Why, Earl?" his master said, his face relaxing slightly.

"I thought it would be fun, if you would take me," he said, his lashes falling and quickly rising, "and you asked me if I found nothing enjoyable. You know you did, sir?"

"Laying it on thick, Earl," his master observed, lying back against the squabs. He was smiling again, not unpleasantly this time. "So I did. Do not look at me like that, Earl. I am not going to hurt you. I had thought when I asked for you that after I had scared

you a little, I might take you with me and let you
have your smuggling. I am not entirely ungrateful,"
he added, "and it might amuse me too."

"What if I had answered wrong?" Simon said, his
face still pale.

"That would have been another story," his master
said, his voice smooth. "But I thought you would not.
You may take yourself outside now, Earl, to your
post." He unlatched the handle of the door, without
stopping the coach, let Simon out and watched him
run alongside the coach and swing himself up onto the
stand behind, with approval.

Simon watched the landscape pass before his eyes,
its beauties if they existed lost on his Northern eyes
which were repelled by its lushness, finding nothing
to hold his memory to in the sameness of the growth,
but glad to be free of the too-seeing eye of his master
and to be able to look about him unobserved. He
managed to establish his directions and assure himself
that since the coach had swung around they were going North. At midday they stopped for lunch, and
James took out his travelling equipment and set up a
fire, and brought out food he must have prepared
early in the morning, that Simon found very good
when he and the other servants were allowed at the
leavings. His master ignored him completely, and he
was glad of that. Left alone, in the soft air, he recovered some of his courage and some of his colour,
enough so that in the late afternoon, catching his master's eye on him, observing him consideringly, he
winked back at him. His gambit of scamp played off.
They made the secret harbour he had been told of after dark, travelling hard through the dusk, and leaving
the coach itself, to take to their horses, no landmarks
visible to Simon's eyes, and he thought perhaps his

master had planned it so, coming out on a headland to see the sea itself stretched out before them in the dark, the breakers rolling in beneath them. His master caused a small fire to be lit, which was presently answered by a small fire lit somewhere out in the darkness at sea. His master made several passes before it, which were answered by the winking distant light. He then came and stood silently beside Simon in the dark, the night wind rising and blowing about them, and after a moment he put his arm about his shoulder.

"Are you having what you want, now?" he asked.

"I do not know what I am having," Simon replied candidly.

"Wait and you will see," his master replied, and removed his arm and moved away. He lit his pipe at the fire, and sat down on the edge of the cliff, and turned back towards Simon and beckoned to him to come beside him.

"How long before they are here?" Simon asked, sitting down. He could have pushed his master over the cliff, he thought, but he had no temptation to do it. It would not serve. He poked idly in the ground with a stick, wondering why he had been called over.

"About an hour, Earl, all told," his master said. "We will shortly start down the cliff to meet them, and receive our goods. Are you enjoying yourself?"

"Very much," Simon said.

"Good," his master observed. "You will perhaps not mind my enjoying myself too."

"Now?" Simon said, shocked. "Here?"

"It is quite dark," his master said. "But you may leave your clothes on, if you like." He unbuttoned the coat of Simon's livery, and slipped his hands under it, against the thin material of his livery shirt, and bringing him slightly forward, took his lips in his and caressed them gently, almost impersonally.

"Still cold, Earl?" his master murmured, after a few moments more of this. "You will learn better, I think, another time." He took Simon's hand, and stood up with him, still holding his hand closely in his, gave it a small squeeze, and dropped it, saying, "Now we ride!"

And ride they did, picking their way down the cliff trail in the dark, the horses knowing their way and leading their riders. The push of oars could be heard now, and as they approached the shingle themselves, the boat touched ground, and was pulled up by figures jumping from it to the sand.

"You will stay back here," his master said to Simon, "and wait."

"But may I not go too!" cried Simon, letting the high excitement he was feeling show.

"No, my pet, you may not," his master said. "You will stand here and watch, as I have said." He smiled at Simon's impatience, and flicked his cheek with a finger. "Hold this for me," he said, and was gone.

There was very little Simon could see in the dark, waiting by the cliff path. Lanterns, low voices, figures moving on the shingle, and then from somewhere to his left, ponies brought out and casks loaded onto their backs, he thought they were casks, and roped and netted bundles. He was left with nothing to hold, except his excitement, and then with a shock, he understood it was that which his master had meant, his nerves tingling in uneasy response. Then he forgot what that must mean, and his excitement returned as he watched the little ponies pass him in the dark, picking their way up the cliff path, and men he had not seen before walking beside them, paying no attention to him where he stood in the dark night, in the darkness of the shadows. The boat was pushing off now, the lanterns dowsed, and there was nothing but the dark silent night again about him, and the swaying of the damp trees behind him in the night wind, the plash of the oars retreating silently, an unshod hoof knocking against a pebble, dislodging it. His master came up beside him and took his hand.

"I have sent James and the other footman ahead to the carriage," he said. "There is no hurry for us to return. Walk with me, Simon, a little way, and I will show you where the ponies were kept. Would you like to see?"

"Yes," Simon said, his pulses racing with an excitement in no way sexual. His master laughed softly, his own pulses beating against Simon's fingers. Their feet sank in and out of the damp springing sand, as they rounded the edge of the little cove and entered another. Here the shore was rockier, and picking their way through the rocks, his Master led the way to a cave backed up into the rock of the cliff.

"A smugglers' cave!" Simon exclaimed. "There is always one! Do you pick the harbour for the cave?"

"Partly," his master said. "There were other reasons, equally good. But the cave was important."

"Why for you?" Simon asked. "I would think here no one would come."

"But they do now. The sea is full of English warships, Earl, looking for French ships of any size, and any contraband."

"What would happen, if you were caught, sir?" Simon asked.

"I? Not very much. A fine, that is all. But I would lose my brandy, Earl, and my smugglers might be taken and their boat. That would inconvenience me very much. The land is mine, but the shingle, of course, is not, where the sea comes. The law would have to find me by sea, or on the shingle. So I keep the ponies in my cove, until I am ready to have them climb the cliff. There is a damned fool Methody of a priest now here hot with his Wesley's ideas from England now, and having stopped the smugglers on the Cornwall coast, or so he thinks he has, he thinks he will stop me. How he has gotten wind of my dealings I do not know, for I doubt he drinks brandy with my wife, but someway I think he has. He came walking here up the shingle all the way October last, and he was very polite when he met me. I walked him a way back along the shingle, and near the house, I asked him to come in, which he did, looking all about him with his curious eyes, and expounding to me on the law and the church until I had the carriage brought round to take him off. He would have wanted to have me come to his services, but I promised him we were already well-supplied in his line, myself and my wife. Then he was wanting to speak to the 'others' on the plantation as he put it—bedamned but he told me he was once in the trade himself until he saw the light, or got grace, or some such high words—I told him flatly I was having no such truck between him and my place, and would discipline anyone caught with him of mine on or off my place. He would enjoy embarrassing me, I think, but he will be hard put to catch me, and if he does, I should not like to stand in his collar, if he is alone when he does."

They had reached the little cave, which seemed hardly more than a windbreak carved into the cliff.

"Is this all?" Simon asked, peering around him in the dim rays of his master's lantern.

"No, it is the false cave. Go to the wall to your

right, and you will find the real cave begins. The ponies stay here. At high tide the water is waist high, and at Spring sometimes higher, in the passage beyond this first room, but it will serve should I need it. Does this interest you, Aston?"

"Yes," he said, looking about him in the dim lantern light. "I told you I liked smuggling. The fire is still going."

"I kept it for us," his master said, taking off his cloak, and putting it on the floor of the cave, by some blankets. "I also left a bottle of the brandy, Aston, remembering you like it. Shall I pour you a glass?"

"If you wish, sir," Simon said.

"I do wish," his master said. "I wish very much." He was silent for a few moments, working with the cork, and then he poured the brandy into two glasses, on a rock ledge where the bottle had stood, and handed one to Simon, keeping one for himself. He stood leaning against the rock, watching Simon drink, sipping slowly himself, and when Simon's glass was half-empty, he crossed to him and refilled it. When Simon half-protested, he shook his head and said, "I wish you to have it. You will drink it to oblige me."

"I shall become drunk," Simon said. "Too drunk to ride a horse, and what will we do about returning."

"Let me worry," his master said, "you will drink the brandy please."

"I think you plan to seduce me," Simon murmured, sipping the brandy slowly under his master's stare. "I can think of no other reason."

"Can you not?" his master asked, his eyes on him, and refilling Simon's glass again and his own. "You have nerve, Aston. Can you not think of other things I might do to you here, where we are quite alone?"

Simon shook his head, and as the hand tipped the

glass, continued to sip the brandy. "No," he said. "There is nothing you cannot do more easily any place and any time you choose nearer home. I wondered myself whether you would come here alone with me, but then I reasoned you knew you had nothing to fear from me."

"No," his master agreed, "I hardly think so. You have rather more to fear from me, I think. I think you have considerable nerve, Earl. What would you do, what could you do, if I came over to you now, as you are expecting me to do, to kiss you, perhaps, for a beginning . . ." as he spoke, he had walked over by Simon, and put his hand against his face, holding it lightly with one hand—"you *are* expecting this, are you not, Aston?—and then, as I kiss you, so," he said, brushing Simon's lips lightly with his, "instead of continuing as you expect, what if I slip my hands down to your throat and press it, so, very carefully, and very gently at first, so that you are surprised, and do not try to struggle, thinking I am joking, but I am not, you see, Aston, I am not at all, for you are really choking now, and yet with the brandy, and the rock behind you, there is very little you can do to stop me, is there, Aston?"

Blinded by the lantern on the ledge near him, and the face looming so close to him, the gentle voice meandering on, Simon hardly struggled at all against the fingers cutting off his breath, partly because they were pressing not only the thumbs against his throat and his windpipe in front, but pressing gently and curiously at the back of his head behind his ears so that even as he was choking, and knew he was, he was also drifting into sleep.

"Are you thinking I am mad, Aston, if you can think at all, or that I was angrier with you about many things than I chose to let you know?"—the voice drifted away from him, and the lips he felt taking his, as he wondered if he was dying, unable to believe it was happening to him, so quickly, and despite the choking, so painlessly. He awoke an indeterminate time later, lying on the floor of the cave, on the blankets which had been arranged, the cloak over him, his throat bruised and sore, and his lips also. He felt sick and slightly dizzy, which he thought must be the effect of the brandy he had been made to drink. His clothes had been taken from him entirely while he had not known it, and he knew that he had been used, and roughly, while he was not awake. He groaned slightly, and moved on the rough blankets, and found his master beside him also lying under the cloak.

"Why did you do that to me?" he asked, his breath still gasping. "Did it give you pleasure, to hurt me?"

"Yes," his master said, "partly, and you are undressed now, Earl, and comfortable, and we are ready to begin."

"Oh my God," Simon said softly, dizzily, "oh God help me. Have you not already done enough?"

"No," his master said softly. "Will you need more brandy to get through it?"

"Yes," Simon said dizzily, "please," taking the glass, drinking it slowly, delaying the moment. The glass was taken from his hand, when he delayed, and he looked about him desperately, at the embers of the fire winking at him like little eyes, and the mouth of the cave behind him, and no one and nothing anywhere to help him.

"You are going to feel now," his master whispered, "I promise it, Earl. And the sooner you do, the sooner we will start back."

"Oh, God help me," whispered Simon, "I am afraid

of what will happen to me if I do." (What will you do to me when you have had all you can get, he thought. Oh, please, do not make me.) He felt the other man at him now, skilful on all points, and he shivered suddenly, with the youthful memories rushing in on him, flooding him, and the effects of the strange choking and the brandy and the manipulations being made on him. Part of the years fell away from him, leaving him exposed and vulnerable. He shut his eyes and the forgotten warmth flooding through him, at that touch, forgetting his danger, he put his own hands to the face of his master, his fingers resting lightly there, and then behind his neck, pressing his master's lips harder into his.

"Earl, Earl," he heard his master's voice saying with amusement, "you forget yourself!"

He dropped his hands, and remained passive then, while his master amused himself, until the intensity of his reaction shook him and overwhelmed him, and he turned and gave himself freely and entirely to the man who had had him beaten and kept in chains. His mature hardness deserted him, and he was left weak and helpless in the force of the brandy and the hands of the man governing him, frightened by the feelings evoked in him, lying quietly finally in the arms holding him still, more seventeen than twenty-seven, the candle long since burned out and darkness about them except for the embers of the fire. His master was gently stroking his hair then, back from his forehead, sweetness enveloping him at the unaccustomed gentle touch.

"You see," his master's voice said, "I *have* taken my revenge, after all, have I not? It pleased you, God knows why, to make my silly wife a little in love with you, and now I have made you a little in love with me. It is ironic, is it not?" His hands gently caressing Simon's hair and face softened the harshness of his words. "Is it not so?"

"Perhaps," Simon said. "You will know. I do not."

"I do know," his master said. "We will return now, and you will return to my wife, and we will see what will happen."

He pulled the cloak back from himself, relit the lantern, and dressed himself, Simon silently following suit. His master stubbed out the last dying embers of the fire, and kicked them apart, and then signed to Simon to follow him, in the night that was still dark though Simon knew dawn had to be near, up the cliff edge on their horses, and back to the coach, to rouse the sleeping coachman and footmen. Simon was left to cling sleepily to his perch at the rear of the coach, as best he could, without a word given him. It seemed to him a fitting punishment for the scene he had enacted, but he was too weary all over to think much about it. They had driven a considerable distance of the way from the hidden harbour before the grey light of dawn appeared.

What became of the ponies and their load Simon did not know. The coach drove straight along the road, that his master maintained well with his forced labour and at one time had tried to maintain with Simon's, without pausing. The man inside alighted at the house, when they arrived in the afternoon, and went in with his footman James, leaving Simon and the other footman to stand at their posts. In a short time he reappeared, reentered the coach, without a glance at anyone or anything, and had it sent bowling again in the direction of the harbour. A few yards from the house, however, the coach turned off the road, and followed a smaller path, into a thicket, and through the thicket into a glade where the ponies were tethered, contentedly grazing, and the men who had led them were engaged in carrying the barrels from the ponies' backs into a kind of storm cellar whose door of laths and turf lay open. Simon watched, his weariness lifting in his interest, while a barrel was broken open and several of the bottles carefully nested in straw inside it were brought out and as carefully stowed in the boot of the carriage. He looked up, to find his master had approached him and was standing near him, studying him. He was cast into sudden confusion, to his horror, blushed fiercely, his ears and his cheeks hot with the rush of blood, and he did not know where to look, under those steady, bright, amused eyes that seemed to see straight through him. He felt again the curious sensation of the years' stripping from him, and standing, a thin young awkward adolescent, inside his browned hulking man's body.

"Earl, Earl!" the man who owned him exclaimed with delight, "you betray yourself. Take care!" He reached up his hand to Simon, for him to take, and to dismount by. "If he puts his hands on me here," Simon thought in surprise to himself, "under the eyes of these men, I shall kill him, whatever they do to me. God help me, I shall." His anger caused his colour to recede, and his eyes to glitter, and the embarrassed youth looking out through his eyes disappeared. His master must have seen the change, for he laughed slightly, withdrew his hand, and said lightly, "Much better, Aston. Much more the thing. Shall we go a-smuggling again?"

Simon struggled within himself, his hesitation deepening the amusement in his master's eyes.

"Come!" he said. "I will not command you. I entreat you. Will you walk with me and see how I store and convey my barrels into my dining room? You have by no means seen all I can show you. Come! We will eat first, and then we will see." He held out his hand, and curiosity overcoming shame and anger, Simon took it and let his master lead him to the fire that was burning and the dinner that had been laid out, and seated Simon beside him. He laid aside all pretence now, ignoring his other servants and his other slaves, and taking a piece of meat in his mouth, offered it to Simon to take.

"God's love," Simon whispered, "you embarrass me. To what end?"

"Take it, Earl," his master murmured. "I wish it."

Simon leaned forward, opened his lips, and bit the meat off delicately from his master's lips, his cheeks crimsoning again under his bronzed skin, his heart beating hard enough to choke him, wondering what limits his master had and if he would use him in daylight in front of his fellow slaves. But having submitted, he was let to finish his meal by his master's side in what peace he could maintain, while the life of the smuggling camp went on about them in the dim green air of the wood, and men came and went, asking and receiving orders. After the meal, the work finished, and the men disbanding, the ponies being led to pastures elsewhere, his master led Simon to the entrance to the cellar, a square door and steps leading down into the ground. His master took a lantern remaining on the first step, pointed to Simon to precede him, and joined him at the bottom of the steps. They were in a fairly large room that was partly full of barrels and boxes, but by no means so many as had come on the ponies. Simon looked at his master inquiringly, and took a step backwards at what he saw in his face.

"Do not hurt me," he whispered. "I will do what you like. Only do not hurt me. And do not let it be seen."

"Follow me then," his master said, taking his cold nerveless fingers in his hand, touching them lightly to his lips. "This way will lead under the ground, into the house, into the cellars there underground and into my room." Despite his fright, Simon looked about him with intense interest, and at the men who passed them, carrying the boxes and barrels on their shoulders, at the various doors they went through.

"Where does that lead?" he asked, pressing his master's hand.

"Into the kitchen."

"And that?"

"Into the store rooms off the kitchen."

"Are you not afraid that the men will misuse this knowledge?" Simon asked, his voice lowered in the dark tunnel they were traversing.

"No more than that you will," his master said, his voice smiling in the dark. "To what end, as you say. A few have tried. It led them nowhere, Aston, nowhere that they liked. These doors are also locked, and James keeps the keys for me, and is my steward."

"Are they hard to find, from the inside?"

"Yes, Aston, but I will show you, if you like."

"No," Simon said, "I would rather not. Someone might see me."

"You should not care. Your place with me protects you, Aston. It is not a thing to be ashamed of. For me to use you, perhaps. To love you, no."

"You cannot love me, sir," Simon said, his voice frightened and low.

"But I do, Aston, in so far as I am capable of that

word. With me it is not lasting, and you may yourself not call what I feel love. Can you love, Aston?"

"No," Simon said frankly, daring, "no, I think I cannot. If ever I did, which I doubt, not now, and not as I am now."

"Then why," his master said, very close to him, "if that is so, do you blush now to see me, like a young girl, when you did not before?" He did not wait for an answer, but opened the door by which Simon was standing, revealing an empty hall somewhere in the interior of the lower parts of the house. "You see, I reveal my secrets to you, Aston."

"And in return?" Simon said.

"In return, of course I want yours." He took Simon's face in his, and kissed it tenderly, pressing his lips against the younger man's immobile and reluctant ones. "But I shall make it easy for you again, Aston," he said. He selected a bottle from several resting in a rack by the wall, took out his knife and opened it, paring away the wrapping and the cork, drank a little himself, and handed it to Simon.

"Drink," he said, holding the bottle to Simon's mouth, tilting it. "You will not refuse me, Aston. I wish it." Simon took the swallow poured into his mouth, choked on it, tried to push the bottle away, and found it hard against his mouth, as his uncle had once done to him. His throat constricted in panic at the memory, and he choked and strangled again over the liquid pouring into his throat, and reached out his hands to push the bottle away. The brandy seemed very strong to him, in his tired state, and he dared not struggle, when he felt his master's lips again on his. He heard with relief the sound of feet coming down the passage, men with more barrels, he thought gratefully. His wrist was taken and he was half-pulled half-led to a stair leading upwards, several floors, his feet like lead mounting the steps one by one, until the man taking him into hell again put a key into the lock of a door, turned it, pressing it back and forth, and swung a door open into an ordinary room such as he might have lived in once, full of sunlight. He gasped, and blinked, and stood wavering in the threshold, while his master strode quickly across the room to the opposite doors and locked them, and back to the panelled passageway entrance and closed and locked it, the lines where the door had been disappearing into the molding.

"It is here," his master said, showing him how to move and press the molding, "but inside, the second door opens only with my key. Drink now, Aston," he said. He poured a glass full of the liquid from the same bottle, and handed it to Simon, watching him closely while he drank. The sunlight fell through the windows, sparkling through the crystal of the glass and the amber in it, as though making the nightmare impossible that was happening to him all the same, Simon thought. His glass was refilled, and refilled again, his master sipping slowly and thoughtfully. When the bottle was entirely empty, he took Simon's glass from him, and as before, put his hands to Simon's throat, caressing it lightly, the fingers feeling again behind his ears, pressing at the base of his neck.

"You said you would not hurt me," Simon whispered, standing still in those hands, frightened, unable to move.

"And I will not," his master said.

"I do not like this," Simon whispered, protesting faintly.

"Hush," his master said, "Hush, now." He put his lips against Simon's, his fingers tightening, the stroking pressures deepening, as before. He could not breathe, and the fingers did hurt this time. He found himself fighting for breath, fighting the hands that were pressing deeper into him. He could not cry out, and the pain was worse, and then he could not move, forced back against the sharp edge of something, and the fingers seeking and probing found their mark and the pain lessened, and he was floating somewhere away. He awoke as he had before, naked and violated, stretched out on the bed, what once would have been the end, and now was the beginning only. He sobbed and coughed, returning to consciousness painfully, his throat bruised and constricted.

"You hurt me," he whispered, his breath coming in panting sobs. "I told you you did not have to hurt me." He ached all over, and the brandy seemed to have had this time no effect on him, except to make him feel sick. He struggled to sit up, and, a hand supporting his aching head, was made to drink something different, and then, as he continued to struggle, he felt hands again at his throat. He collapsed, moaning slightly, as the hands tormented him, and then released him when he lay quiet. The second different burning drink began to have its effect on him, combining itself with the first, and taking away some of his tiredness and much of the pain. He lay back, relaxed now, his limbs too stripped to move, opening his eyes to look at the man beside him, and then shutting them. He was moved slight in the bed, his knees bent, a pillow pushed under the small of his back, arching and lifting him. His master then proceeded to play with him, with coins flattening his eyelids, the flat of a knife run up and down his darkened thighs, the point touching his ribs, flattening his tongue, the rounded haft thrust up him from below, his erection taken from him, re-

created, taken, a heavy weight laid upon his stomach
and pressed hard. He lay still, weeping soundlessly, as
the indignities were done him, and then the toys and
objects were removed from him, and his feet and pel-
vis let down, and there were only his master's human
lips pressing him. He sighed in relief and gratitude,
and kissed them back, and folded his arms about the
human form. When his master had quite finished with
him, he took a diamond pendant from his dresser, that
he himself sometimes wore, and put it about Simon's
neck, fastening it, the stone lying small and cold on
his breast.

"Wear this," his master said, "for me. Will you, Aston?"

"Yes," Simon said faintly, "if you wish it, sir."

"It is the mark of my favourites," his master said. "I
do not give it lightly, Earl. Do not ever take it from
you."

"Why me?" Simon said faintly, the little stone
pressing heavier, the slender threads of gold holding it
burning his neck like heavy iron.

"Because I love you, Earl," his master said, "and because the courts convene tomorrow, and I must go to
town to sit on them."

"You are also the general law?" Simon asked.

"I am," his master said.

"I wish you would take me with you," Simon murmured.

"I cannot," his master said, unclasping his arms. "I
will take you back now to my carriage, and we will
return home the usual way."

"When do we go a-smuggling again?" Simon asked,
presuming and daring to presume in his lightheaded-
ness.

"That is one secret I do *not* tell you," his master said, not offended.

"If you are the general law," Simon said, "I see now why you know you would suffer only a small fine. Can you not smuggle as often then as you like?"

"No, my dear," his master said. "There is not only the civil law, but the military law, and that at sea I cannot control. Must it be smuggling, scamp? Will nothing less content you?" He took Simon's clothes then, his wife's livery, looking at it thoughtfully, and handed it to Simon.

"Am I to wear these still?" Simon asked, making no motion to take the clothes.

"I am a man for domestic peace, Earl," his master said. "You will wear them for a while yet. Do not anger my wife, Earl, while I am gone. We like to take each other's pleasures, Earl. You will dress now, and then help me to dress."

When Simon's fumbling drugged fingers had accomplished this, he led him down the stairs, Simon's brain reeling like his feet, his master chuckling slightly and steadying him with his hand, and down the long passage under the lawn across to the thicket, the tree roots pushing through the roof and weaving overhead, and then up into the glade. Before he pushed the door open again, he took Simon's shoulders in his hands and pressed Simon's lips, unresponsive again.

"Cold, Earl, ice again?" he whispered. "You are wise. I like that in you, Earl, and I think you know it."

Simon shivered under his hands, not fighting or resisting him, and his master laughed, and touched the diamond where it lay below his throat, through his shirt, and released him reluctantly, and opened the slanting cellar door. The way to the carriage seemed long to Simon, and he looked at the footman's stand with tired apprehensive eyes, wondering if he could hold to it and what would happen to him if he could not. But when the footman who had remained with the carriage opened the door, his face impassive, and his master indicated he should get in, he wished for the footman's stand. He managed to pull himself up and into the carriage without assistance, his strength quite gone out of him, too tired to wonder about it. His master sat down on the seat beside him, and brought Simon's head against his shoulder, onto his breast, as though he had been a child, his chin resting against Simon's hair, and held him closely to him. The coach lumbered its way in the darkness, well sprung, but hitting fallen sticks and rocks the one footman could not always see in the dark to run before and remove. The hands holding Simon were strong, and firm, holding him from the jolting, and the arms kind and warm. Languor stole over him, and a curious peace, and the sudden desire to relax always, not just now, but always, and let this man care for him in his own strange ways. The hands were gentling him now, as if he were an infant or a colt or a dog, the long fingers weaving in and out of his hair making it into elflocks, pushing them back for the dry cool lips to touch his forehead. He raised his head then and his eyes met his master's, quietly looking at him, quietly appraising, and he lifted his lips a little as those lips bent to meet his, and kissed them without passion, briefly. He withdrew his lips then, even as his master did, his head resting against that shoulder, his eyes fixed on that face.

"Do you love me, Aston?" his master asked, the words falling quietly into the darkening coach.

"Yes," Simon said. "Yes, I do."

"I thought perhaps you did," his master said quietly. "I think I should not have, had you not. I wonder that you do."

"I wonder too," Simon said, "but I do."

"It is not, I think, quite the way that I love you."

"No," Simon said. He was conscious of a wish, very strong, very sudden, to give this strange older man his name, and to end the use of a name he had never had, but a last reserve held him, and saved him from that, and instead, without speaking, he lifted his head again a little upwards, and met his master's lips with his own. He did not break the caress, nor did his master, until a jolt in the road broke it for them. And then he put his head back very quietly on his master's breast, and felt his master's hand against the side of his face, holding him gently to him.

"How strange," he thought tiredly, "that we should love those who hurt us and use us to our harm." He turned his face a little, his lips into the hands against his face.

"Shall I stop the carriage?" his master asked.

"Yes," Simon said. He was removed a little from his place of quiet, while his master leaned out of the window and directed the carriage to halt. The mood left him, though, while they were walking away from the carriage, a little way into the woods. It returned slightly when his master unfastened just his easement and Simon's, and let their full selves brush against one another, as they stood, very close now, their lips just touching. But when he had to disrobe more completely and position himself, the mood left him entirely, and he thought himself mad. The drugs were beginning to leave him, and his senses clearing, and he knelt on the ground, feeling like a fool, the sticks and pebbles piercing his hands through the cloak his master had spread, waiting for what he knew would be bad, and that was worse than he thought for, writhing slightly, the tears pricking behind his eyelids, but above all bored and ashamed. He stood up quickly when he was allowed to, nothing left of his own desire, and pulled up his breeches, his face averted.

"You did not like this, after all," his master observed.

"No," Simon said, his face averted, his voice low and flat.

"No, what?"

"No, sir, I still do not."

"But you thought you might."

"I suppose so," Simon said miserably.

"It is a start," his master observed. "Had I not asked, I would have had you, I think?"

"Perhaps," Simon said. "I do not know. You have done this to me so many times," he added bitterly, "entirely against my will, I do not see why you should care now whether I like it or not."

He felt light fingers in the dark touch the chain about his neck, and then they were gone, like a whisper, in the dark, the little chain still about his neck, weighing heavier.

"Well," his master said. "We will go back and go home now. You may stand outside now."

It was late. No one was about, except the keepers of the gates and the doors. His mistress was asleep. Simon left his master, taking the hand given him to kiss briefly in his and, under the ironic gaze directed on him, bending his head over it, briefly, and went to his bed in the small room his mistress had given him, so that he might come out to her unobserved. "I will feel better tomorrow," he thought, "and then I will think about these things."

Chapter 14

IN THE morning, though, he had no chance to think about anything. The rap on his door awakened him, as it had every morning since his residence in the house, when he was in his own bed, for him to rise and wash and dress himself, to be ready for whatever calls were made on him. He answered the bell to his lady's room, imperiously rung, bringing with him her morning chocolate, as he had found she liked him to do. It was not the chocolate she wanted this morning. She knew he was back, she had been told by her first morning maid that the master was returned, and it was something besides chocolate she wanted.

He locked the door at her command, and went behind the screen to put on the dressing gown she kept hidden in her closet, though no secret to anyone, and came out to her and over to the bed where she lay lost in a sea of white frothing ruffles, with a reluc-

161

tance he had for some weeks put aside and which she had forgotten he had ever had. "I am not going to get through this," he thought, "I have had too much," and he did not.

She lay, the froth pushed aside, like a nymph exposed on foam, smiling at him, her arms outstretched, and his answering smile was like a leaden sky, as he tried to meet the enthusiasm of her greeting.

"Oh, Aston," she cried, enfolding him to her, "I have missed you so. My most cruel husband to take you from me! Have you missed me as I have missed you?"

Try as he would, he could accomplish nothing satisfactory.

"I am very tired, Madonna," he said finally, apologetically. "I have not slept all night, with the travelling. I am sorry, I think even the rods cannot effect it, but you may try if you like."

"You need the rods!" she exclaimed. "When you have been away from me a week, is it not! It is not I who will use the rods, Aston, but the ropeman on you."

"I cannot stop you, my lady," he said tiredly. "I am sorry. I am very tired."

Her fingers that had a moment before been twined lovingly about his neck felt now at his throat, and he knew now what they looked for. But he had thought to remove the little chain from his neck, before he came to her.

"Aston," she said, "is it my husband who has made you so tired? You did not use to tire so easily, when you worked the horses and took those women. Is it my husband?"

He hesitated, not knowing what to say, and she interpreted his silence correctly. She let fly a string of imprecations on the head of that absent person, explicit and exact, but her anger against Simon subsided. "For him to take you from me and to mistreat you, Aston," she said, "it is too cruel!" She continued to caress him a moment longer, and then she excused him, to sleep, she said, and rest, and make himself strong. He smiled at her weakly and unhappily, the situation he had led himself into with its complexities he had not anticipated near to overwhelming him. He wanted to be entirely by himself, but he could not expect that. He slept for an hour, and then my lady had to have him to drive her across the way to take tea. He pulled himself together, pulling on his coat, fastening his lace, and made the required effort, falling asleep on the footman's stand while she took tea. He was expected to make light dalliance in the carriage with her, on the way home, with talk and flirtation, but it was beyond him. The heavy silence he had lived in for years was sweeping over him again. If they would only leave him alone, he thought desperately. Service he could manage for them both, if they wanted that, if they would only leave him otherwise alone and not probe into his spirit, such as it was, and into his feelings, which he did not want to have. It was his fault, he thought, for speaking, and playing with them at all, but he had known no other way to break out of the empty ignorance he had been kept in. He had indeed broken out of it, now, he thought wretchedly. He followed my lady up the hall, his eyes blank, and into her room, at her desire. He exerted himself this time, seeing no reason why he should not succeed, but his essay was no pleasure to her, and her tender mood turned shrewish. She took the rods to him, forming an erection in him, but he could not hold it.

"My lady," he said, his voice flat and without charm, "if you will but wait—"

"If you wanted me," she flamed, "with your mind, you would want me *there*."

"No, my lady," he said, patiently, his voice very tired now, "it is not so." But the weeks in the house had removed him, particularly this past week, farther from the stud slave. What she had was the Earl in truth in her room, not the first effects that had charmed her, of his re-emergence. He was not aware of it himself; but her presence and her expectations were arousing in him a new disgust that his tepid efforts to be what she expected could not overcome. She looked at him uneasily, unsure, and then she laughed slightly, and sent him away.

"You are tired," she said, her own voice flat now, "as you said, this morning. Go and rest, if you must. But I have never known a man of your station to be tired."

He bit back the retort that rose to his lips, and redressed himself, while she watched him, her breath rising and falling rapidly, her eyes hard and slightly suspicious. He saw the look, and the danger it held, and went across to her and made himself take her in his arms and after a moment to put his mouth to hers. He kissed her eyes, and her eyebrows, and her throat, and then her mouth again, trying to blanken his mind, saying huskily, "Bear with me, Madonna." She was slightly mollified, and he felt her yielding in his arms, but the effort of undressing again and the uncertainty was more than he could undertake. He kissed her again quickly, and then her hand, and went quickly to the door where he took the leave she had granted him previously.

He did not see Alyx in the hall, and had he noticed

her, he would not have known her. Her hair was strained back, and unwashed, tied unbecomingly with a knot at the back of her head, and her stuff dress was a dull mousy colour, the tucked-up apron she wore dingy and not white at its beginning. She had come for the slops, and was dressed accordingly, an empty bucket in one hand, a can of water in the other for the upstairs. But if Simon, coming from the room did not see her, and would not have known her, she did see him, and she did know him. Dressed in livery with a high collar and lace at his throat, the little cape falling over his shoulders, his head thrown a little up, though unsmiling, the tired lines dragging his features into hard patterns, she knew him at first glance. She stared, unbelieving, her eyes widening, and the child stirred in her womb, turning. The empty can in her left hand dropped unheeded with a clatter to the floor. He looked at her then, wide eyed and staring at him, and he still did not know her. She was clutching the can of water in both hands now, that were shaking so the water was spilling over the edge, and then as he turned away, she whispered his name, "Simon," and he saw she was swaying and about to faint.

He knew her then, of course, for there was no one else to know his name. He turned back and caught her as she would have fallen, the hot water spilling over them both. He shut his eyes and knew the feel of her in his arms, and knowing the danger, he could not release her, but held her tightly against him.

"Alyx," he whispered, "Alyx!"

"Yes," she whispered, the tears streaming down her face. "Yes, it is I. Oh, Simon, Simon." She was clutching him now with her hands, running them over his face, and he bent and kissed her lips. He could not help himself, he found. He put his hands quickly then under her apron, against her belly that he felt faintly rounding, one hand now against her back.

"Yes," she whispered, "I am. Oh, Simon," she whispered half-crying.

"Alyx," he whispered, "pull yourself together, for God's sake," he said. "This is too dangerous, for you and for me," and then he saw to his shock she had actually fainted in his arms.

He put her quickly from him, onto the ground, aware of the opening door behind him, and looked in the water can to see if any water remained. He was shaking the drops on her face, when he felt a ringing slap to the side of his face, and saw his mistress standing beside him, her face contorted with fury. She must have rung for help, he thought, before she came out to him, for he heard feet approaching hurriedly. He wondered how much she had seen or heard, but it did not matter, he thought, for she knew who Alyx was. She had told him so. Nevertheless, he did essay, ignoring the two footmen who had come running, as she called again for help.

"Madonna," he said, "this girl fainted, in your hall—"

"You spoke to her, Aston," she snapped, her voice savage and quivering with rage. "You spoke to her, outside my door, and you *know* the rule! I know you know it!"

"Yes, Madonna," he said, his tired face whitening, "I know it. If you heard me I must have spoken. What would you have had me do? Let her fall and leave her on the floor?"

"Yes," she snapped, "I would!" The overseer was in the hall now, and two female servants, and she pointed to Simon with a long quivering finger. "Take this—this—stud of yours!" she screamed, her voice rising in fury. "He is not safe! He has broken the master's rule, he admits it, and has spoken to another servant in the house, to this female girl, and he *knows* he may not. Will you take him or will you *not?*" she cried to the overseer, her voice rising again to a scream. "Or shall I report you too?"

"I do not know what you would have me do, my lady," the overseer said uneasily. "My lord is not here."

"Do?" she repeated, her eyes blazing. She spoke very slowly then, as though for his benefit. "This man, this stud, has come upstairs in my hall and has spoken to one of my maids. I will have him whipped for it, and whipped now. I do not need my lord for this, I assure you. And I will see it myself done now. Do you not know your own business? I tell you he is dangerous, and yet you leave him standing in my hall before me."

"Should we not wait for milord to judge this? He is your footman, my lady, he may be in the hall," the overseer said uneasily. Simon stood there, looking far from dangerous, the livery hiding his muscle, his eyes fixed on the overseer pleading, ignoring Alyx, who the maids were trying now to revive.

My lady rounded on Simon and demanded flatly, "Did you speak to this maid or did you not speak to her, Aston?" Her voice using his name had no warmth in it. "Remember, I heard you."

"I spoke to her," Simon said dully.

"And you knew you had only to call me, to knock at my door, which you remember, you had just left, and I would have myself called for help. Did you not know this?"

"Yes," Simon said, "I knew." He looked at the overseer in despair, who had come over to him now, and had reached for his hands, to bind them with the strap he carried for such cases in his pocket.

"And have I not had you whipped before for less than this?" she cried.

"Yes, Madonna," he said. The little name stung her into further fury, and she lost control of herself entirely.

"You knew her!" she cried, her voice rising. "You lied to me, Aston, you lied to me, all the time."

"No," he said. "No, Madonna, God's truth, I did not." She stood before him, her hand raised, and then she slapped him. The footmen who had come caught his arms, and tears rolling down her cheeks with emotion, she slapped him several times more, with her open palm, the flat sound ringing out in the sudden silence, the footmen holding him rigid between them.

"You knew her," she whispered, "you knew her in the dark, and you know her now, and she knew you. It is not allowed, and you know it, and I will teach you to know it." She caught her breath, sobbing with rage, her dress loosened at the neck, opening too wide in the force of her emotion. Simon, watching her, his eyes narrowed in disgust, prayed silently, to what or to whom he did not think. "I know your excuses now," she said, "I see them. I see them very clear. You will not do service again to anyone, Aston Smith, for when I have had you whipped, I shall have you castrated, this night before I sleep. I shall watch it done, and this—this woman, shall watch it too."

Her face was livid with rage, the veins swollen and throbbing in it, and one had burst, darkening her cheek. He shut his eyes against the sight, swaying slightly in the hands of the footmen whose hands were laid on his arms. He did not dare look towards Alyx, afraid for her, afraid of what she might show on her young face, or say. He need not have been afraid, however, for she was lying quite still in the maidservant's arms, her eyes closed and her face still. She had heard all the voices, and what they said, and not seeing any way to help Simon, it seemed to her the best thing to do. Her pulse had gone quite away with shock and fright, and to the maid servant chafing her hands she did seem to be in a faint.

"You may do what you intend, Madonna," she heard Simon say, tiredly, "I cannot stop you, as you know very well. But you are punishing me wrongly for nothing I have done. I know what you think, and I know why you think it, Madonna, but what you think is not true."

She came very close to him, and motioned the footman back, and laid her hands on his bound ones. "Prove it me, then," she whispered. "When I have had you whipped, if you are my true knight, prove it to me, on my body, that I am wrong. I would be glad to be wrong, Aston. Or if you will prove it now, Aston, I will pardon you. I so want to be wrong."

He had only to smile at her, and he knew it, but he could not. He shook his head, and removed his bound hands from hers, detaching hers from his quietly. "I cannot, Madonna. I wish that I could. I cannot promise you now what I could not do earlier. If it was impossible then, it is twice so now. You have shamed me, Madonna, and I have not deserved it. But if you will wait a night, until tomorrow night, I will do then what I can."

"I saw how she looked at you," she whispered, asking for reassurance. "I saw. I saw it all."

"There was nothing to see, Madonna," he said. "I was myself not looking when I came from your room. The girl is pregnant, one can see that. I alarmed her, coming suddenly upon her, and she fainted. You make too much over this incident, Madonna. There is nothing to make."

"If she is pregnant," she said, her eyes narrowing, "she is pregnant by you."

"Perhaps," he said. "By one of the four. I do not know, Madonna. I have told you. Such things are done in the dark, and nothing is made over them. If it is so, it is my master to blame for this, not me, Madonna."

"Perhaps," she said, her eyes very narrow, "but she knew you, Aston. I saw her face. How could she know you?"

"You will know, Madonna," he said wearily, "I do not. I have been much at your service, in this house. She may have seen me anywhere."

She turned from him, suddenly weary herself, pulling her dress together and collecting herself. "It is after all the first time," she said, to the overseer. "I perhaps make too much of it. He is indeed my footman, one of my footmen, but you will whip my footman, Mr. Jarvis, for speaking to one of my maids, without my permission. Do it here, Mr. Jarvis, and quickly, and then let him go."

She sent one of the little maids to fetch her riding crop, and Jarvis had one footman make a back, and the other catch Simon's hands and stretch him across it, holding him. Alyx was sitting up now, her face white and wide-eyed.

"Oh, my lady," she said, her voice trembling, "please do not whip your gentleman because of me. Truly I did not mean to faint, and to annoy you and give the gentleman trouble. I am sick every morning. It was the slops, milady."

"Little minx," Simon thought appreciatively, ducking his head to hide the grin spreading over his mouth. She was worth it all, he thought suddenly, his spirit flooded with springtime. The overseer was asking his mistress how many cuts to give, and while they arranged it, he turned his head to one side and looked toward Alyx and winked. He saw the quick answering flash in her eyes, though she did not change expression, and then he turned his face away, and felt the whip cut his buttocks, where they had pulled his breeches down. "Well-done, Madonna," he thought, "if there is danger, make me ridiculous, in those eyes. But you are far out in this, we know too much, my Alyx and I."

His veins filled, and his weariness left him, thinking of Alyx. "I must love her," he thought. "I did not know it. I had forgotten." He put his head down on the footman's back, and let himself remember. Not the tired drab girl in the stuff dress watching him being punished, and incidentally at the same time forced into an erection, but the warm piquant voice speaking in the dark to him, and her sweet body his hands had had to go to, regardless of the danger. He had not seen her for weeks, and in his schemes he had somehow forgotten her, who alone was real. His whole being was filled with springtime like spring freshets, pouring through him, washing and cleansing. He felt he could move mountains and endure anything. He bit the coat on the back of the footman he had been pulled across, felt him jerk and cry ouch; the whip stopped, his hands were unstrapped and he was allowed to get up and pull his breeches up, hiding what had happened to him. He looked up and saw the maid's eyes on him, and he grinned hugely at them all, turned, knocked at his lady's door, which she had gone into and shut.

"Madonna," he said falling on one knee before his departing audience, "I implore your forgiveness!" The lilt was back in his voice, and the sparkle in his eyes. "Peccatus Sum," he said, beating his breast.

"Aston," she exclaimed, but not displeased, "you forget yourself! Hush, and get up! Hush now!" as he continued his litany, his eyes rolling up. She began to giggle, and she gave him her hand to rise.

"Are they gone?" he whispered.

"Yes," she said.

"Then let me come in, Madonna, and I will show you how truly sorry I am, and how glad I am, and you will be too, you did not have me castrated."

She opened the door wider, and he came in, stars and springtime sweeping and flourishing about him, and caught her in his arms, squeezing the breath out of her.

"Aston, Aston," she cried, laughing and gasping in his arms, "shall you be whipped *every* night?"

"Behold and judge," he said, taking down his breeches carefully, and first he showed her what she had given him, all sides, and then he gave it back to her with good measure. And they were very happy that night, after all, though their reasons were not the same.

Chapter 15

THE BRIEF contact with Alyx had cut the disturbing scenes with his master. He had felt his child in her belly, and the faint swell covering it, and he was alive again to the urgency to take her and the child out of the place quickly they had been cast into. He knew now what he had to do. He would make contact with the Methody in the town, who did not like his master, promise him anything, even conversion, to persuade him to read the lines and record them, bring Alyx and himself to the minister, where he did not know, and then wait for the smugglers and go out with them. The diamond his master had given him he thought would suffice. The difficulties and the dangers in these actions he did not dwell on. Or how he was to leave the house, or she, hedged in and restricted as they were. He made love joyously to his mistress, his powers returning to him, laying her suspicions to rest. But she did not remove the girl from her service, which puzzled him, whether he had convinced her better than he thought so that there was no need to, or less. In fact, he met Alyx frequently in the halls after that, and he did not know whether she had always been there and he had not seen her, or whether she was purposely being set in his way.

He was desperate to speak to her, but he did not dare, there always being someone a short way away, or his mistress, or doors and windows too near them. He shuttered his eyes, his face wooden, when he passed her, and the times he did dare glance at her, he noticed she did the same. He wondered then if she was angry with him, or jealous of his doings with his mistress and hers, and he remembered her dismay at his revelations and his proposals and her refusal of them initially, and wondered if she would be governed by him in his plans, could he effect them. He had thought some time before that his mistress had a devil in her that he would do well not to arouse, and he wondered now if she was delighting to tease him and to test how vulnerable he might be. Was it common female devilry and curiosity, he wondered, or a general jealousy, such as she had once shown, or prurience, or was it directed malice, and towards whom? He could not tell. He knew that his mistress now realized that Alyx was one of the women who had been with him, for she had as much as told him and so he could not help knowing. He continued there his pose of careless indifference. And he knew Alyx knew without question why he was now my lady's footman. He had in fact himself told her in the hut that he serviced his mistress, from time to time, but incomprehensibly to him his mistress had had her maid summoned to come into the room while he was with her, broad

waking and broad naked in broad daylight, to bring
them glasses and wine. Alyx had set them down on
the table by the bed, her hands shaking, a blush rising
in her pale cheeks, her dress rising and falling over her
bosom.

"She knows you," his mistress observed aloud, her
gaze travelling indifferently. "It is clear, Aston, that
she does. And it is clear too that she does not like to
see you here with me. It is not allowed, Aston, is it,
such knowledge and such feelings? How does she
know you, that it is you and you were with her?"

"I believe, Madonna," he said apologetically, flicking an indifferent glance towards the trembling child,
his age and his experience protecting him now from
any such betrayal, no longer caught off guard as he
was that first night, "that you told her so yourself. I
am sorry."

"You are sorry!"

"Yes, Madonna. My master will not be pleased, and
I would not have him displeased, with me or with
you." He looked at her meaningly, and she bridled
slightly, and put her hand possessively on him.

"You do not care, Aston?" she whispered.

"I, Madonna? Why should I care? Or you? I have
been at stud for five years. You know that. And in all
those years there is only one woman who has touched
my heart." He spoke truthfully, but as he spoke, he
put his own hand lightly on her belly, and she took
his words as he meant her to take them.

"Prove you do not care, Aston," she whispered,
"what she may think. Take me now, as you were
about to, while she is here. I have been jealous of her,
I admit it, Aston. Let her be jealous of me."

"I would not shame you so, Madonna," he whispered, turning slightly to her.

"Shamed? How can that be?" she asked in astonishment. "Before my maid? If I do not mind, and I do not, why should you? You can have no feelings, Aston, can you, except those I wish you to have, and hers need not concern us. She knows well enough what men do." He realised again, as he had before, that outside his relationship with her, he did not exist, or any other feelings he might have; and that she looked upon the girl similarly, as an annoyance to her, or as a useful and movable fixture, or an amusement, but in her own right, nothing. "Come, stud," she whispered, "work! Take me, now, before her; or take her before me."

"Madonna," he said slowly, slowly lowering his mouth to hers, "you can be quite wicked."

"Yes," she said, amused, "I suppose so. I must make a special contribution to the church."

He grinned, at this, because it seemed what he should do. He had not lost his erection, on Alyx's entrance, despite his shock and his horror to be seen so, because of her presence which he found exerted a countering effect upon him. He ignored Alyx then, standing near enough to touch him. He knew she was there and that she had not gone away, for she had not been dismissed. My lady's thighs had fallen apart, and he turned into them and filled them, and for a moment then, he did forget there was anyone else in the room, the five years' habits proving very strong, and the responses trained into them. When he had finished, and she had finished, he rolled away from her onto his back, his eyes open and unseeing, Alyx a blurred shape beside him, hearing the rapid rise and fall of her breath. He heard his mistress dismiss Alyx, and not turning his head, knew she had gone, and then he turned to his mistress savagely and filled her with delight.

In the afternoon his mistress who, though amused, had not been joking, did make a visit to the church, and did make a special contribution.

"I also thanked God I had you, Aston," she murmured, looking up at him both shyly and with triumph. They were walking through the church gardens, through the high boxed hedges in the twilight that was gathering.

"I thought only Methodees required such contrition," he said, bending to brush her lips with his.

"No," she said seriously, as always, her dark brow knitted in hard concentration, "Mr. Alwyn is not our parish minister, you are mistaken. It is Mr. Dennison, and he is most understanding."

"He must indeed be," he murmured, brushing her throat with his lips.

"You must not, Aston," she whispered, her voice and her bosom fluttering like the white moths that were fluttering about them. He caught one, and put it down the neck of her dress, and held the neck together watching it flutter against the soft material.

"Why not?" he whispered. "I thought I would give you more reason for contrition."

"Some one will come," she whispered.

"Then I will do it standing up," he said, "and they will think it only a small matter for contrition, not a large one."

"You cannot," she said, fascinated.

"You will see that I can," he said, and leaning against the tough springing hedge, he showed her he could. "Of course," he whispered, "if you wore undergarments when you went out with me, I could not."

"Someone is coming," she whispered urgently. "Aston, stop now and come out." He did, obediently, and she pulled the front of her dress down hastily.

"Is it Mr. Alwyn the Methody?" he asked.

"No, I don't think so," she said seriously. "His church is in the harbour, not here, but even Mr. Dennison would be too much to meet. Oh, Aston, you should not have."

"Well, did I not prove my point?" he asked, storing up her words loosely dropped. "Or should I prove it again in the carriage?"

"I think you should prove it again," she said, so he did, and hoped he had put all her suspicions now to rest.

For two days after that he did not see Alyx, and the first day, shamed and relieved, he became tense and uneasy, wondering why he did not and what had become of her. He passed her that third afternoon, walking behind my lady to her berlin, Alyx coming before them, towards them. As she passed, his lips formed the words silently, "I must see you," but she gave no sign she had seen, her cheeks flushing, her eyes quickly lowered. He returned that evening, and took the horses around to the stables, where the groom took them, for he had taken my lady out alone that day, and walked slowly back to the house. He sat down on the footman's bench between the outer and inner doors, and leaned his head back, and after a moment the inner door opened, and Alyx slipped in beside him and saw down on the bench beside him. He could not look at her, but he reached out a hand toward her, and she took it in hers.

"So that is how it is done," she said quietly.

"Yes," he said.

"I must have looked like that, and you."

"Yes," he said.

"How ugly," she said, "and how ridiculous."

"Yes," he said.

"It went right in," she said wonderingly. "I wonder I made such a fuss. It is clearly meant to go."

"Yes," he said. He looked at her then, and saw the tears were slipping down her cheeks.

"Alyx," he whispered, "Alyx, Alyx, love, don't cry."

"I am crying," she said, "because she shamed you. I cannot help it.

"And because," she added, "because I wish she *had* made you do it to me."

"I could not have," he said, "though I had died for it, with you before her."

"No?" she asked quickly.

She had dropped his hand, and she was gone then, before he could turn or speak, the door swinging behind her. He sat there a moment, and then he moved over to the fountain in the courtyard, and washed his burning face and dry lips, and let the wind fan them dry. He could not bring himself to go into the house, until he was peremptorily summoned.

He did not see Alyx again for a week, and in that time he tried to keep pace with his mistress's demands, and her quick rising, quick falling, suspicions. She frightened him, and he did not know from day to day what new excess she might think to ask. The simple explanation occurred to him that without knowing it yet herself, that she was tiring of him, and he might lose his access to the house and have never spoken to Alyx of what was always on his mind. He passed her in the hall that day, and she went by him quickly. Heedless, then, of danger or eyes, he ran after her, and caught her, his hand on her shoulder.

"Let me go, Simon," she said, swinging around, trying to shake his hand.

"No," he said, "I must see you."

"Let me go," she cried in an angry frightened whisper, and he did not know she was frightened for him.

"Not until you promise to see me," he said. "I cannot meet you. You must meet me."

"All right," she said, looking around with frightened eyes, "but let me go!" He took his hand from her shoulder, and she backed away from him quickly. A door was opening, and a cook maid with a tray of bread was coming out. Alyx bent quickly to tie her shoe, and Simon turned and held the door. When the hall was empty again, Alyx looked up and said "where?"

"Meet me at the fountain before you go to supper," he whispered, and went quickly out of the door himself.

He was kept late, because his mistress stayed to take tea with friends on her afternoon drive. The sun was setting as he gave the horses to the groom. He sat by the fountain, as he often did, and cooled his face, the light wind of the summer evening picking up, and rustling the leaves over his head. The shadows were lengthening and he heard the bell ringing for supper, and after a moment he stood up, and looked about him and then walked to the back of the fountain where the shadows were deeper and the stone cast a shadow and the small trees planted about it. He wondered if Alyx had come and had gone, before he had come, or if she would come at all. And then she was there. She was in his arms without a word, and as his arms closed about her, and his lips found hers, his resolves left him and he could not speak. They clung desperately together, like children, making little sounds and murmurs of endearments, and his prudence and his words deserted him entirely, as he felt her body yielding against his. They slipped down together to the ground in one movement, her lips never leaving his, and as she had said, "it was clearly meant to go in."

His mistress saw them standing at her window, the casements open to the soft wind of evening blowing the white curtains gently in and out. She could not see their faces, but she knew the livery her footmen wore. She came herself, and parted them, putting her hand on Simon's shoulder. He turned and saw her, and she knew from the look in his eyes, even in the lingering dusk, that had she been alone, he would have killed her. But she had not come alone. She had wisely brought the overseer and four of his strongest men, and as Simon looked at her with murder clear in his eyes, she called them, a smile fixed on her lips, and had them pull the two apart.

There was nothing to be said, no accusation needed, no denials possible. For a few minutes she stood there screaming at the two, until she was hoarse, reviewing his conduct in those weeks since his return and the new reasons she saw for it, and the false advantages he had taken, and the misuse he had made of her pardon and her favours and her trust. The overseer, taking charge, his voice quiet, instructed the men he had brought what to do. Two of them held to Simon's arms, holding him back from his mistress, hooking each a foot before his ankles, and the third took the straps the overseer held out and wrapped them around his wrists the fourth pulled behind him. He did not submit easily, for he did not doubt what was to come to him as a rogue stud once they had him, but once his wrists were bound he stopped his struggling, and looked to Alyx, and saw the overseer had taken her and brought her to her feet, her dress down now, having her hands bound like his. He smiled at her then, fleetingly.

"You may speak to her, Aston," he heard his mistress say, her voice now a hoarse whisper. "You might now as well. Perhaps you have something tender to say."

He ignored her, and the hands on his arms loosening, he went quickly to Alyx, and bent and kissed her. "I shall win clear of this coil somehow," he whispered for only her to hear. "I doubt not I shall. My plans are almost made, and when they are and when I do, doubt not I shall come for you, love. Be ready for me, love, and be of good cheer."

He spoke with more courage than he felt, for he did not think he could live through castration, although he knew some men did. He was after all not a horse, and he was old, and he did not expect them to be gentle with him.

"You will tell me what you said," his mistress said to him, "for I heard the part."

"I have told her to be of good cheer, Madonna, for nothing lasts very long," he said.

"I shall make this last," she said then. "I promise it, Aston. I shall make it last, and you will cry to me for pardon before it is over, and I shall not give it."

"Perhaps, Madonna," he said. "It should not be hard, if that is what you wish to do."

"I trusted you, Aston," she whispered, her voice broken and hoarse, her eyes burning.

"You should not have, Madonna," he said, "for I am a slave. You can never trust a slave. Remember that." He spoke frankly at last, for he knew his credit with her was irretrievably gone.

"You told me you loved me," she whispered.

"I think not," he said, "but if I did, I lied. I do not love you, Madonna, and I never have."

"Take care, take care!" she cried, in the whisper left of her voice.

"Will it help if I do?" he asked.

"No," she said. "It will not help. You have broken the law, and these men have seen."

"You brought them to see," he said.

"Yes, Aston," she said, "I brought them to see."

She walked up to him then and with her own hands adjusted his clothes, her hands lingering, her face sad, but her eyes when she raised them to him accusing for more than his act and implacable. He said nothing more, though his eyes met hers steadily. They had played the scene through so many times now, and all the accusations had been made and answered, until there were none left to make, and all his assurances shown for the lies they had been.

She moved away from him then and gave him over into the hands of the overseer.

He was shut in a room while my lady dined and the overseer took supper, and then he was brought out by the overseer, and two burly like-faced field workers he did not know, and taken down from the house and its gardens and environs, back to the slave quarters, and beyond them, to a wide dirt courtyard fenced with tall stems of the cane where he had been before. He had thought he might have the night, but he saw he was not. The lady was hot for it, he thought bitterly, as he looked about him with incredulous horror at the arrangements that had been made for him while she supped. Torches were set about the square, smoking and casting lurid shadows that jumped and lengthened over the fire that had been lit, and the wooden block beside it, a common butcher's block, and a butcher's plain hacking knife lying there, its whetted edge gleaming in the firelight. He shivered, and was glad it had been sharpened, for he did not want to be hacked and sawed at. A black kettle that had been hung over the fire was steaming. There were other objects on the block whose purpose was not clear to him, and after his first fascinated gaze, he turned his eyes away, and then he wished he had not, for he saw it did not matter how cleanly they did it. Across the limb of a tree that hung across the fence into the courtyard a rope had been thrown, a noose knotted in one end, and a table and a bench for steps, set below it.

"Oh, God," he thought, "must I die for so little?" He looked at the overseer, his eyes stricken, and he thought the overseer looked embarrassed. He does this all the time, Simon thought, he whips us or has us whipped, and starves us, and if we break the laws he executes through his master, he sets us in a noose with some embarrassment at doing it, and that is all. He looked wildly about the enclosed yard, at the huge impassive black faces about him, their eyes shining in the torchlight, and the embarrassed thin face of the overseer, with his pistols at his belt.

"Do not hang me," he whispered, his pride gone. "The law does not demand that for what I did. Do not hang me on a woman's whim. Wait until tomorrow at least, or wait until the master comes, if it is the law, and let him judge me."

"When my master is gone, my lady is judge," the overseer said. "I cannot help you, Aston. It has happened before to studs and I warned you of it."

"Oh, my God," he whispered, his eyes on the noose, swaying slightly in the night wind, sweat pouring down his face and glistening in the firelight, "do not let her hang me."

There was a noise at the gate to the enclosure, and the overseer left him in the hands of the blacks, and went to unchain it, letting in his mistress, still in riding dress. She paused, and turned, and he saw his brave words to Alyx were to no effect, for she had been brought down with his mistress, in the hands of two maidservants, needlessly and cruelly, to witness what they were going to do to him. And then he remembered her part.

"You cannot whip her," he said, his lips dry and shaking, to the overseer who had returned. "You cannot! She is going to have a child, and she is too young, she is just a child. You cannot!"

"If we do," the overseer said, without comfort, "you will not perhaps have to see it, and if we do, by then you will not care. Think now of yourself, Smith, and if you can, pray, you young fool, for I shall have to do what my mistress commands me."

She came over now, her face set, and her eyes hard, and with her own hands unfastened the catch at his throat and loosened the cape at his shoulders that she had put on him and took it from him. She held it in her hands a moment looking at it, and then at him, and then she folded it and laid it aside in the hands of a foot servant she had brought with her.

"You will take the rest of my livery, Mr. Jarvis, from this man," she said then, and stood back a few steps, her eyes intent and narrowed, and watched while his hands were unstrapped so that the sleeves of his shirt and his jacket could be taken off him.

"No," she said, as the overseer would have restrapped his hands, "do not," she said. "I want him whipped first, and I want to watch. Give me now the rest of my livery. Let him take it off himself."

His hands shaking, he took his shoes and stockings off, and then his breeches, and stood before her, frightened and helpless, in the midst of the small group of people standing about him watching him in the flickering lights.

"I could always make you do anything, Aston, by whipping you or threatening the whip, could I not? Are you still so afraid of pain?"

"Yes, Madonna," he said. "I would do anything in my power to avoid it now."

"There is nothing in your power to do. You cannot unsay your words or undo your acts, Aston, and there is nothing else I want, except to hurt you now, as you have hurt me. That I loved a slave who did not value what he had hurts me, Aston. It cuts like the whip and the knife, which at least I can make you feel, and I shall. I hope you die hard, Aston," she whispered, the viciousness in her voice flicking over him already like the whip, and he winced under it. "Your neck is strong, and I hope it will not break, and that you strangle slowly. I hope you take a long time to die, and that you know all the time that it is happening, and that you pray for death before you get it, Aston. I will watch you, Aston, all the while it is happening to you, I will watch your face, Aston, and not let them cover it, so that I can see you while you are suffering. And I will hold the piece of you they cut from you in my hand while you are dying, and tonight perhaps I will use it and remember you. And then I shall have you put out of my sight entirely, Aston, and forget you."

"Must you kill me, Madonna?" he whispered. "The

rest perhaps I have deserved, but have I deserved that?"

"I always kill my studs," she said, "when they cease to please me. Did you not know that, Aston? Did no one tell you? Or did I forget to tell you? How careless of me to forget. You might then have been more careful. There is no man walking on this place, or on this earth, Aston, who can say he has had me."

"Except my master your husband," he said then, all hope lost.

"No," she said, "not even he, Aston, not even your master my husband."

He stared at her, his face bleak, his skin cold with fear, as she turned away from him. He still cared then, but shortly he did not care.

"I will have him whipped first," he heard her say to the overseer, and felt relief flood him that the knife and the rope were not yet to come.

"To what end, my lady?" the overseer said. "Do not torture the poor man further, but end it now."

"I have said I will have him first whipped, and I do wish it and I do intend it," she said. "You will please have him put up and attend to it."

"My lady," the overseer said, embarrassed, "if he is whipped first, he will likely erect; it would be better to use the knife now, as he now is. I am not meant for a butcher, my lady, you should not ask it. As he is, there will be less blood."

"I am myself not so fastidious," she said, "but if you mind, then keep him from it. Tie a string. I want him whipped."

So Simon had the indignity of a string tied tightly by the nervous hands of the overseer at the base of his stem, the pain shooting up causing him to wince and to stagger, and then he was dragged to the whipping

frame, where he had been many times, and strung up
to the hooks set in the top of the frame by his wrists,
his ankles tied to ropes threaded through two hooks at
either end of the base. And so he hung spreadeagled
in the air, resting on nothing, and felt the whip crack
into his back and wrap around him like his mistress's
fingers, and retreat, and then return crashing in
against. He swayed in the ropes pulling him apart, and
waited for the next lash to hit him. He had never been
whipped long, when he was put in this rack, for he
had not been able to endure it long. He had always
given in. But he was not asked now to give in, only to
suffer. The veins stood out in his forehead with his effort not to scream, as the blows continued, and then
he could bear it no longer, and he began to scream,
strangling and choking. He heard what seemed to be a
woman screaming somewhere far away, but he could
not hear her very well, with the blood pounding in
his head and ears, and the pain was such now that he
did not care. In the corner of the yard by one of the
torches he could see the noose waving gently back
and forth, and he wished for the knife and the noose
to come quickly, as the overseer had said he would, to
end his suffering. He was fainting now between
blows, each cut pulling him briefly awake with the
new surge of pain. It was like a rhythm, like the
waves of the sea on the smugglers' beach, pulling him
in and out, and in and out, and then the rhythm
abruptly broke, and the swing of the lash stopped.
He hung in his bonds, hemorrhaging, choking, and
coughing, and felt a cool hand reaching to his mouth
to stop the blood. The yard was strangely silent, after
the tumult and the noise of the whip and the screaming. He opened his eyes and looked down into the

face of his master who was standing below him, looking up at him.

"You should not have taken off the pendant I gave you," his master said to him, his voice quiet in the courtyard. "Did I not warn you?" Then he turned away to the overseer and the blacks, looking at them and at the array of instruments laid out. He walked over to the fire, where the kettle was boiling, and tipped it so that the steaming water poured out into the fire, extinguishing it, and looked around at the small group of people staring at him.

"Who has dared command this done to my servant, in my absence?" he asked. He picked up the knife and handed it to the overseer. "Please to cut the man down, Mr. Jarvis. I wonder at what you have seen fit to do, in my absence. I do wonder indeed."

He watched them release Simon, first one hand being cut loose, and then the other hand, and then his feet. When they stood him on his feet, he could not stand, and they supported him between them as his master took out his penknife and with his cool dry fingers cut the string that had been cutting tightly into his flesh.

"I wonder you thought you would need the knife too, Mr. Jarvis," he said dryly. "I do indeed wonder. Did you not know, Mr. Jarvis, that this man was mine, and not yours and not my wife's, to dispose of to your liking? My dear," he said, turning to his wife with infinite courtesy, "if my servant no longer pleases you to be your footman, he will not trouble you longer with his presence. You need exert yourself no longer in his behalf." His ironic eyes left her and swept over the rest of the little circle and came to rest on Alyx, her face puffed with tears, her dress torn where she had struggled with the two women holding

her, her hair loosened, her hands still strapped together in front of her.

He stood for a moment looking at her, and then he
held out his hand without a word to the overseer,
who put the knife in them, and with his own hands
cut the strap that bound them.

"Why is this girl here?" he asked at large. "I cannot
think it necessary. Mr. Jarvis, I left this girl, who is
breeding, in your care, to be used gently in the house.
If she miscarries from this, you will have much to regret. I shall see personally you do regret it." He took
his cloak from his shoulders and put it about Alyx's
trembling shoulders, and fastened it. He put his hand
under her chin, and lifted her face, looking into her
frightened eyes.

"Be still, child," he said, his cool voice gentle, "and
do not fret. You are not to be hurt. No one here will
touch you. Did they bring you here to whip you too,
child?" She did not answer, her eyes wide-fixed on his
face. "I wonder anyone should dare," he said softly.
"I do wonder indeed." He took her hands in his, and
raised her, where she had fallen as he spoke onto her
knees.

"Peace, child," he said, "I have said you are not to
be hurt."

"Nor him?" she whispered, catching at his hands.
"You will not let them hurt him any more?"

"I will have none of my servants, of those men and
women belonging to me whom I have bought for my
own use, hurt except by my command. I would hope
this would be remembered. This man and this girl are
expressly my own," he said, looking straight at his
wife, "and I have never given either to you that I
remember for your use except on loan. Indeed I do
not remember it otherwise." He looked down at the

girl clinging to his hands, who had fallen again to her knees, and he said, his eyebrows lifting slightly in surprise, "Did I not tell you to go into the house?" He tried to disengage her hands from his, but she held to him tightly, her eyes frantic with fear. "Do not send me away yet," she whispered.

"There is no need for you to stay here, child," he said. "There is nothing that is to be done here."

"You will not believe what they tell you?" she said, holding to his hands. "I beg you will not! You will not hurt him when I am gone, or punish him any more? I beg you will not."

"I have asked that you will not fret, child," he said, "and that you will go into the house. Do you think I do not know how to care for my own?" He patted her hands, disengaging her clinging fingers, and caused her to come to her feet, lifting her with the pressure of his hands. Then, as Simon had done, he put his hands to her waist and felt the child under it, and patted her rounding stomach gently with his hand. Then he turned to the two women who had brought her, and gave her back to them, telling them to take her with them back into the house.

When she had gone, he walked to the limb of the tree and pulled the rope from it and coiled it loosely about his arm, and walked slowly back to the center of the court where Simon still stood supported between the two blacks. His wife who had been struck silent by his sudden entrance now rounded on her husband, as she saw him remove the rope.

"Will you not even hear what this man you call yours has done! Must you make me, and also Mr. Jarvis look like fools before the blacks? You are unjust, August!"

"He is come to justice now, my lady," her husband

said, his gaze he briefly directed on her both cold and quelling. "I do implore you to be quiet." He lifted the noose and put it around Simon's neck, an end trailing on the dusty ground between them, and watched the stark fear that came back into Simon's dazed eyes, pricking them into stark consciousness. He pulled his arms from the loose grasp of the blacks, and fell onto his knees before his master, his face raised pleadingly to that stern one.

"My lord," he whispered, using the address without being aware that he did, "you will not hang me?"

"If what you have done deserves hanging, by my laws and without justification, in my eyes, yes, Aston," he answered not ungently, looking down on the frightened eyes dark with pain staring up at him mute and helpless with agony and new fear, but with a sternness more implacable than his wife's emotion, "I will, and forthwith now, myself. But I would first learn what you have done, to so incense both my wife and my overseer against you. And I would advise you, Aston, to tell me strictly what is true now, for you will not later have the chance to change your words."

"I have not deserved it, my lord," Simon said with trembling lips, "I have not. I beg you will not."

"So you have said," his master observed, his face unsoftened. "But what is it that you have done? You will tell me yourself, and I will myself decide what the act merits, and if you are indeed a rogue stud who must be put away."

"I—I spoke with one of the women of the place, while you were away," Simon said, despairingly, his eyes fixed on his master's face and on the rope whose end he had picked up as Simon hesitated and held now idly in his hand, flicking it over.

"When did you speak, and where, Aston?" his master asked.

"At noon," he said, "in your hall."

"Knowing that it was forbidden to you?"

"Yes, my lord," Simon said. "I knew it. You had told me."

"I thought that I had," his master observed. "And I thought then that I had even explained to you, and requested my overseer to explain to you, why it was forbidden to you, so that it should be entirely clear to you before you undertook to breed my women for me.

"You have broken then knowingly this one of my laws," his master commented. "Did you do else besides?"

"I—I took one of the women who work the place behind the fountain in your garden tonight," Simon said helplessly, humiliated.

"You took her? In your arms? And joined with her, I believe my wife has said. Is this so, Aston?"

"Yes, my lord," he said, his eyes mutely pleading.

"In full copulation, such as might give seed?"

"I have said I did, my lord," he answered, a slight flash rising in his eyes, not unnoted by his master.

"I would have it entirely clear," his master observed. "You did this, knowing the law and the penalty in law, as I have set it and established it here?"

"Yes, my lord," Simon said. "I did know."

"Knowing to do it meant castration?"

"Yes, my lord," Simon whispered, and then, unable to help himself in his fear, he whispered, "I could not help myself, I did not mean to."

"I would say, Aston, that to say that does not help

your case at all, rather the opposite, Aston. Was the girl herself willing?"

"You, yourself, must ask her," Simon said.

"I shall. But I take it she was not unwilling. May I also take it that she was the girl who was here tonight, or do you remember?"

"Yes, my lord," Simon whispered. "It was."

"Now I would have you think well how you answer me, Aston. Had you seen this girl before, before you took her in full copulation behind the fountain?"

His throat dry, but with some slight spirit, Simon raised his head almost impatiently and said, "Yes, my lord. I have told you, that I had spoken to her, in the hall of your house. She looked to me to be fainting, and I—I assisted her."

"And were you seen?"

"Yes, my lord. I was seen, and I was whipped for it."

"Yet you took occasion even so to see her again, or did you not recognise her when you took her in copulation tonight?"

"My lord, I have told you that I had seen her before."

"This girl, Aston, I will tell you, is breeding. I will also tell you that you have been with her in that way in the hut. And I am asking you now, Aston, if you knew this, if you knew that you had been with her before, tonight when you took her?" His eyes were steady and without expression. "I would have you think well, Aston, before you answer me."

Simon was silent, not knowing what he should answer, the rope heavy about his neck, the fire in his back burning him and making him dizzy, the silence lengthening, and then he raised his head and said, his voice flat and hopeless, "Yes, I did know."

"You knew?" his master asked, his brows lifting. "How did you know?"

"I knew because your wife told me," Simon said bitterly, "after I had met her in the hall by your wife's door."

"My wife told you," his master repeated reflectively. "And then, Aston?"

"I—I had gotten a taste for her," Simon said at last. "I told your wife I had not, but—but I had—and when I knew who she was, I—I wanted to have her again, and so when I could I did."

"Knowing she might be breeding?" his master asked gently, his voice frightening in its quietness.

"I—I did not think, my lord," Simon muttered. "I saw her at the fountain, and I wanted to have her."

"So you took a girl I had bred to you, Aston, knowing who she was, knowing what I had done, and knowing my laws on such matters. What else did you do, Aston, besides this?"

"Nothing, my lord," Simon muttered.

"Nothing?" snapped his master sharply.

"I have told you what I did," Simon said wearily. "You have asked me and I have told you."

"And you do not think you deserve to be hanged for what you did?"

"No, my lord," Simon whispered, the terror returning to his eyes, "I do not think so. I beg you will not."

"Your wishes, Aston, cannot affect me. I beg you will not beg me." He turned to his overseer. "And is this all the man has done?"

"Yes, my lord," the overseer said.

"And did you think it merited death?"

"No, my lord, I did not," the overseer said.

"Yet you were willing to put this man whom I paid

money for to death, and would have done just that had I not happened to return?"

"Your lady, my lord, wished it, and I believed she must have her reasons." He paused, and then he said hurriedly, "I looked for your mark, my lord, and there was none. So I saw no reason then to deny her her judgement, in this matter, in your absence."

"I see," his master said. "I think I do indeed see." He walked to Simon, and slipped the noose off over his head, and gave it to one of the blacks to coil.

"I have heard enough," he said. "There is no hanging matter here. Whipping, yes, but he has been whipped sufficiently, Mr. Jarvis, quite sufficiently. For the other, as it happens, I do not at this time wish my stud gelded, although I do not fault your general judgement. But Aston," he said approaching his man, "let me warn you that you not repeat the nature of this offence a second time, for I will not interfere again in the law's course. Mr. Jarvis," he said, turning away to the overseer, "you will have my man taken now into your quarters to be cared for."

He stood erect, and watched Simon attempt to walk, and stagger, and the larger black pick him up on his shoulder. Then he smiled and walked across to his wife and held out his hand.

"My dear," he said pleasantly, "you must have been surprised to see me. Am I home early? The sessions finished today, and I did not wait. How glad I am that I did not."

"August," she said furiously, "I pray you, do not mock at me!"

"Believe me, my dear," he said, "I am not mocking. I am indeed glad I came home. Mr. Jarvis," he said, turning to his overseer, "I shall expect you to wait upon me in my office in the morning."

He took his wife's hand and put it through his arm, holding it there, and walked back to the house in her company, passing Simon and the blacks who were waiting for the overseer without a second glance.

Chapter 16

WHEN HE was recovered, Simon waited upon his master in his office where he had been summoned. He was wearing his master's own black livery, that he had been fitted for and that had been sent to him, and the tiny diamond on its chain was pulled out over his shirt and his jacket plain to view. Under his coat, still tender to the touch of the material, his back had almost healed, the new scars standing out in ridges over the criss-crossing mesh of many faint white scars from his many other such whippings at other times, though none so severe. He had not seen his master since that terrible night, and he approached the door to the office, his heart beating unsteadily under the black stuff of his coat, and entered, outwardly poised, inwardly torn and uncertain, when that voice called him, in answer to his knock.

He walked across the rug with the easy assurance,

not unnoted by his master, that was still unconscious
to him, and that nothing that had happened to him
could take from him, for the room was after all the
kind of room he was accustomed to. It was the places
he was now kept that drew the startled, surprised look
from him even still.

"You walk to the manner born, Earl," his master
observed, watching him. "Almost, almost, sometimes
almost you persuade me to wonder a little."

Simon said nothing, tongue-tied by emotion, and far
from feeling the assurance he showed.

"It is perhaps the clothes," pursued his master. "You
wear them well, Earl. They become you exceedingly.
More, I do think, than my wife's. Do you think you
will like to wear them, Aston? Will you like to take
my service?"

The question startled Simon, and his eyes widened,
his upcut thin nostrils quivering, and he stood uncertainly, no possible answer open to him. His master
smiled.

"I half expect to see you paw the ground, Aston,
and stamp. Do I offend you, Earl?" He held out his
hand with an easy familiarity. "To think what was almost done to my stallion. I shudder, to think, Aston.
How could you have been such a fool? Take my
hand, Aston, I am offering it to you. You may not refuse it." Simon took the cool fingers in his, and then,
to his own surprise, as much as his master's, he
dropped to his knees as he had in the courtyard, and
brought the hand to his lips.

"Earl, Earl," a voice near him said, above his head,
still cool, still amused, "all this because I did not hang
you? You make me wonder almost, almost, if you did
not after all deserve it. But if you are grateful you
may show it to me another way, another time. I have

brought you here this morning to this room to talk to you, Aston. Otherwise it had been another room. I take it, Earl," he said, removing his hand from Simon's, and putting it on the head bent before him, bringing the head against him, and laying both his hands lightly on the springing soft black locks pressed against him, "that you do not like to wear livery for anyone, not even for me, but that you will do it if I ask you?"

"You do not need to ask me, sir," Simon said, turning his head slightly under those hands. "You may require me."

"Not entirely, Aston, not entirely. I may force you to many things, but you must want to serve me to serve me well."

"I was afraid, sir," Simon said, not answering his master's unasked question, "that I had put you in disgust of me."

"And should you care?" his master asked.

"You must not ask me these questions," Simon said helplessly. "I do not want to lie to you, sir, but you ask me to feel things I cannot feel and to promise things I cannot promise. If you can sometimes forget you have bought me, sir, I cannot ever. I will serve you because you ask me to, but you cannot ask to repose trust in me, sir. It is not in the nature of a slave."

"You are wearing my diamond, Aston, I see," his master remarked inconsequentially. "I do not wear my heart on my sleeve. Wear it inside," he said, taking the little chain and slipping it under the folds of lace and silk at Simon's throat. "How much you must love me, Earl, to say such things to me, and how much you presume upon my love to dare." He took his hand and brought Simon to his feet, and with his hands moved his unresisting face towards him and kissed his quiet unresisting lips. "I acknowledge the truth of what you say, Aston," he added thoughtfully, "and that is why, Aston," he said, taking his hand and leading him to a chair by a small table, and seating him, and then taking himself an opposite chair, "when some weeks ago I considered adopting you, I rejected the idea out of hand. It is something to have brought you to this measure of obedience, but it is not enough, for as you say, you do not forget the means by which I have achieved it. You do not ask me why I should have considered adopting you?"

"No, sir," Simon said with a twisted smile. "If you wish me to know, you will tell me."

His master looked at him appreciatively. "Earl, Earl," he said softly, "how I do love you. I have been hard put to wait, but I see you still sit somewhat uneasily. Did it never occur to you, Earl, to wonder why I did not let them tame that offending member of yours, Earl. It is of no particular use to me in my pleasures, and for you to lose its abilities would have given my wife considerable pleasure. You had clearly deserved it, Earl, there was no question of that, and I have not spared other studs when they turned rogue, as eventually they all do."

"I was too frightened to wonder, sir," Simon said. "As you know, I do not stand pain well. And afterwards, I was too sick."

"I think you are not yet entirely yourself," his master observed.

"No, sir," Simon said, smiling faintly, "but I shall be. Your overseer was surprisingly kind."

"He was kind because I ordered him to be. Did you think perhaps I enjoyed merely the chance to overset my wife? Believe me, Aston, if you did, it was not so. Your danger was that I should give over my own wishes and my own pleasures to humour her. But in your instance I was unwilling to, and I have been hard put to return her into humour. I could have wished, Aston, you had not angered my wife. In fact, I believe I instructed you that you take particular care that you do not. You have caused me embarrassment and put me to considerable trouble. Why did you do what you did, Aston? You so nearly ruined us all, and all my plans."

"I told you," Simon said, helplessly and yet defiantly, "I told you when you asked me. I could not help myself. I never meant to do it. God help me, I never did."

"I do hope you have not gone rogue," his master said, his eyes on him thoughtfully. "I keep wishing, Aston, you could reassure me on that count, but each time I ask you only disturb me more." He rose, and rang the bell. "Aston," he said, "you will wait for me, until I return. I will not be long."

Simon sat uneasily, waiting, and after he had waited perhaps half an hour, another footman in his master's livery came into the room, and told him his master had an unexpected visitor with business, and that he was excused, and would be recalled after luncheon. He had come to take him at his master's wishes to his new quarters where, as his master's new personal servant, he was to stay.

He led Simon not out through the door he had entered but upstairs, and into his master's bedroom, next to my lady's, which opened onto a wide veranda, on which, as he passed, he saw out of the corner of his eye Alyx sweeping, and through a smaller door into a smaller room, opening onto the veranda also, as well as to his master's bedroom and to the hall outside, and having access to the courtyard stairs off the end of the veranda. The freedom and the openness of the doors and the windows and the air and the light were like nothing he had had since he had been put on the ship, and it intensified his captivity and servitude as nothing had. His mind, he thought, was not working clearly. He felt the room about him like a trap, but he could not see how there could be one. When the footman had gone, and left him alone, with the doors open and unlocked, the windows open and the sun and the air entering them, he waited. "If Alyx goes into my mistress's bedroom," he thought, "I will not speak to her." And then he thought, "If she goes, I cannot speak to her." He could hear the soft noise a little distance away, and he did not know what to do. The air was otherwise perfectly still. The heat of noon was descending, with its quietening stillness. The house except for the servants seemed to be at luncheon. He was not himself called until later, and there was nothing for him to do but wait. No one was anywhere about but Alyx, and she was unaware of his presence. He could not bear not to see her, or to speak to her, and he could not bear to be whipped again, or punished further. He stood, undecided, and the sweeping sounds seemed to be receding, and he did not delay any longer. He walked to the door, that was open, and stood inside his room, just at the jamb, and called softly her name. He heard the sweeping sounds stop, and silence as though she were looking uncertainly around. He called her name again, and he heard the broom drop, and she was running toward him, and had flung herself into his arms. "Simon!" she cried, her voice hardly more than a whisper, the tears flowing down her face, holding to him, her lips hunting for his and finding them.

"Hush, love, hush," he whispered. "This is so dangerous, and I cannot bear to be whipped again just now. Go get your broom, my love, that silly broom, and come outside my room and sweep. I have to talk to you, and there is no time for anything." He held her away from him, his face heavy with love, for just a moment looking at her as though he could not see her enough, and then he released his hands from her shoulders, and walked back into his room, his face wrenched with strain, and stood inside his room just by the open window. After a minute she had come with her broom, and though he did not dare look at her, he heard the sounds of the sweeping near him, and knew he could have touched her, had he put out his hand.

"Simon," she whispered, "I did not know what had happened to you."

"Hush, love," he whispered, speaking softly and quickly, his voice hardly a sound, "there is not time. I have perhaps been taken into our master's service, but it is very difficult. I think I have found a man who can marry us and I think he will. When I can make the arrangements, will you come with me?"

"They will never let us," she whispered, frightened.

"We will not ask them. Alyx, will you come with me, if I can do it?"

"Is it what you want?" she whispered.

"Yes," he said. "Will you come?"

"Yes," she whispered, "if you want it."

"Go sweep then," he said. "I will find a way to tell you when I do." He stood at the window, his eyes unseeing, listening to the sound of the broom going away, his face blank with love and worry, and then he turned and saw his master standing in the open door watching him.

"It was then," he said heavily, "after all a trap for me."

"Yes, Aston," his master said. "You will forgive me, but I had to know. I do not wonder that you should love her; I wonder I should not have known that you must. Why did she call you Simon?"

"It is my name," Simon said dully. "One of my names."

"I prefer it. I will also use it," his master said. "Do you love this girl enough not to hurt her, Simon? Or to hurt the child she is bearing?"

"Yes," Simon said. "I think so. What must I do?"

"You must not see her again, or speak to her," his master said, "and you must let her forget you. She is very young, Simon. She will forget easier perhaps than you."

"Am I to promise you this?" Simon said heavily, torn with fear.

"No," his master said. "You told me, I believe, that I must not trust you or your promises. You are not a rogue, Simon, as you have just proved to me, and you have still your control, enough so that I believe if I tell you what you must do, for her safety and your welfare, you will do it. You will come down with me now once more to my office, Aston Simon, and I will tell you why." He took Simon's hand, and brought him out of the room, and then led the way, Simon following.

"I told you, without surprising you, which I thought curious, Simon, that I had once briefly considered adopting you. Did you understand me, Simon? It seemed to me you did not. I meant adoption of you as my heir." He watched Simon attentively, and did not see his set face change. "The idea, I see, would not have pleased you."

"No," Simon said. "It would not have."

"Why, I wonder," his master said.

"Because I would not have wished to give up my name for yours," Simon said briefly.

"Smith?"

"Nor do I wish to take anything from you that I can help accepting. I can help that, I think."

"I have made a fool of you, Aston Simon Smith," his master observed mildly, "but must you try to make me angry?"

"I am not trying to make you angry," Simon said, "God help me. I simply do not wish to be your son, and I cannot believe you ever wished it."

"I do not wish you to be my son now, certainly," his master said, smiling slightly, "as I shall show you tonight. But it is true that when I bought you, I had something of that undefined in my thoughts. You quickly showed me, however, what you have since told me, that your ways were too set, and that you were, young as you were, already too old, that wherever you had come from to me, you could not forget it. By son, you see, Simon, I mean simply my legal heir. I have none. By a defect of nature, I can have none, and though I put you to my wife, by a curious coincidence, I found the fault, had I put it to the test with her, not wholly mine. When I saw you, you see, Aston, clearly bred to a different life, a solution to my problem occurred to me might come, one way or another, through you. But the children you have bred for me, I could not accept. Nor could I accept you, even had you been willing, such ideas are storybook ideas, and now ironically, you tell me you are not." He looked at Simon, quizzically, but Simon sat silent. "I could yet change my mind, Aston Simon. It is not yet too late, and I have in these last weeks felt towards you, such feelings as I might have had towards a son."

"Then I say, 'God help your son,' if you had one," Simon said. "I am not willing to fill that place for you," and then, as he saw the older man's face not angry at his foolish and audacious words, but moved and hurt, he was moved himself, and he fell as before on one knee before him, and took his hand. "My lord," he whispered, "oh, my lord, forgive me. But if you cared for me, as you say, you would let me go home."

"Where is this home of yours, Simon?" his master asked.

"I have told you," Simon said, "but you would not believe me."

"When was that?" his master said. "I do not remember."

"When you first had me whipped," Simon whispered, "because I would not speak."

"I do not believe you, Aston Simon," his master said. "I did not then, and I do not now. I have some knowledge of the world, though you may think I do not, removed here from that world on this island across an ocean. And when you persist in this implausible and foolish imposture, I do not wonder your parent had such an embarrassment removed. But let me tell you this, Aston Simon, if I did believe you, and if I had believed you then, I would have acted no differently toward you, then or now. And I wonder that you could wish to go back, when life has closed whatever gap you left, and has gone on, as it inevitably and always does. You are better off here, Aston Simon, and you might one day, if you could see it so, own a great part of this island."

"I will not take your name," Simon whispered. "I

will never do it. And I do not want any part of your world, though I die for saying it. I can bear anything from you, even the whip, even the rope, except for you to take from me what I am. I do not want to die, but if I must die, when I must die, I will die still that. And I love you too much, sir, God help me that I should, to deceive you now in this way and pretend to you on this subject."

"My poor deluded fool of an earl stud," his master said, "there is no question of your dying, now. God forbid it. And I do not, as you say, care for you except to my own uses, for there is no question of your going home, now, or ever. Put it from your mind entirely as you must put this girl from your mind. And be content, if you can, that I find some pleasure in your company, and that you will not, if you watch your tongue and your actions and do not anger me too far, die in the fields. I am not capricious like my wife, and I do not pull men from them, only to throw them back when I tire of them. Why must you cause yourself such useless pain?"

Simon was silent, wondering that he had spoken at all, cursing himself for the sudden weakness. He had had only to pretend, but he could not, on the subject of the land and its heir that he understood too well. He smiled a little twisted smile, endeavouring to find some lightness and to make such recovery as he still could. He rose awkwardly from his knees, and stood before his master.

"I am sorry, sir," he said penitently. "I have these spells, as you say. I was hit on the head in the ship, they tell me, and sometimes I think I am still confused."

"Aston, Aston," his master said, "coming it too

strong now. When were you at Eton? Or was it Harrow?"

"I forget now," he said truthfully and lightly. "Too long ago to count. And they could not bear me very well either. I was not there very long."

"I wonder you did not tell me you were kidnapped when you ran away from school?"

"I wonder too," Simon said. "I suppose I did not think of it. Shall I go, now, sir?"

"No, Aston Simon, I have not finished. I brought you to my office to tell you why you must forget my very charming maid servant, and when I do, I think you will agree it is best, and not force my hand. I am not after all surprised you should feel as you do, for I bought her for you, to breed with you. When I saw her, Aston, I knew, as when I saw you, what she was, for whatever reasons she had come into the hard circumstances where I found her. As with horses, one can only get what one has. So I bred her to you, Aston, to get from her and from you, the child I cannot myself have. If this child she is bearing now is male, I will take him into my house and raise him as my son. I will adopt him as my heir, and educate him well, and train him to that position."

"And if the child is a girl?" Simon asked, his tone flat, concealing his dismay.

"I did not, after all, have you castrated," his master said mildly. "At some time, there will, I think, be a son. Had you expressed yourself less strongly, I had thought of you still as the child's guardian, Simon, and my heir by default. But I see that will not do. Perhaps it would never have done. The child's natural mother must never know, I think, and except for your interest in the child and its mother, I should not have told you. Now, of course, I have. An impulse, and perhaps an unwise one?"

"Are you telling me that if I try to speak to this girl again, if I make any opportunity where I may have told her this, that you will later put her out of your way?"

"Something of that sort, my dear," his master said. "But she is much younger than you, and I will see you have the women you require. She will forget, when she has had many children, and you can forget, if you will."

"And you have told me this," Simon said, "to insure I stay away from her, because you think I care."

"Something of that sort," his master agreed. "It is best that she not see the child or you again, and yet I do not wish to lose her or to lose you."

"What of the child?" Simon said. "What if he should have other thoughts and other ideas? Children sometimes do—"

"He will have no choice."

"And I—" Simon said with difficulty, "how am I to feel?"

"*You?* I should think you would be pleased."

"And if I am not—" Simon said, with more difficulty.

"Then, when that time comes," his master said, "if it does, I shall see you cause me no difficulty. Had I not thought you would like the idea, I would not have told you of it. You need not otherwise, you see, Aston, have ever known of it."

He looked at Simon's face, and then he said gently, "What possible difference can it make to you, Aston? What possible difference. Do you require of this child that he suffer like you, and be whipped like you, and when he is grown, be set out, ignorant and brutalized, to set seed in black women? Or to work cane? Or dig canals? You will not see the child there, or know its fate. Would you not rather be glad that I should want the child, enough that I will care for it and raise it well?"

"Yes," Simon said dully, "I should be glad. And if the child is not a boy, if it should be a girl?"

"I have no interest in a girl," his master said briefly and indifferently. "Now Aston-Simon," he said, "dear Earl," he said, the briefest flicker in his eyes, "you will tell me if I must hurt you, or if I may trust you. You made it, you see, my dear, so that I did have to give you my confidence, but you have not received it as I might have hoped. If I pull this bell, that door will open, outside my office, and three of my larger men will come and hold you, while I blind you, Aston, with tongs I shall heat, and while I take out your tongue. You can then of course not drive me or do my errands, or amuse me as you do with your talk and your stories, but you can still get children for me, and still amuse me, if I still want you, in other ways. I hope, Aston, you can reassure me, but I wonder if you can."

"Don't pull the bell," Simon said, his voice hard with desperation, his eyes straight on his master. "You don't need to. I give you my word I will never speak to that girl of anything you have told me in this room, or to anyone else of it whatsoever, anywhere, at any time."

"Well spoken, Earl," his master said dryly. "And on what assurance and authority do I have this?"

"On my word as Earl," Simon said briefly. "That should suffice. It always has."

His master looked at him, and said slowly, "By God, Smith, almost you make me believe you. Almost.

I will take your word. I notice," he added dryly, "you have not said you would not try to see my little maid again or speak to her at all."

"If you do not get your boy," Simon said, his voice as dry, "and you put me to her again, I cannot promise to see nothing or to be entirely mute. But I will tell you this. What taste I had for her, I find I have lost. I have no longer the least desire to see or speak with her. Besides," he said, "if I do, I see you will surely know, my lord. Your hand and your eye are everywhere, to save and to chastise, at your will and your discretion. Who am I in the face of this to assert my will?"

"Who indeed?" said his master thoughtfully. But he did not pull the bell, or threaten Simon further. He stared at him several seconds longer, Simon meeting his gaze squarely, and then he dismissed his servant to his room.

They did not discuss the episode again. That night when Simon had gone to bed, his master opened the doors between their rooms, and called him in, naked except for the little chain about his neck. His master removed it and laid it carefully by, and when he had finished with Simon, not requiring much of him, with care toward the tenderness of his multilated back, he replaced it about his neck, and kissed him with great tenderness. He did not comment that Simon stood unresponsive, but he said, his fingers still on the little chain, "Do not take my chain off again, Aston-Simon. I will not give it to you a third time."

Chapter 17

As HIS freedom of movement increased, as his master's personal servant, doors open to him that were closed, his time his own except when at his master's personal demand, subject only to his master's orders, Simon felt the web of circumstances closing in on him, tighter than the little chain about his neck which they symbolised. So long as his back was tender, his master had not drugged him and had not forced his emotions, with the destructive effect on his will, which still remained his own. But he dared take no steps now except the final ones.

He had met the Methody priest. It had been one day when he had accompanied his master to the Harbour.

"Do we go a-smuggling again?" he had asked gaily, and had met his master's quick stare with bright eyes. He was quite recovered now from the whipping he had had, and from the scene in his master's office, to all outward effects. He behaved as though he had forgotten both, and he wondered if his master had.

"Scamp!" said his master affectionately, his hand familiarly at his waist, moving as Simon's smile glinted towards his easement. "Do you think to enjoy smuggling still?"

"I cannot drive!" he said, protesting faintly, letting the horses jump, like himself. The hand stayed as it was, and he breathed hard, and decided it was the moment, and he must let himself go. He looked at his master, his eyes dark, his breath quick, as the hand stroked him softly, and wondered if he would be choked. "You know I did," he said, "and you said you would take me again."

"Did I promise it?" his master said.

"I do not know," Simon said, fretting the curvetting horses skilfully, "but you said you would." He gave them their head at the turn, and they left the road abruptly and took off for the thicket. "See," he said, "even the horses want to go," he said, slipping a glance out of the corner of his eyes at his master. He saw the look on his master's face that had so frightened him once in his master's room, and he thought, "it is going to happen now, any moment now," his throat dry and contracting, the horses no longer pulling at him, but pulling at the soft grass they had found instead.

"Drop the reins, Aston," his master said, his voice urgent and hurried. "Let them have their heads."

He did not protest, but lifted his throat to the hands that reached to take it, and his lips to those lips. "Be gentle," he said, putting his arms about his master, "and take me smuggling with you then." He threw his head back, the fingers tightening on his throat, the rail of the open carriage he was driving through the woods through the unchanging seasons, pressing into his back. But the back of the carriage impeded them both, and the narrow seat, and the hands hurt him very much. He lost control, and began to thrash in them, moaning for his breath, and pulled himself free, jerking in the air in quick breaths, his eyes shut and then opening to see the hands reaching for him again.

"Give me something," he gasped, all gaiety gone, "do something, I cannot bear it." He gave himself into the hands again, but he still could not lose consciousness, and he dragged himself free again, leaning back, gasping and sobbing for breath.

"Do not fight me so," his master said. "Put your head in my lap, and it will come."

"Have you nothing to drink?" he gasped. "It is not the same."

"I cannot wait now," his master said. He reached once more for Simon, pulling him against his knees, twisting the loose reins around his neck and jerking them tight, wrapping them over his hand, and with both arms holding the struggling choking young man to him. The seconds passed, and Simon's struggles intensified instead of weakening, disturbing the grazing horses and causing them to rear. He did not know his danger, but his master did, releasing the reins instantly off his wrist not to have his servant's neck snapped. He had to let Simon go to hold his plunging thrashing horses, and while he brought them under control, Simon caught his breath and watched his master's skill with appreciative eyes.

"I have dropped a rein," his master said, when he could, more calmly. "Fetch it, Simon, for me."

Simon did not move, eying him warily and the rein he held, and his master smiled at him, his eyes quizzical. "I would be sorry to hang you, Simon," his master said. "I think you would take it hard. It will not do, now, will it?"

"No," said Simon, "it hurts too much."

"I was going to the Harbour tomorrow for the powders," his master said.

"Then take me now," Simon said, "and after you get them I can bear it better. Is it so far?"

"No," his master said, "it is not so far." He looked at Simon curiously, but Simon showed no embarrassment for the brief unsuccessful seduction, and flashed him a quick brilliant smile as he leaped down from the carriage to pick up the rein, and under his master's eyes, push himself into his easement again. The years were rolling back again. He was going for broke, how far and where he did not know, before the Autumn Storms began, and as when he had been a young boy in the hells, ready to blow all he had on a single chance, he was exceptionally gay. His friends then would have known the signs, but his master did not know them, and only watched him, as he urged the horses on, springing them, with interest and then appreciation. Their legs were pressed together in the seat, for Simon was after all not a young boy, the flesh warm, and aware, and the movement of the carriage and the promises ahead, made the ride itself a kind of seduction, in easy stages. Simon was panting hard when he reached the harbour town and gave the reins to his master to drive them down the narrow streets he still did not entirely know, to a part of town he had never been in with his mistress. He watched his master go into a door to a kind of seaman's inn, and then come out, and drive to another, and then yet another. In the third he was gone for the longest time, and Simon got down from the carriage seat and walked the horses slowly and looked about him curiously and alertly. He was keyed like a string to his highest pitch to take any chance whatsoever offered to him, and he found it in an urchin wharf child who was passing aimlessly, straddling the kennel of the street, stubbing his toes as he walked on the cobblestones, and jumping on the mounting blocks, until he reached the one by Simon.

"Hi, you!" said Simon, whistling softly at him. "Want to earn a bit of something?"

"Walk the horses?" said the child knowingly.

"No, easier than that," whispered Simon. "Do you know the Methody Mr. Alwyn? By sight, I mean?" The child who had first shaken his head nodded it vigorously. "Could you find him?" The child looked doubtful but a mention of a shilling he thought perhaps he could might.

"I wish I might hold them horses," he said wistfully.

"No," said Simon, "it would be worth my skin." He grinned at the urchin who grinned back at him knowingly. "Look, now," he said to the child. "You run find Mr. Alwyn as quick as ever you can, after you see where this carriage puts in for the night. And you tell him where we stabled, and tell him if he want to ken a thing about the smugglers I can tell him what he'd like to hear. He is to give you a shilling for it, and you bring him, when you find him, to the place you saw us stopping. Tell him," he said, "not to ask for me or anyone, but you describe me to him and this carriage. Can you do that? And you tell him to wait where you take him until he hears something seeming to go on inside, and then let him come in, and after that he will know what to do."

The boy's sharp eyes were fixed on him, the aimlessness gone. "Be you one smuggler maybe your-self?"

"Maybe," Simon said. "Can you do it just as I said?"

"Tell me once more," the child said, and with one eye on the low-lit door, Simon repeated carefully in the same words his message.

"Ay, can do that, maybe," said the child.

"Maybe won't get you any shillings," Simon said. "And don't let my master see you, he is a rough one. Tell this only to the Methody priest, mind you, no one else."

The child flashed a quick gap-toothed smile, and darted under the bellies of the horses, and skittered off in the dusk. Simon watched him go, and continued walking the horses up and down. It was not very good, but it was the best he could think of to do. He hoped it would serve. After the child left, a party of seamen came by, into the inn, and then the street was deserted again, and after a while longer his master came out, looking as well pleased with himself as he ever showed.

He walked over to Simon, where he stood by the horse's head, and put his hand over Simon's on the rein, his eyes glittering in the light from the Inn, and Simon knew he had what he had gone for, his own hand shaking under the hand covering it in frightened anticipation, but his eyes dancing, and his face looking surprisingly young and gay.

"You were gone so long, sir," he said, "I thought to walk your horses. Have I pleased you, sir?"

"Yes, Simon," his master said. "That was well done."

"I wanted to please you, sir," he said.

"Did you, Aston-Simon?" his master asked, his hand tightening on Simon's trembling one.

"Yes," Simon said, "I hoped if I pleased you you would take me to see the smugglers here, if you found them."

"What, Aston Simon," his master said softly, "still wanting smugglers? What a child you are, after all. There is nothing to smugglers, they are ordinary men doing a business, that is all."

"I thought I was to see them," Simon said, letting his face fall and his disappointment show.

"And so you shall, if you please me well," his master said, taking his hand from Simon's and putting it briefly to his face. "Tomorrow night, I will take you."

"But they will be gone!" Simon exclaimed. "I shall please you so much better if you will take me tonight," he said ingeniously, "for then I shall be excited and it will not be hard."

His master laughed, and said under his breath, "Scamp."

"Take me and give me something to drink," said Simon, his excitement rising and showing in his voice and face, as he saw his master undecided. "And while you are making me a little drunk, point me out a smuggler!"

"I think I will," his master said, smiling at his eagerness. "But who will watch the horses?"

"Then bring him to me here, if I may not go inside with you," Simon said. "Could you not do just that? And have a glass brought to me of anything that is strong, so that I will not know when you hurt me?"

"I had thought to do that at the Inn, Scamp," his master said, "after we have dinner. By God," he said suddenly, "I will do it, Scamp. I will have the captain to dinner with us." Simon's startled look of dismay was comical, had he seen it, but he did not, having hurried off to the Inn.

"I have overshot myself," Simon thought. "It will all happen too soon." But he resigned himself, and pulled his spirits back up to meet his master and the seaman he brought with him.

"So you wanted to meet a smuggler," the seaman said, his eyes sharp in the dark under his shaggy brows. "And now you have, what do you make of me?"

"I think my master was right, and that you are just an ordinary man, after all," Simon said impudently. "I suppose one must see you in action to know, and my master will not let me do that," he added regretfully.

"Will he not, now?" said the smuggler, amused, "a likely young man like you. It is a raw shame."

While his master had gone to fetch the Captain, Simon had folded and sat on the cloak he had flung in the seat, and now while the Captain declined the dinner invitation, and Simon sipped slowly the hot glass of brandy he had been brought, his eyes fixed on the Captain. His master missed the cloak, and could not find it, and went hurriedly back in the Inn to look for it there.

"By God," the Captain said, "you have an impudent tongue, young fellow. And I know you are sitting on my lord's cloak. What did you want?"

"I want to talk to you," Simon said, "and I could have my tongue cut out if I am seen doing it, or if you say what you saw and what I have just said. How can I do it?"

"Tonight?" said the Captain. "After hours?"

"No," Simon said. "I have got to go and be raped."

The captain whistled slightly, and slapped one hand against the other.

"Look," Simon said, "I can pay you."

"Can you?" said the Captain. "That puts a different complexion. *I* will find *you*, mate, not you me. Look for me. And have a good time, mate. Your master's coming now. Here's your cloak, m'lord," he said. "Your boy was sitting on it all the time, and did not know it." He pulled it out and handed it to Simon's master, and walked off a little way with Simon's master, talking. Simon watched them, his face drawn, and then he could not bear the suspense, and jumped down from the seat and began again walking the horses.

"Still wanting to please me?" his master said, coming up behind him, his hand on Simon's shoulder. "Did you finish your drink? Shall we go?"

"I am sorry about your cloak, sir," Simon said. "Are you very angry with me?"

"No," his master said. "Only a little. Have you anything left in your glass at all?"

"Only a little," Simon said.

"Then give it to me." He reached into the cloak's inner pocket, and felt with his fingers and brought out a little white packet, whose contents he partly emptied into the glass. "You shall drink this for me, Aston-Simon, and make amends."

Simon took the glass, made a swift prayer, and swallowed it, grimacing at the bitter taste.

"Faugh," he said, "it is all over my tongue." He recognised what it was. He had had something similar when his uncle had drugged him years before. "I know what this is, sir."

"Do you, Simon? You do surprise me. And the captain saying you were no more than a milk babe."

"Did he say that, sir? And I thought I was very

knowledgeable about the smuggling. Did he not come that night into your harbour?"

"No, Simon, this Captain is not my brandy smuggler. But he runs the Blockades for a new company, the East India Company. And he is very knowledgeable indeed, but he does not run with ponies."

"Oh." Simon sounded slightly crestfallen, and then his voice brightened. "But he is all the same a smuggler, and that is perhaps more dangerous than the brandy smuggling and the ponies."

"It may well be, Simon. Do you enjoy danger?"

"No," Simon said, "not really very much. It is you, in the smuggling, who runs the danger."

"Then I wonder why you would speak to the Captain in my absence?"

"But did you not bring him to me so that I could?" Simon asked, his voice surprised and anxious. "You *are* displeased. I thought perhaps you were."

"Scamp," commented his master, his voice softening. "Come, you do disarm me. Let us have our dinner. Shall we have it brought to our rooms, at the Inn, and you shall eat with me, or shall we take it downstairs in the parlour?"

"What would please you, sir," Simon said.

They were met at the entrance to the Inn by a groom, but his master sent Simon around with the groom to the stables to see that his horses had taken no harm from their wait in the sea air. On his way back, a hand hooked his arm, out of the dark, and he stopped, and saw the smuggling captain had kept his word.

"I am not certain you did not tell my master what I said," Simon said.

"You still have your tongue, lad."

"I may not long," Simon said. "Did you tell him?"

"If I did, lad, I would not tell you, but happen I did not. Your master is not one easily put over, lad. You run a dangerous game."

"I know I do," Simon said, "as you yourself do."

"Well, quick now, the offer?"

"I wear a diamond," Simon said, "and I will give it to you, if you will take me off the harbour on my master's land in your boat."

"You do not want much," the smuggler said.

"If you bring me to the French island, I will give you the diamond," Simon said, "or if you put me on a French ship, either one. If you bring me yourself through to England, I will give you any price you think to ask. I have a title there and much property."

The seaman drew in his breath, and then he said, "How do I know this is so?"

"You cannot know it," Simon said, "but I am telling you it is so. And in any event you will have the diamond." He fished it from his neck and it glistened whitely, even in the dark. "Don't try to take it from me," he said, "or I will have to tell my master; he will see shortly it is gone."

"When shall I come?" the smuggler said.

"Wait off that harbour for all this week, starting after tomorrow night, with your lights dark. When I make through, I will make a light, and do not answer it, but come in for me. And I will have a second person with me."

"But I don't know the harbour," the smuggler said. "You forget. I don't run ponies."

"It is the northern end of my master's property, where the cliffs are on this island. My light will bring you in."

"Look for me," the Captain said briefly. "I will be there. And enjoy yourself," he added.

Simon smiled his slight twisted smile, in the darkness.

"Get me out," he said, "and I promise you will never regret that you did. I have to go now. I have stayed too long, and as you say, my master is not one easily put over."

He found dinner waiting in their main room in the upstairs of the Inn. He served his master, and drew his bath, and then while his master was bathing, instead of eating, he went to his master's cloak and hunted for the packets. At first he could not find them, and he thought they were gone, but then in the inner lining of the inner pocket, his fingers touched them. He drew them out, his own fingers trembling, one eye towards the door of the smaller second room. He did not dare take any single one, so he shook a little from each of the packets, making twice the amount he had taken first, and making again a swift prayer, put the powder in his mouth and swallowed it with the help of some water from the basin. Then he took his supper and threw it out the window, off the plate, poured himself a second glass of brandy and swallowed that quickly, and at his master's call went in the second room to rinse his back, and help him from the bath.

"Did you eat well, Earl?" his master asked, his eyes on him.

"Yes, my lord," Simon said, "it was a good chicken wing." He could feel the drugs taking him, but for the moment they increased his perception and his spirits.

"I left you more than a chicken wing," his master said. "Be just. But there is one thing more." He held out his arms for Simon to put the dressing gown on him, and then to Simon's horror, going into the next room, he poured a second envelope of the powder into a glass and added brandy to it and gave it to Simon again to drink.

"I have had some already," Simon said, in an effort he knew was futile. "Did you forget?"

"I did not forget, Simon. You will drink this also for me."

"God help me," Simon thought, and because under those eyes he could do nothing else, he drank.

He lost his footing, as he lifted the glass, and staggered. His master caught his arm with the glass, and lifted it again to his lips to finish, holding it there until he had.

"It is the effect now of the first you are feeling," his master said. "Do not be frightened, Simon. You may sit in the chair, if you like."

"I cannot find the chair," Simon said weakly. He smiled faintly, as his feet slipped again, and then he saw his master looming towards him, out of a kind of darkness. He put up his hands as though to ward him off. His hands were caught, that felt like lace ribbons, and had less strength, and then he felt the hands release his own helpless hands, putting them at his sides, somewhere far away from him, and move as before to his throat, holding him up by it. He opened his eyes and saw the candles were still lit, approaching him out of the room that was wavering about him, as large as men or as angels, he thought, with halos, smiling again, receding and approaching and receding. He wondered that the lights were still on, and hoped his neck would not snap, as his feet would not support him.

Something, he thought, this time was surely working, for though he knew the fingers had tightened around his neck again, and the mouth was pulling the air from his lips, this time he felt neither panic nor pain, only an enveloping discomfort that was irritating but not wholly unpleasant, and then as the pressure increased, he felt nothing at all.

Chapter 18

HE AWOKE to find his lips still in the grip of another person's mouth, and he struggled to no purpose, and tried to open his eyes, and could not, and felt the lips working at his, and he was surprised because they were blowing air inwards, instead of sucking it from him. He moved his own lips under them, and felt them lift from him, and then return with renewed vigour. He sighed, and let them do as they liked, breathing gently with them. He became aware then of a babbling of sounds like high voices in the air about him, but he could not make out the words. The lips left him, and he continued breathing without them, and someone lifted his head and pushed a spoon, it seemed, through his teeth, and made him swallow what he recognised to be something tasting very like lukewarm coffee.

"How strange," he murmured, when he had stopped

choking from the liquid, but it did not seem that his voice made any sound. He had barely recovered from the first than a second spoonful was pushed down him, and then after he had stopped choking, a third. He was tired of choking, and so this time he swallowed, with the help of the fingers massaging his throat, and some time after that, and several spoonfuls more, he found that he could open his eyes. He moved the lids upward with an effort, and saw a strange face bending near his, very concerned. He stared at the face, uncomprehending, and then turned his head a little way, and saw the face of his master, the muscles pinched in his face as though he were frowning, and behind him several other faces, pressing in. He closed his eyes, then, and turned his head away, feeling very sick, and let himself slip away again into the sleep that was pulling him down as into a long well. He was not allowed to stay, though, for like hands, a voice was drawing him up, calling his name over and over again, and then he felt a light slap at the side of his mouth. His eyes flew open in outrage, and he felt the spoon between his teeth again. He was furious to be disturbed now, and bit the spoon with his teeth, but the spoon knew its way in and emptied its contents down his throat again, but not coffee this time, but a warm broth. He discovered now he was hungry and he did not fight the spoon, and after he had had several spoonfuls he became aware the sounds in the air had gone, and the air around him was still. He opened his eyes again, the lids fluttering up this time, and saw again the strange face, but the other faces had gone, even his master's. As he said the word in his mind, he realised who his master was and who he was himself, and where he was, and that he had taken too much of something, but he could not remember what it was or why he had. Then he realised the face bending over him was speaking, and he tried to understand the words.

"I am Mr. Alwyn, Simon. Can you hear me? I am Mr. Alwyn. You sent for me, did you not? I am Mr. Alwyn, Simon. Why did you send for me? Can you speak? Can you tell me?" Over and over the words kept repeating, and then he did remember.

He tried to sit up then, but he could not at all, and he gave up the effort. He could not find his breath to speak, but he formed the word "alone?"

"I have sent them all away, Simon, your lord too. Do you know who I am?"

"Yes," Simon said, giving a faint smile, "the Methody." His voice was a thread of sound, almost inaudible.

He felt his hands taken, and the minister lifted his head and cried "God be praised!"

"I must talk to you," Simon said, forming the words painfully. "But I can't." He smiled faintly, apologetically, and mouthed the faint words "I took too much." He relaxed, shutting his eyes, the slight effort too much for him. He felt again the spoon at his mouth, this time with coffee, and he managed to swallow it and several spoonfuls more.

He was remembering now how he had sent for the minister, and his plans, but he had not planned to be unable to speak at all. He had not taken that into account. He wanted to know so many things, but he could not make his tongue work to ask them. And there was no time, he thought. "Do not go away," he whispered, and shut his eyes in exhaustion.

The faces changed, but the hands working with him did not. He opened his eyes and saw his master's and closed them quickly, so that his master could not read in his eyes what he had done and was about to do. He wanted to go back to sleep, but the hands about him would not let him do that, and made him sit up, and tried to make him walk, when he could not feel his legs, or use them himself, but he was naked and cold and he was let to lie down again, and more of the coffee, hotter now, and the soup, that was hot, given him that he was made to do it. Then the voices seemed to leave again, and the face of the Methody Mr. Alwyn was bending over him again, taking his hands warmly and firmly in his.

"Simon," he said, "your master has left to speak with the Governor. If you want to speak to me alone, you must try to speak now. Are you a smuggler yourself, is that it? And wanted to repent?"

"God, no," said Simon, weakly, and his lips twisted in the faintest trace of bitter amusement at the look of disappointment that crossed the priest's face. "I am sorry," he whispered weakly, "but perhaps when I can talk better I can put you in the way of one." He paused, panting, realising he had no breath and no strength to waste. He turned his face away from the spoon being put again to his lips, and then yielded and drank it and caught the minister's hands with his. "I want you to marry me, father," he whispered. "It is not allowed such as I, but I must have the ceremony—and the papers—" he paused, and waited for his breath "—to protect my child. Please." Something of his desperate urgency and the sincerity of his desire communicated itself to the priest.

"Did you take what you did to bring me to you?" he asked.

"Yes, father," whispered Simon.

"So rash," the priest murmured. "Did you know that you nearly died of what you took?"

Simon brushed the words aside, ignoring them, with a slight turn of his head, his eyes fixed on the priest. "Will you do it?"

"Your master does not like me," the priest said.

"I know that," Simon whispered. "I sent for you because I did. It will be so very hard, father," he said. "But I thought—you might."

"Who are you, my child?" the priest asked, looking intently at the white face staring up at him, expressionless except for the urgency of the eyes, the distinguishing line of the bone showing clearly through the tight skin.

"I am Simon, Earl of Halford," Simon said.

"And the woman?" the priest asked, no flicker of surprise passing over his face.

"Alyx de Vere," Simon whispered. "A transport, father. She is seventeen—I think."

"Is she here?" the priest asked.

Simon shook his head, fighting for breath.

"How shall I come to you?"

"You cannot," Simon whispered. "I must come to you." He paused, feeling a strange sensation inside him, swelling, cutting off his breath. He fought it with all his will. "Wait every night on the West shore just where my master's land begins. If in a week I have not come, you will know," he paused and fought for breath, "I could not come. Will you do it, father?"

"Yes," the priest said, and saw though the young man's eyes were open, staring at him, his breath had stopped again. He bent over him, and put his lips again to the blue rigid ones beneath him, and began to breathe into him as he had done before, without effect. His eyes intent, as he worked, he saw the pillow under the young man's head that had been put there when he was being fed, and pulled it out, onto the floor, and continued to breathe into his lips.

"I will do that," Simon's master said, who had approached without being noticed. "You are tired, father, and have no breath yourself. The Innkeeper is bringing more hot bricks, and you will arrange them." He sat down on the bed, bending over Simon, putting his hand under his armpits, lifting him slightly, bringing him up to meet his own lips that he lowered, pushing his breath into him, and then lifting his hands slightly with his hands, as though releasing it. He took his mouth away briefly, and said shortly to the priest, "Press his stomach with your hand, each time I take my mouth away." They continued working in unison, silently, not pausing while the new hot bricks were wrapped and put at Simon's feet that were cold in the warm bed. The Innkeeper's wife brought fresh hartshorn which she spilled over the pillow, and a feather, which she burnt, making Simon's master sneeze.

He looked down then, his rhythm broken, and saw that Simon was breathing without him, slowly and shallowly. He paused and drew the breath into his lungs again, and then watching closely, he moved into the rhythm of Simon's breathing adding his own stronger breath and stronger rhythm to it. After a time, Simon's eyes that had closed when his breath first returned, opened slowly, and saw and felt his master. The priest had at Simon's master's wish lifted his arms and put them about his neck, clasping them loosely, and holding them there with his handkerchief he wound about the wrists that could not hold. Simon moved his arms slightly, tightening them about his master, and returned lightly what seemed to him his master's kiss, and then he relaxed, his fastened hands resting on his master's neck, and let the strange relieving kisses of those familiar lips continue as they would.

Some time later, near an hour, Simon's master left Simon and escorted the minister to the door politely but firmly. He had his luncheon brought to his room and sat beside his servant who was sleeping deeply, watching his uneven but continuing breath. Simon slept all that day, and into the night, waking about one, his mouth and lips parched and feverishly dry, but his head clear. He stirred, and his master was at once by him, feeling his forehead and his pulse, and lifting his head offering him cool water.

"How are you now, Simon?" he whispered, lying him back down, flat.

"I am so very cold," Simon said unhappily. "Are we still at the Inn?"

"Yes, Simon," his master said. "You have been sick, that is why you are cold." He tucked the feather bed more closely about his servant, his hands very gentle.

"You gave me too much of the powder," Simon said, opening his eyes and then shutting them. "It made me feel very—odd. I did not want the second."

"You remember that?" his master said, worriedly. "I must have, but I do not see how I could."

"Perhaps the smuggler gave you the wrong powder," Simon said, and shut his eyes again. "I am sorry, sir. Have I been asleep very long?"

"It does not matter," his master said. "You have had us all very worried, Simon. When I could not wake you in the night, last night, I woke the landlord, who had gone to bed, to find a doctor, and a harbour priest who was passing by came in. He is experienced in such things, and he saw what had happened, and he did know what to do. I was very grateful to him, for

I could not find a surgeon until much later, and he might not have done so well as the priest."

"I thought it was you who helped me," Simon said, opening and lifting his eyes.

"That was later, Simon. We had thought you were better, but you surprised us. I think you were fed too quickly, or perhaps the coffee was too strong, Simon. I had forgotten, but seeing the Methody reminded me, I had seen the smugglers do that once to a man with too much water in him. Do you remember none of this?"

"Very little," Simon said. "I remember you. I could not breathe or speak and you came to me."

His master took his hand, and sat by him, holding it, and did not answer at once. Then he said, "The Methody believed you were dying in sin, and he insisted on being let in to you. Do you remember none of that? And the Governor had heard there was a smuggler dying at the Inn, and insisted on talking to me."

Simon shook his head, and closed his eyes. "I am so sorry, sir," he said presently, his voice very faint, so that his master had to bend to hear, "that you have had this trouble over me. Are you very angry with me?"

"For what, Simon?" his master asked in surprise.

"For the powder making me sick, and my causing you so much trouble. Could you have what you wanted before I was sick?"

His master did not answer. He bent a little closer, and pressed Simon's lips very gently with his. "No," he said, removing his lips at once, "I am not angry with you at all, dear Scamp." He lifted the candlestick to move it away from the bed, and saw, as he raised it, tears glistening on Simon's lashes and on his cheeks. He was surprised, and took his silk handkerchief and wiped them away. "There is nothing to weep about, Simon," he whispered. "I am not angry, I promise you." He pressed Simon's lips again gently with his. "Go to sleep, Scamp," he said. "I have sent for my carriage, and tomorrow, if you are better, I will take you home."

"Where will you sleep?" Simon asked. "I am in your bed, I think."

"Another has been set up, Simon," his master said. "I shall do very well."

"I am so very cold," Simon said, "and this bed is so very large. Could you not sleep here, too, or move me there? You will not be comfortable, sir, in a set-up servant's bed."

His master did not answer him, but when he had undressed he pulled the feather bed back, and lay down beside Simon and took him closely in his arms and held him. Simon put his arms about him also and clung to him weeping silently, the tears falling down his cheeks again, and onto his master. Try as he would, his master could not comfort him until finally he threatened to leave the bed. "I cannot stop them," Simon said. "I am so weak and they will come. I love you, sir," he whispered.

"But you will not be my son," his master said.

"No," Simon whispered. "I am someone else's." He put his lips to the older man's again, too weak to move. They slept all that night in each other's arms, but like father and son.

Chapter 19

IN THE morning when Simon woke, his heart as heavy as his eyelids, the bed was empty beside him, the feather bed pulled up about him warmly. He found he could sit up, though he was still very weak and dizzy and his heart thudded painfully in his chest when he moved, like his head. He made himself pull himself up and out of bed, and walk to the press where his clothes were. He put them on, resting between each effort, and then holding to the pieces of furniture, and to the door, and then to the stair rail, he made his way down the stairs and into the coffee room where his master was breakfasting.

His master looked up, surprised and concerned to see him. Simon tried to smile, and achieved a sickly grin, and took the chair his master pointed him to gratefully. After breakfast, he found he felt better, and in the coach on the way home he sat up part of the way with his master, and slept the rest of the way, waking to find his head in his master's lap, as they were entering the gates.

His master was shaking him, and telling him he must sit up, and he did, and saw they were approaching the house. There were many servants, with curious eyes, more than required, who met them, or stood where they could, watching. Alyx was among them, at the door, and as he passed her, Simon, walking slowly, turned his head slightly and said, his lips just forming the words, "Tonight, the stairs, my room." He turned his head away from her, and saw ahead of him in the mirror his image and his master's, but his master's eyes not on him but on his lady who was approaching.

"To be caught by an old trick," Simon thought, his heart missing a beat. But if his master had seen him, he gave no sign. He had taken my lady's hand in his and bent his head to kiss it, and putting her hand through his, was walking now apart with her, his tall head bent to hers. Simon waited behind them, until his master turned and dismissed him, to supper and to his room. He passed by his mistress, but she ignored his presence as she had since the night of his whipping. He might have been thin air.

He was excused from attending his master at supper, or when late in the evening he came in to be made ready for bed. His bell was not rung, and after a time, he fell asleep, on his own bed, in his own room, his door left ajar, should his master call him. He did not wake until the servant who had helped Simon's master undress came to his door and spoke to him and told him that his master wished him.

"You should have called me," Simon said, his eyes heavy with sleep. "It was my place to help you, not his."

"I thought you should sleep," his master said, taking his hand, his eyes very grave and very tender.

"What may I do for you now?" Simon asked.

"You may sit by me, dear Scamp, if you will, a little. Here," he said, indicating the stool at his feet. Simon sat there, his head against his master's knees, his master's fingers roaming in his hair, and after a time, reaching to his throat and pulling out the little chain. His master did not speak, and Simon, waiting, grew very drowsy, and fell asleep, sitting on the stool and toppled sideways off of it. "My lord!" he cried, in dismay, finding himself on the floor. "Forgive me! I did not mean to fall asleep."

"You are tired," his master said. "I am selfish to keep you, dear Scamp, from your rest. No," he said, "do not protest. I am going to sleep myself shortly."

"Will you want me tonight?" Simon asked.

"I would be cruel indeed if I did," his master said. "Tomorrow, if you feel better, you may wait on me in the morning."

"You are kind, my lord," Simon murmured.

"No, Scamp," his master said, drawing him towards him with his hand, "not kind, only tired like yourself." He kissed Simon's lips, and paused, and kissed them again, and then he dismissed him. "Close your door, Simon," he said. "I will not need you tonight. I will sit up a while longer and read, and I would not disturb you." Simon bent his own head, and kissed his master's hand, and then, pausing, his master's lips, and turned his back on his master and his master's room, and withdrew to his own.

He moved about as though he were undressing, and then he lay down on the bed, in his clothes, unhappy and uneasy. Could he have called his enterprise off for that night and laid it for another, he would have. But, he thought, if he suspects me, of anything, he cannot think I will try to do anything against his wishes tonight, for truly I am not fit to. And he could not call off his plans. He could not reach Alyx, and if she came, he could not lose the chance. He might not see her again, or be able to speak if he did. He could not read his master's mind towards him, but he thought that if the scare of his poisoning had alarmed his master beyond suspicion, his wits would recover soon enough and he might have embarrassing questions to ask of his servant. If he were to go, he must go, before that happened, and while he was still free to move at will, and thought to be too weak to move anywhere.

His master's light stayed on for an hour, and then went out. Simon waited yet another hour, until the sound of deep breathing, when he stood next the door, relieved him. He went then to his own door, which he had left ajar, opened it without any sound, and slipped through it. The veranda was empty, and he walked in his stocking feet, his shoes in his hand, over to the steps, and went down them, still without any sound. They were solid, and the wood supported by stone and wood pillars did not creak under his weight. When he reached the bottom step he looked quickly about, and saw no one, and stepped into the shadow of one of the pillars, underneath the steps, to wait.

The little moon on the wane had risen, and the air grown damp and chill, before she came. She paused uncertainly, hiding back against the wall of the house, under the stairs, until she saw him as he moved out towards her. He did not say a word, his finger to his lips and hers, but took her hand, and led her cautiously, along the house, until they found an open window, which they crept cautiously through, and

into the dining room and down the narrow stairs into
the kitchen passageway. He had gone into his master's
room while he took supper, and taken the keys he
thought he had seen him use on the passageway, out
of his drawer where he had once seen him lay them,
the second pair, not kept on his general ring, and
now, Alyx with him, he pressed the panelling of the
wall, as he had seen his master do, and after several
tries, the panelling moved under his hand, and slid
back and inward against the wall, revealing the second
door with the lock just beyond. He took the key now
in his hand, praying it might fit and might turn, and
without effort, it did. The well-oiled lock released the
catch silently, and he pushed the second door open,
pulling the panelling to behind him, and then the
door, relocking it.

The girl with him had not said a word, and now he
laid his finger on her lips again, and taking her hand
again, led her forward, slowly in the total darkness of
the passage that clung around them like soft enfolding
cloth. He had no sense of direction in the pitchy
black, and he knew there were many turnings and
side passages. He let his hands feel the walls as he
went, holding the girl's hand in his. He wondered if
she was frightened. He knew he was himself. If he
made a wrong turn, he could not trust his memory to
put him forward again, and not to set them walking
backwards again into the house. It was cold in the
passage, and their hands were both trembling with it.
They passed under a vent, a round barred circle set in
the ground above them, the outside light entering in
faint rays through it, Alyx's face pale in the light
beside him. He had not noticed the vent when he was
there before, but he could not think of any wrong
turning he might have taken. When the wall had

fallen off, for a turning, he had gone the length of his arm leaving Alyx to hold the last wall with her hand, and then when his arm found the beginning of the wall on the other side, leading straight ahead, he had pulled Alyx to him. His memory was good, and he saw in his mind as on a map held before him the passage as he had travelled it in the lantern light with his master. He could hear a faint dropping of water now, somewhere in the passage, and the frail dangling tree roots he remembered before brushed his face like spider webs. He put his finger to Alyx's lips, to warn her not to scream, and put her hand up to one and whispered, "It is only the root of a tree." He thought now they had passed under the lawn, where his master sometimes set his dogs loose at night, and past the high walls of rock and spiked iron that he had not thought Alyx could climb, and perhaps he could not have either, and were approaching the thicket and the clearing. He hoped so. He was tiring, and his breath was coming hard, and he thought she must be too. The way seemed interminable, and the second half longer than the first, boxes barring their way now, and filling him with fear the smugglers might surprise them. He thought they must have been walking for more than an hour, though perhaps it was not so long, when he felt the ground rising beneath his feet, and watching for them, felt the steps carved in the dirt, and braced with wooden supports. He led Alyx up them, took his second key, put it to the door, and found it would not turn. His mind in a panic, not knowing what to think, he forced himself to try again, with both keys, and discovered he had interchanged the keys. He put the right key now into the lock, and it turned, and he opened the door made of turves and laths, pushing it outward, stepping out fearfully himself into the clearing and bringing Alyx with him.

There was no one there. He could have laughed for joy and relief, looking around him, in the little glade. The trees loomed up over his head, a few stars sprinkled in the uneven circle of sky they left above their heads, the branches blowing gently in the gentle night wind. It was warmer above ground than in the passage, and though it was dark night still, and the scrap of moon falling lower, it seemed light after the total darkness of the passage. He put his finger again to Alyx's lips, and wondered briefly what she might be thinking, as they stood holding hands in the little glade, but he was too busy listening, his ears pricked, to wonder much. Clear in the night air, and not very far from him, he could hear the sounds of the ponies browsing. He pulled Alyx's hand and began to walk in the direction of the sound, towards the fenced pasture where the smuggling ponies were grazing. He did not have bridle or rein or saddle or rope, but he knew how to handle horses, and without any difficulty to speak of, he had brought one to Alyx and seated her on it, and shown her how to twist her fingers in its shaggy mane, and then he caught one for himself. The gate was locked, but he knew Alyx could ride, and running back a little with his pony he took the fence with a jump that surprised all the ponies, not just his, and looking back, saw Alyx follow him, and slow her pony to a sedate walk, beside his.

For the rest, they had no difficulty. He set his course by the little moon and the pole star, that he had checked by the house, where he knew his directions still, and set off with Alyx leisurely towards the sea.

It was a long way, and dawn was close to breaking

before they reached the edge of the woods that led down a grassy headland sloping evenly to the sand and the sea. It was far too exposed a place, he thought, but he had never seen it before, and it was the only place he could think of where the priest might meet them that they could both find. He could see a quarter of a mile away the tall outside fencing about his master's grounds, and he rode with Alyx slowly along the shingle, at the water's edge where the wet sand erased their tracks, filling with water behind them and dissolving, towards the fence that rose higher before them like prison bars, too high to go over, and extending through the shingle and the sand, out into the ocean itself, mounted on a sea wall. He had not expected this, and had not realised how well he was kept in on his master's place and the outside world kept out.

He did not expect the priest to meet them that night. His master had stayed awake too long, and Alyx had been delayed in coming, and the passageway had been more difficult to make their way through than he had thought in the semi-light of the lanterns it would be. But he rode up to the fence, and sat on his pony, Alyx beside him, peering through it. He stood there, waiting, not daring to make a signal or a light for he did not believe the priest would come, and watched the sky over the breaking sea lightening. It was a beautiful sight, the sea birds beginning to wake, the sea freshening, and the taste of salt blowing from the spray onto their lips and on their eyelids. And then, as he was thinking he could not stay longer, he saw a figure that had been sitting unnoticed rise and walk briskly towards them.

Simon looked at Alyx, and whispered, "It is the priest, Alyx, he has come. Are you ready?" She nodded her head, but she did not speak. He slid off his own pony, that his legs almost touched the ground on, like a child's pony, and helped her from hers, and holding the manes of the ponies in their hands, they walked up to the bars and stood waiting for the priest.

"You did come," Simon said gratefully. "I was afraid that you might not, or that you might have left already."

"I thought you could not yourself come so soon," the priest said, "but you had asked me and I could not let you come and then not find me. I have been here all night since sundown, waiting. Let us not risk this ceremony being stopped now."

"Whatever comes now," Simon thought, as the priest, without wasting time in words, took out his book, and papers he had with him which he put at the back of the book, "the child is protected so long as it lives. It will have its heritage, if it can reach to it." He looked about him, and there was no one else in sight. The pale sky was turning rosy, and the little waves were still, only ripples stirring their surface, as they flowed in, and receded, the wet sand turning rosy too, reflecting the colours of the sky and the sun that was not in sight, far to their East. He sighed, relief flowing through him, easing his tiredness, and took Alyx's hand in his.

"Don't let go the pony," he murmured. "We might never catch them again."

The priest was speaking to them now, gravely conjuring them, and then using their names which Simon had given him. He made his replies, without hesitation, unsmiling, and Alyx made hers, slowly, his eyes on her, and hers on him, wondering. He saw the child she was carrying stir inside her, the side of her dress moving with its motion, and he put his hand holding hers there, and kissed her, as the priest adjured them to do, and it was finished.

"So simple," Simon said, "now it is done. Father Alwyn," he said, turning to the priest, "if I win through myself to my home, I shall build a chapel for you on my land. Will you protect these papers for me, which I do not myself dare to carry with me? If we are caught today before we take ship, I do not want your name involved with us. Will you keep them for me here, and if you have to return to England will you make a copy and register it with the Bishop in London? He will know my name," he added, unsmiling.

"I will send him a copy by mail," the priest said, "and one copy I shall keep here, that I will not register while I am here, and I will take a copy with me if I should leave the island." He took their hands in his and said, "God bless you, my children, and keep you, and bring you out of your perils safely. And do not stay here any longer, so that He may."

"I hope He may," Simon said soberly. "About the smuggling—" he paused and looked at Father Alwyn. "These are smugglers' ponies. But I do not know how that will help you."

"I know very well what they are," the priest said, a smile lurking in his eyes. "And I do not know what I can do about it either, except to hope they smuggle you safely out, however your way to go. I never thought to pray for smugglers. Go on now, with you," he said, "go on." And turned, his black gown rustling over the sand, and walked hurriedly away from them across the sand, down the southern beach.

"Simon," Alyx whispered. "Is this true? Has this happened?"

"Yes, Alyx," he whispered. "It is entirely real, and

entirely valid, and I mean it with all my heart. Up you go now," he said, helping her back on the little beast. "We must find a place to lie safely, until dark, and I do not know where it shall be. We cannot make the little caves I know of."

He guided the ponies out into the sea's edge, where their tracks would not show, and then in the gathering quickening light, he urged both ponies on, faster than he thought safe for them or for the child, until an hour later, in broad daylight, they reached the line where the cliffs began to rise. Then he helped her dismount, clumsily, so stiff she was near falling, and smacked the ponies hard on their rumps, and sent them cantering back towards the South.

"We shall have to walk now, love," he said. "We could be too easily seen if they stayed with us."

They picked their way along the edge of the shore close to the rising cliffs, their feet slipping in the soft dry sand that was harder to walk in and that made their feet ache, over the debris the sea had brought in. The sun was higher now, but not over the cliff's edge, where they walked in shadow. His eyes were alert for any place they might go to hide in, during the light. The tide was beginning to roll in again now, and he thought the sand they were walking on might soon be covered, which would be helpful if dogs were put out for them, but that might also drown them. His eyes scanning the cliffs beside him, he saw an opening well above their heads, but no way even for him to climb to it. So they walked on, silently, too tired to speak, hungry, and frightened.

"Oh, God," he prayed silently. "I am doing my best. I am doing all I can. Is there no place where we may rest?"

The shore was rockier now, and harder to walk on.

They made their way between stones when they could, and around them when they could not, and then when the sea grew deeper, they climbed over them, scratching their hands and knees, until finally there was no sand at all, only the sea, and the rocks, and dead trees and pieces of mast that had been washed up or blown down from the cliffs towering above their heads.

"Simon," Alyx said, when she had slipped for the third time, "Simon, the sea is coming in, isn't it?"

He nodded, listening for any sounds of voices or dogs, but he heard nothing, only the noise of the waves moving against the rocks.

"Are we going to drown, Simon?" she whispered.

"I don't think so, Alyx," he said, trying to smile, "I never thought I was meant to drown."

"But you meant to ride the ponies, didn't you?"

"Yes, Alyx," and then he said, "I think it is all right, Alyx, but if you like, you might pray. I am myself praying hard. And look for any place, any ledge, on the cliff high enough to be above the water and not so high we cannot reach it. Like that," he said pointing, "but that is too high."

"Would it be better we were caught, Simon," she whispered, "or better that we drown?"

"For you, that you are caught," he said. "But myself, I may choose drowning. I hope we will have neither. We have won so far, love. Look!" he whispered, and pulling her after him, crying now, as she slipped and stumbled, he began to climb the rocks, taking her with him, until they reached the top of a very large one, and in the top of it they found a hollow, washed out, curving back a little way under the stone's edge.

"We could be seen," she whispered, "from the top of the cliff."

"Yes," he said, "if they look just right, but the lip will shield us."

"When the sun comes overhead, it will be very hot. Should we go on?"

He shook his head. "From here I can see quite far, and I see nothing better, or half so good. Those caves are very fine in the wall, but the way looks crumbly, and they are too high even for me. And look, love, at the water. It must be near noon. I think it may even cover the rock, so we may not have to worry about being hot. See, there is a little pool of water still left, but perhaps this tide will be lower."

The rock, which was several rocks, perhaps a cliff fall, at a turn in the land where they had fallen together and been fused together, rose up on all sides of them like walls, and they could hear the water beating at the sides about them, and rising through the little cracks and fissures. The sun grew hotter, and the water rose higher, and reached their feet, and their waists.

"Are you afraid, Alyx?" he whispered.

"A little," she said. "It is so very uncomfortable. Do you think, Simon, we shall ever one day be comfortable and safe together?"

"I hope so, Alyx," he said. "I think we may. I think someday we will look back at this time, which I think we can never tell our grandchildren about, they would be so shocked, and remember it with pleasure, because we loved one another and our child enough to endure it and hardly to complain." He did not speak his own thought, which was that in comparison to what he might be feeling by nightfall, the hard rock might seem high comfort.

The water was rising steadily higher inside and outside the rock, but Simon was not worried about that so much as the effect of the cold water on Alyx for so long. He could see the high water mark on the cliff, that he had been watching uneasily all morning, and did not think they would be entirely submerged, and that the rock walls would hold them from being swept out to sea. The sun was warming the surface of the stone and warming the water caught in it, and Alyx suddenly lifted her head, and said "Simon!"

"Yes," he answered. "Simon, did you never go swimming in the sea?"

"Many times," he said, "on holiday."

"If we forget why we are here," she said, "and just look about us, is it not very like being on holiday?"

"Very like," he murmured, and took her in his arms and held her, and kissed her. They clung to the edges of the rock, and floated, and watched the sea life, and as the day wore on, the water receded, and left them wet and hungry and shivering in their small castle. They climbed down then, from their too exposed height, and walked slowly along the receding tide, thirsty, in the midst of water, and no water anywhere accessible they could drink. The sun blazing on them full from the West, its rays muted by the Autumn clouds, dried their clothes, and Simon took his tinderbox from his coat, and found the water had dampened the tinder, and set it on a warm stone to dry. The long day wore to its close, and the cool of night began to take its place, shadows lengthening, small sounds of evening echoing in the stillness.

"Even the longest day ends," Simon said. "How sad, Alyx, that the first day of our marriage should seem so intolerably long, as this one has." He took her in his arms, in the shadow of the cliff, and kissed her gently. "To be with you all day," he said, "and hardly to be able to kiss you." He smoothed her hair, and she smiled tiredly at him, and he smiled back at her as tiredly.

"It is not much farther, now," he said, "and then we can sit down, I hope, and wait for the boat that is to meet us." They walked very slowly over the rocks, in the dusk, tripping over driftwood and submerged rocks and shells, protected somewhat by their sturdy servant shoes. They were too weary to talk. Simon stopped from time to time to listen, but he heard no sounds except the water.

"I think we are near now," he said. "I am going to walk ahead and see if anyone is looking for us here."

"Can I not go too?" she said. "If they are, I would want to be found, if you are."

"Yes, but I do not mean to be seen or heard," he said, "and you make twice the noise I do. Wait here, I shall not be very long."

But he was quite long returning, and she grew very frightened, in the dark, by the sea on the shore, and cold in the rising wind, before he appeared out of the dark beside her.

"There is no one there," he said. "I have lit my signal fire. That was what took me so long, Alyx. I could not find dry material, and the salt would not burn. But in the end, the tinder caught."

"What did you use?" she asked.

"My coat," he said. "There was really nothing else. It did not burn long, and I hope it was seen. Come now, love," he said, "keep your courage only a short while longer."

He led her on, around and up a curve in the shore, and they were standing on the edge of the harbour, protected from the rocks, and the waves and the wind by the curving descending walls of the cliff that

marched out into the sea. They stood on the edge of
the natural wall they had mounted to, and looked at
the harbour, and out to sea, where they thought they
saw a small shape in the dark waters moving in
towards them.

"Alyx," he whispered, "Alyx, I think it is the boat
from the ship!" He led her down the rocks, and onto
the sand of the harbour shore, where they stood listening, his arm about her shoulder drawing her close.
And as they listened, quite clearly they heard the
sound of oars, muted, but pulling through the water,
and the creak of the oarlock. He stood there, tired
and dazed, unable to believe that he had achieved
what he had set out to do, watching the boat coming
now into sight, and now pulling up onto the shore,
and the captain he had met, and two sailors jumping
from it into the shallow waters and splashing ashore.

Simon went to meet the captain pulling the diamond from out of his shirt and over his head. The
chain he intended to keep for passage, and he pulled
the diamond from it, putting the chain in his pocket.

He held it out to the captain silently, who took it in
his hand, examined it, nodded, and taking out his
handkerchief put the diamond carefully in its center,
wrapped the edges over it several times, and put it
into his own inner pocket, buttoning down the flap
carefully. "It will do," he said briefly. "I will take
you." He directed a third seaman to pick Alyx up, to
carry her to the ship, and had started towards the
long boat himself with Simon, when he stopped short,
stiffening, with a startled grunt. The report of the gun
came almost at the same moment, firing from the edge
of the high cliff over them, shocking the quiet of the
little harbour, bringing them all to a horrified stand-

still, watching the captain slowly falling onto the sand beside them.

Simon was the first to move. He did not need to look to see what had happened, or who had fired the shot. He walked slowly across to the seaman holding Alyx, not afraid of being shot, and took her in his arms from those of the seaman and kissed her, as he set her down. He ignored the commotion about him, everything left of him concentrated on the girl before him he had made his wife and whom he did not expect to see again.

"I tried, Alyx," he whispered. "It was the best I could do, but it was not enough. Some day perhaps all the same you will go home, and when you do, my mother or my sisters will receive you." The seaman who had held Alyx had recovered his scattered wits, and he was running now, behind them, as hard as he could towards the boat, when the gun cracked again, and he fell into the dark water, thrashing and choking in the little foaming waves.

"You will please stay exactly as you are," Simon's master's voice said coldly and clearly across the dark space still separating him and the little group.

He will not shoot me or Alyx, Simon thought, not to kill us, at least. But he stayed all the same where he was, motionless, as he was directed. He did not want Alyx to see him shot, and there was nowhere now he had to go. He waited, silent now, his arm about Alyx, until the men his master had brought came up with them, and had taken him from her, pulling his arms behind him and tying his wrists together, so tightly he winced despite himself. They did the same to the two seamen who were still standing near him as if rooted to the sand, their amazed faces lifted in horror to the cliff's edge where the shots had dropped as if from heaven, but Alyx they left unbound, thinking, Simon thought bitterly, looking at her weary frightened face, they did not need to.

He stood with the men holding his arms, the boat half-beached, rocking behind him against the waves, the dead captain at his feet. He had not known his master would overreach him, but now that it had happened, he was not surprised, and he knew he had expected it. When his master came up, he did not move, not even to turn his face. His master bent down and turned the captain over, and felt in his pockets until he found what he was searching for. He rose then, and walked around the captain's body to Simon, and felt into his pockets until he found and retrieved the chain.

"I told you, Simon," he said, "that if you removed my chain again, I would not give it to you again. And I will not."

Simon was silent. There was nothing to say.

"I hope," his master said then, when he did not speak, "that you did not think that affecting scene last night would sway me to be lenient with you, for you will be disappointed. And you have, I think, been disappointed enough already, no?"

"No," Simon said then, "I did not think it. I do not expect you to be."

"Did you not know, Simon, that I must find you? How could you be so foolish and so unwise? I have known all day where you would come tonight. I am not entirely stupid, Simon. When you were gone this morning, I understood your interest in smugglers. So I did not waste my time or anyone else's, rushing about after you, until night came, and then I came here. Did you have a pleasant day?"

"No," Simon said briefly.

"A pity. I had thought you might at least have had that. And now I have a long boat and two smugglers living and two smugglers dead for the Governor and Mr. Alwyn. That should please them, and show my righteous indignation. Have you anything else you wish to say to me, Simon? I would say it, if I were you, while you can."

"Yes," Simon said, "but I cannot say it here, before these people."

"No?" said his master. "A pity. I wonder why you cannot."

"Because you required my word of me," Simon said, "and I have kept it, and I will keep it yet."

His master looked at him sharply then, but he only said, "You shall tell me later tonight, then, if you still wish to."

He left Simon then, and started to walk away, leaving the rest to follow him, but Simon called after him sharply, "Sir!"

He turned, and looked inquiringly, but did not move to return.

"Do not make her walk, sir!" Simon said.

"She walked here. She can walk back."

"She will miscarry, sir! She has had too hard a day. Look at her!"

"Then you may carry her yourself," his master said, "if you think she requires carrying."

Simon walked to his wife, his hands still bound, and bent, and picked her up, speaking softly to her to clasp his neck, and hold to him, but her weight and the child were too much for his strength, and before he had reached the path up the cliff, he had had to stop and put her down.

"Sir!" he called. His master turned. "Sir, I cannot! I beg of you!"

"Is it all that you beg?"

"Yes," Simon said. His master nodded to one of the stronger men, who picked the wilting girl up in his arms, and carried her up the steep path, Simon stumbling and falling into the dust, and picking himself up to stumble on. No one helped him, or offered him a hand. At the top of the hill, there were the remains of a camp, and several horses. His master rode, as did his men. He put the dead seamen over one horse, and Alyx he put in front of one of his men, but Simon and the two smugglers he put on leading strings attached to the horse carrying the dead smugglers that was led by the man carrying Alyx before him. When he reached his carriage, he had Simon and Alyx put inside, Alyx beside him, Simon and one of the men on the seat opposite him. The smugglers then he had taken up on horses, and carried behind the carriage.

Simon tried to stay awake, but he could not, and he fell asleep, sitting up, and fell to one side, against the side of the carriage. The fall woke him, and he tried to sit up again, his face dazed with sleepiness, his eyes meeting his master's.

"Yes," his master said, "I would sleep, while I could."

The words brought him broad waking, and he looked across at Alyx, asleep now against his master's shoulder, his arm about her, while she slept unaware in her sleep where she was or who was holding her. He was going to cry, Simon realised to his horror, and he turned his face away again, as far as he could, against the cushions, and after a time, despite his master's words, he fell asleep again, falling this time backwards as the carriage jolted on, against the man put to guard him, seated beside him, his tear-stained face full in view of his master's in the lamp-lit carriage.

It did not move him, as Simon had known it would not, and had therefore turned away to hide his weakness. He woke, not very much refreshed by his sleep, when the carriage stopped before the women's quarters, not at the big house. It was late at night, and his master took his arm from around Alyx, so that she did not wake, and went himself to the door of the quarters. When he came back, he had two women with him who between them lifted Alyx and carried her inside.

"Do you see how you have harmed her?" he said to Simon. "Was she not better as she was, left alone, inside my house in comfort?" He stepped back inside the carriage, his face remote, and the carriage went on, where Simon knew it must, though he had hoped for the night to collect himself, to the courtyard where he had suffered at his mistress's hands. There was no one else there. Everyone else was asleep, except for the men with his master. But it did not matter. His master knew well enough that by morning the word would have spread and that whatever was done to him that night would be quickly known and that part of his punishment served to its use. He did not know which was worse, he thought. To be hurt before people, and to be hurt alone, with no one there, except the persons hurting him. He rather thought it was worse to suffer alone, in the dark, and more cruel, when the person hurting him might easily stop if they would, but in the end it was much the same. The dead men were unloaded from the horses, and put down for the time on a bench by the gate. The two smugglers were taken over to the stockade at the side of the courtyard and locked into the small rooms made into the wall, and a guard put by the door.

It is my turn now, Simon thought, watching, and it was. His wrists were untied, and he was strung up as before into the whipping frame, his wrists already raw and sore, his weight and the rope cutting into them unbearably, but he had to bear it. There was nothing else to do. His master stood in front of him, watching him, his face impassive, while a whip was brought, and then he was whipped. It is as simple as that, Simon thought. One takes a person and puts him up and whips him, and he wishes he were already dead. And then he could hear the strokeman, to his surprise, counting the strokes. He fixed his attention on each number as it was called out. He hoped for fifty, but fifty passed, and the regular fall of the whip continued. Then he prayed for one hundred, but one hundred passed. At two hundred, the strokeman's voice stopped, and the fall of the whip ceased. He was still conscious, and though he felt he had no back left, he knew the whipping had been less severe than his mistress had put him to. He wondered why, and what he was to be kept for. He heard his master speaking to him, from a long way off, and he brought his wandering wits into focus.

"You had something to say to me, Simon?"

He stared blankly at his master.

"Say it now, if you do, Simon. There is no one else here, who will hear you, and you will not see me, I think, again."

The words brought him back to full consciousness.

"Yes," he said. "I do. I did not take the boat the first night, if you looked for me, because there was something else I had to do."

"Yes, Simon," his master said, "I was there. I did wonder where you were, but just a little. I thought when you did not come I knew."

"No," Simon said. "You were mistaken. She is too near her time. I went south, through your tunnel. You will find your keys in my shirt, wherever it has been put, or one of my pockets. Your tinderbox is still on the beach. I did not like to steal from you."

"Did you not?" said his master.

"No," Simon said flatly. "We went south, on your ponies, I will not tell you where, and when I came back to where you found me, I had married the girl you found with me."

He saw emotion for the first time cross the man's face standing before him, disbelief, doubt, and principally surprise. He saw the man step toward him, but he did not flinch, for he could not move any more.

"It is true," he said, "and valid, and I have taken care for the safety of the record. I cannot stop what you do to me, sir," the old address slipping out, "you will do what you like, but know this. If you take my child when my wife bears it from her, if you do that and if that child is a boy, you take him from his legal right and his heritage, to succeed to my seat as Seventh Earl of Halford, which he must now do as my son. I do ask you to think well, if you have any conscience, if what you offer him can replace what you will take from him."

"Is this true?" his master asked.

"Yes," said Simon. "Otherwise I would not have told you."

"I do not believe you," his master said.

"Then you do not believe me," Simon said, his voice weak now, and faintness sweeping over him again. "I have told you." His head fell forward, the pain on his neck muscles snapping him back to consciousness, and then falling forward again.

Chapter 20

HE WAS still there, in the morning. The slaves were brought to see him, and then he was cut down, and put in one of the small stockade rooms. His back was not dressed, and he was given no food and no water. By evening, when he was taken out, he was in a high fever, and the overseer on his own account took charge. He had Simon brought into his room, and his back dressed, and he gave him water, a few sips at a time.

"Am I to die?" Simon asked, when he could speak.

"Not at this time," the overseer said.

"Am I to be cut?"

"Not at this time, either."

"Are you to do anything to me? Hurt me, I mean?"

"Why do you ask?" the overseer asked curiously.

"I just want to know," Simon said. "I don't want to

let you make me feel better if it is to make me feel worse when you do it."

"I am not going to hurt you, unless you make me. I am going to put you to work."

"Thank God," Simon said, and he wept. His master had after all been merciful, for whatever reasons of his own. And he had whipped him, which Simon knew had to be done, quickly and finished with it, and though the number of strokes was reputable, he might easily have had more. 1000, he thought, would have killed him, though it was done all the time; 500 even. He had no hopes now, but he wanted to live even so and to live unmutilated, for no reason except that he did.

The overseer kept him, under close guard, in his rooms until Simon's fever left him. He did not speak to Simon again, and would let no one else speak to him, nor would he answer any more questions. As soon as he knew Simon was in no danger of dying, from any of his escapades, his back still raw, he put him in the farthest field, with a mute whose tongue *had* been cut out, to ride the mules who pressed the cane round the winch, and when his back was better, to drive them as they brought the canes up in bundles dragging behind them. The mute was twice the size of Simon, and he had been made to understand Simon was to be kept. Simon looked at the mute, and the mules, and the cane, sized the situation up in his mind, and accepted it because it was all he could do.

He did not know when his child was born, no one told him and there was no one to ask, whether it was a boy or a girl, whether it had lived or died, or how Alyx had fared and was faring. In time he learned the answers to the last two. It could not have lived, and been a boy, because some unkept quantity of time later, he was again brought to Alyx, as stud. The overseer came to him, and informed him curtly and bluntly what he was to do, and how he was to do it.

He was not told the woman was Alyx, but he knew before he was put to her who it had to be, and why. He was warned not to speak, and he thought she must have been warned too, and he did not speak. Partly because he was afraid to; they were not alone. The escort and the overseer did not leave them, but waited, and took him as soon as he had made seed and given it. And partly because to speak was to invite despair. Once he might have been humiliated to take her as he had to now, but now, as he lived in the life left to him, it was the only alleviation to the bleakness and loneliness of his days. He was brought there to her for several nights, how many he did not tally. Their lips and their fingers spoke for them, in the dark, and showed he knew and she knew the past and what was left them in the present. Then she conceived again, and he did not see her again, and so as time went by, endlessly and meaninglessly for him, he knew either she had had the son his master wanted, or that she was dead.

He did not see his master again, as his master had said he would not. He lived in the hut in the field, and never left it for any reason. At first, the contrast had hurt him, having lived for some months again in a house in some comfort, but he had spent ten years in discomfort and he became used to it again and his memories began to recede. He did not try to hold them. There was nothing to hold them for. He worked cane with the mute, in the vast lower field, and sometimes he saw other workers in other fields, but never to speak, and he did not want to speak to them. He did not try to escape. If he could not before, he could not now. He had seen men torn apart by dogs, and he did still fear pain. If he were slow, the mute impartially held his face in the pulp of the cane, and let the mules walk over him; and he had himself once seen when he was younger a man thrown into the black syrup made in the giant pots, in another field. The first week he had been kept chained to the winch, and he had after that shown no reason to the overseer, who from time to time looked in, why he should be chained again. When the mute rutted, he took Simon as the only solution available. Simon could not help this either, and though he was frequently hurt, it was not by intention and in time he toughened to that too. In this way over three years passed. Browner, more muscular, bearded because he could not shave, he passed his thirtieth birthday, and did not know the day, or think of his age. Then, without cause, without warning, one night he began to dream again, and sometimes to remember what he had dreamed. He dreamed of many things: his mother, a visit to the sea, his first hunt with his father, a schoolboy friend, his room in his house, the land about his home, rolling, the fields in different colours on the hills, the groves of trees, and the air and the light there. Then one night he dreamed of Alyx, and that dream was not of anything that had happened in the past.

She was in a white room, with white curtains blowing at the windows, and outside the window he could see the fields of his home, beyond the lawn, stretching into the distance, and in the fields were the hayers of summer with their scythes and rakes. The room was full of light and air, and a moist freshness that was a summer morning in his home, and everything was clean. The room, the bed, the curtains,

Alyx herself, her skin, her hair, and the white gown she was wearing, and the white ribbon in her hair. He was clean too. He was shaved, and his hair cut, and his skin clean, lying in the clean white bed in a white nightshirt with ruffles such as he used to wear, with sheets that were white and pressed and smooth against his face. The dream was so real that he woke, and finding it was a dream, he tried to dream again, and when he fell asleep again, half-waking, half-dreaming now, the white and gold panelled door to the room opened, and a maid in a pink and white striped dress with a large white apron and cap, such as his mother's maid had used to wear, came in with a breakfast tray for two. He could smell the toast and honey on the tray for Alyx, and on his, apricot marmalade from the trees on the south wall, the kind he had for special holidays. Fresh eggs in little cups, and pots unopened and steaming: tea with milk he thought. Alyx came from the window where she had been standing in her gown and sat on the edge of her bed and ate her breakfast with him. On her tray was a pile of white stiff envelopes—invitations—he had forgotten there were such things—she opened two, and laughed, and turned to him, and he to her, and they had set the trays on the floor, not waiting for them to be taken away. Her eyes were on his, laughing, filled with lights, not sad, not frightened, not tired and heavy with pain and the cramping of the child within her as he had last seen them. She lay down beside him and shut her eyes, her lashes sweeping her cheeks—he had not known her lashes were so long—her cheeks delicately coloured, flushing pink now as she lay back against the laced pillow, her hair loose about her face, and her lips in repose, faintly parted, looking as though they were about to smile, or speak. He bent to kiss them, and her arms were about him, and his hand moved to lift her gown, and he woke smiling, the dream fading into clouds of gold and pink and cream in the sultry early morning air. He saw her again several times more in his dreams, always in his home, always fresh, immaculate, inviting yet eluding his actual touch, once on his terrace, by the small columned pilasters and the white urns, having tea, with his children beside him. He saw them so clearly, a little girl like Alyx with chestnut hair, who was six, perhaps, and a little boy, younger, very like himself. They held out their arms and ran to him, and for a moment he held them, their sweet flesh warm and soft melting against him. Were children like that? he thought. One's own? He did not know at all. He woke, surprised, torn by longings he had not known to feel.

He knew that he was never going back. He knew that he had been put in the far-off lower field where few people ever went, for anything, to live and die forgotten and hardly productive, doing the lowest labour, outcast, except when his heredity that showed so clearly in his face served to further the purposes of the man who had sent him there. That man's voice echoed in his ears: "Do you believe I mean what I say?" "Yes," he had answered. "I hope so," that voice had said. He heard his own voice saying once in those days when he had worn his master's mark: "I think you could be kind—very kind—but I do not think you often are. I think you do not very much like to be thought kind." And from forgotten days of his educating: "Those who have power to do harm and do none . . ." It was there, he thought, goodness lay and all that was virtue in men, and in women too. That virtue lay beyond him now, for he had no power to do anything, and there was no virtue in his refraining from doing harm. If he tried to do harm, he would only be hurt worse than he had been, and his obedience and his dutifulness were not qualities to be called any virtues, only the inability to do otherwise.

His dreams pulled him back from the pit of his middle years on the plantation, into which he had been willing to fall again, not to feel the pain of remembering. He recounted his dreams in words to himself, in his mind, silently, and then, there being no one to hear when the mute was not near, aloud, to himself, surprised to hear the sound of a voice, even his own. He set himself then to recount to himself everything at all he could remember, from his earliest days upwards, conversations he had had, books he had read, until he came to his years of dissolution, and those, with their wastes of the things most precious to him now he could not bear to recount. Nor could he bear to remember or recount any scenes with his uncle before or during his kidnapping, or any part of his life thereafterwards, until he had entered the room of the breeding hut and found Alyx. Those scenes, those conversations he did try to remember, all that he could remember, but not his forced service with his mistress, or the abuse he had taken from his master. Like the scenes with his uncle, he knew them too well, and they gave him no pleasure to recall. But leaving the awkward grotesque passages he had endured from his master, he remembered their quiet scenes, and the affection that had grown up between them, and how he had wept the night he had deceived the man in his rare kindness. He knew now, though then he had not been certain, and though his master had never said so much, after he had recovered his escaping servants, that his master had somehow known something of what Simon was going to do, and had given him the opportunity to destroy his credit or to draw back of his own will.

He was cutting cane in the marshy part of the field, his hands toughened now and no longer sliced by the sharp ribbons, his bare feet moving unafraid in the muddy water, for, as his master had told him, there were no snakes on his island, even though St. Patrick had never come there to his knowledge—he was cutting the cane, feeling the wind on his bare back, and the rustle of the leaves against his bare thighs, a piece of cloth knotted about his waist and through his legs, remembering about the snakes—when his name was called and he looked up to see the overseer. He was surprised, for the overseer did not speak to him, only looking in to see that the two men were well, and that the hut was supplied. He raised his head, and heard his name called again, and he stepped forward out of the small thicket of cane that had hidden him, and walked out of the marshy ground onto dry ground, to meet the man who had called him.

"Simon," the overseer said, "you are wanted. You are to come at once."

"Who wants me?" Simon asked, coming towards the overseer to follow him as he moved off, not waiting.

"The master," the overseer said. "You are to come to his house, Simon, at once."

"Three years," Simon thought, "or is it four, now? And I am to come at once? Like this?" he said. "I cannot."

"No," said the overseer, turning to look at him, agreeing, "I think you cannot either. We will go by my quarters, first, and you may shave if you like—"

"I do like," Simon said, "very much."

"And I must find you something else to wear."

"At once" proved to be several hours later, after Simon had bathed, and cut his beard and mustache away, and shaved himself clean, and the overseer had cut his hair, roughly, and washed it, and then cut it again. Simon stood in the center of the overseer's room when this was done, clean, but naked, a towel wrapped about his waist. The problem of what to put on seemed insuperable. Simon had no clothes, and the overseer's did not fit him. He took finally a length of undyed shirting, that had not been made up, and measured Simon, and with a knife cut off enough that folded, slit, and belted, with a piece of rope, made a rough tunic to his knees, the open sides folded in.

"You will do," the overseer said. "And with this the fact you have no shoes does not so much matter. It is rough, but one knows you now."

As he walked across the courtyard after the overseer, Simon was assailed by doubts. His smock reminded him horribly of the smocks used for executions. The overseer's tone had been cheerful, and he had assumed, not thinking why, that he should be glad to be called. But as he walked across the courtyard past the fountain, the fears increased in his mind, and he wondered how he could have thought he might be summoned for anything good.

"Wait," he said, sudden nausea sweeping over him. He paused by the fountain, and looked about him. "Why am I sent for? Do you know?"

"No," the overseer said. "I was merely sent to find you and bring you here."

Well, he thought, if it is bad, I shall know soon enough. And nothing bad lasts forever, it only seems to. He sniffed the fragrance of the flowering bushes about the house appreciatively, noting with pleasure the variegated foliage of the trees, and followed the overseer inside in his bare feet. He was kept waiting for several minutes in the hall, his bare feet dusty on the cool black and white tiles of the floor, and then the door to his master's office was held open to him.

He walked in, and at first he thought the office was empty, and then in one corner, on the floor, he saw a child sitting on a rug, fitting together chipped pieces of tile into a design on the floor. He did not have to be told who the child was. He knew. He might have been looking at himself, at that age, and he knew the age, two years, three years?, though he could not tell exactly. The child was too busy to look up, and Simon stood staring, until he heard a door pulled to behind him. He turned, and saw his master had come in.

Chapter 21

His MASTER, like himself, was three years older, more now perhaps, but he looked unchanged, his light auburn hair mixed with grey still falling lightly to his thin erect shoulders, the blade of his thin beaked nose cutting his face above his thin drawn lips, his dark grey eyes piercingly alert hooded under the arched line of his brows, his face with its stern grooved lines still complexioned like a child's. Simon as always felt short beside him, and gross now after his years in the cane. He stood unsmiling, his eyes and his mouth bleak, and saw in his master's eyes that he was not gross, the sinewy muscles rippling down his arms and legs polished like carved wood by the sun, and exposure where the short sleeveless smock exposed them.

His master walked to him, where he stood at rest, waiting, and pulled the unsewn sides of his smock aside, revealing his side, burned like the rest of his body to the colour of dark tea, except for the white broad line where the cloth he wore in the fields protected his loins, the muscles of his powerful flanks rippling as he stood still while the liberty of looking at him was taken by his master. He might, he thought suddenly, have been standing again on the slave block, to be bought, and when his master sighed slightly, and pulled the side of his smock together, he wondered if that was where he was to go, now that his master had his male heir. He could not avoid indignity or exposure or impertinence or presumption or pain, if his master wished to deal them to him, and he stood quietly in his helplessness, his dark eyes alive and burning now in his browned face, his lips parted slightly from his white teeth, his breath coming quickly in helpless anger under the calm appraisal of those eyes. He turned his lifted head a little away, not to see them while they looked at him.

Then his master walked away, as if a curtain had fallen on a play, Simon thought, but which play he did not know.

"A beautiful child," he said, "is he not? I was right, you see, about the breeding."

Simon did not answer, his head turned away. There was nothing to say.

"You are angry, Halford," his master said. "I do not blame you, and I will not tease you. Take your child. He is yours."

Simon looked now at his master, his head thrown up in startled inquiry, his flared thin nostrils quivering, looking again much like a startled highly bred horse, the look that had first caught his master's eye, and his master sighed again.

"I have said I would not tease you, Halford. May I still call you Simon? I have been away, it is two years now. You would not know. I listened, you see, to what you said to me, and from time to time I thought about it. When this second child was born, male, as you see, I paid a long delayed visit again to my home, and to yours, Simon. I thought, you see, I would check out your story, that I had not believed, and I found it true, as you first told it to me, under the lash, after all. There was no question. I found your mother, Simon, and saw your picture, and knew I had the proof myself in my hands that the story the man who presently goes as Halford told me could not be entirely true. I did not, of course, tell him that. Will you sit down, Simon, and not stand looking at me as you are? I will call your child to you presently. Like yourself, his attention can be hard to get. Have you heard what I said?"

Simon stood looking at his master still, silent still, his feet rooted where he stood, his hopeless eyes wary. He had heard, but the story was not a surprise to him, any part of it. He remembered too well his master's flat statement, that the truth of Simon's story would have made no difference to him, and would make none.

"Then, Simon," his master said, "if I may call you that, I remembered something else you had said, and I checked the possible places of registry in London, and I did find the record of your marriage, as you said it would be, where a Mr. Alwyn had sent it, signed in his name. It was a fortunate thought, Simon, for the man's church and all his papers were destroyed in a fire here, and the man himself much crippled. He is blind, I believe, Simon, and he cannot speak, and he cannot walk or use his fingers which are broken. It is believed a matter of revenge by the friends of two smugglers he brought to trial. I am not a kind man,

Simon, to those who attempt to thwart my purposes."

"Poor brave man," Simon said then. "I have much to atone for, to have brought him into my affairs, when I knew better than he with whom I was dealing. I was as ruthless in my wishes as you in yours. Did you manage to destroy the London record?"

"I did not try to," his master said. "I had not looked before, you see, Simon, to see if your story was true, I had merely acted to prevent it, if it was."

"So you did to him what you said you would do to me," Simon said, his hopeless eyes looking at his master, not accusing. "Why?"

"I had not his word," his master said, "and I could not expect him to give it or to keep it, after his promise to you. And I was angry, Simon, but I could not bring myself to change or mutilate the remarkable animal I still had in you. To do so was after all not in my interests." His eyes swept over Simon again, and this time, under his tanned skin, Simon felt himself flushing.

"My interests rule me," he said to Simon gently. "You know that. But I have also a brain, Simon, and it tells me what you told me was true. Do not frown so at me, Simon. I do not, you know, have to tell you these things."

"No," Simon said. "I am wondering why you do."

"I said I would not tease you, Simon, and yet I do." He took a paper folded and lying on his desk and handed it to Simon. "You may tear this up now. That should tell you why I do."

As Simon stood there, not moving to take the paper, he tore it quickly in two himself, and laid it on the desk. "Your paper of purchase, Simon. A legal quibble, and not worth much to me or to you. I find after all I cannot keep you, suspicioning and now knowing what I do. Your motives after all were only my own. I am going to send you home."

There was no boy left in Simon, despite his blush before those eyes, and with the tearing up of the papers, no servant. He, himself, stood quietly in the room, and said, "I do thank you."

"You do not ask about your wife and your child?" he said, his brows raising slightly. "I will of course send them with you, Halford. To lift the sentence off your wife will be your own affair."

"What Halford asked put on," Simon said, his voice very quiet, "Halford may ask taken off, I think."

"You would, I suppose," his master said, "return with half an English army to take them, if I did not send them."

"Probably," Simon said, a slight smile rising in his eyes.

"And ruin my land. They are not worth the risk. But you must know, Simon," he said seriously, "it is only because of them, because of the boy, that I let you go. Otherwise, I should keep what I have."

"You are difficult to understand," Simon said. "I am grateful, and I am not going to try."

His former master shook his head. "Not so difficult, Simon. I saw your land, and I did not like the man who had it, or his children. And he has no sons. I have not told you. You have also a daughter. You will find them waiting for you on the terrace, when you have met your son."

Chapter 22

HE LEFT the island on an English man-of-war, with Alyx and his daughter and his son, parting from it and from his former master, without rancour and without a backward look. With him he took the priest who had made his marriage, to keep the promise he had made to him, hoping he might somehow still find some use in it. He had gone through his last weeks in his master's house with outward calm and with no inward emotion. He had greeted Alyx gently, and kissed her forehead, looked at his daughter who looked a little like his sisters and more like Alyx herself, in miniature, and who did not know him. They had been standing by the railing of the terrace porch, in the light brown stuff gowns of the slave women and their children. The little girl, he saw, did not know her mother, and the little boy, who was dressed in the clothes of his station, did not know either of them. The little boy had shown polite interest, and wanted his nurse and to go back to his game, and the little girl had cried. He did not try to touch them, or to speak to them then. But when he left, though the boy cried bitterly and fought him, he did not take the child's nurse with him. He could not bear to take any part of the scheme of the island with him, any reminder of the life he had had to live himself.

He had found the last days uncomfortable, while he was fitted for clothes and shoes, and dresses were made for his wife and his daughter. His polite reserve, which it was now acknowledged to be his right to have, carried him through them. He took dinner with his master and his mistress in the evening, without his wife, who was not yet pardoned and therefore in his master's eyes not eligible. Nothing that had happened might have occurred, from the tone of those formal courteous meals. He had been there all along, but no one had thought to see him as he was. The change, he thought, was in their eyes, not in him. That his former mistress could meet him as she did, addressing him as my lord with only the most distant sparkle in her eyes, did not surprise him. He had seen it done many times in society. Bodies do not remember pleasure or pain long, except where the spirit is touched, he thought, and the mind can forget what it will, where the spirit is not touched. He was given a guest room, as was Alyx, and the children with their nurse. It was not his house, and not his rooms, and he did not go to them.

When the ship was in harbour, and he had taken his leave of his master and his mistress, the reserve set up between them was still unbroken. He took his mistress's hand and kissed it briefly, formally, under the eyes of the ship's captain. He turned then to his master, and held out his hand. The older man took it, formally, no pressure from those fingers now, no look in the eyes, veiled now, except polite, acceptable interest.

"I do not expect you will return again, Earl," he said, his voice slurring the last name slightly with his old inflection.

Simon looked at him sharply, and saw in the older eyes, looking at him sadly now, a lurking gleam of amusement behind them. He smiled slightly.

"No," he agreed, "I think I will not. But you must come to visit me, sir," he added.

"Do you mean that, Earl?" his former master asked.

"I do," Simon said, "and I will hope to entertain you as you have entertained me."

"I shall surely come then," his former master said, the amusement deepening in his, answered in Simon's. "Good luck, Earl, good voyage!" He turned away, to shake hands with the children, and to bend to kiss the little boy, who put his arms around his neck. He held the child closely to him, and then picked him up, on his shoulder, and changing his mind, walked aboard the boat with Simon and his family that was to carry them to the man-of-war. He sat with the child in his lap, talking to him, showing him the waves, until the sailors were ready to go, and then he put the child down in his father's lap, and let the sailors help him from the boat. "I shall perhaps leave my land all the same to this boy," he said. "You cannot, I think, stop my doing that. And then you may tear down all my quarters, Simon, and my stockade and the courtyard, and see how well you do without them." He stepped across the water to the sand, without waiting for Simon to answer, and walked a short way from the boat, and stood with his wife watching the sailors push off to start for the ship. Simon raised his hand to him in a gesture half-salute, half-farewell; startled, felt the sharp tears pricking behind his eyes; and turned to his wife, whom his former master had ignored in his farewells.

That night, in the close confines of their single cabin, the children asleep, the little boy still with the tears on his cheeks where he had cried himself to sleep after the wrenching from his home, Simon took his wife, because it was his right and expected of him, not because he wished to. The child's grief had unnerved him, he had not expected it or thought to think about it happening, though he saw now he should have. Beyond the child's grief, beyond the voyage, lay his remeeting with his uncle and his reclaiming of his lands, and his name, and if necessary, the proving of his identity. He did not know what he would do when he saw his uncle again, what he would say, how he would act, above all, though, what he would do. The prospect did not elate him, as once it would have; it was instead a cause of strain, in the face of which passion and the gentler emotions, even those of his son, seemed irrelevant. But the thin wall that had arisen between Alyx and himself by their change, in habits not only of dress, could not, he thought, continue or be allowed to wait to be broken until he or she felt such emotions again as he had felt in his dreams in the cane. They would come, he thought, if they were to come again, later, when their situations more nearly resembled those he had dreamed. Or if they did not, if they were the stuff of dreams and belonged to dreams, they had their living to do. Courtship was not among his plans or in his thoughts. She was his wife, and they should both know it, he thought, indeed that they must, in its simplest form.

They had hardly spoken, he preoccupied, she embarrassed, not knowing what to do, their difficulties removed, and all barriers separating or preventing. There had been first the curious formalities of farewells, and then supper with the Captain and its formalities, and then the settling of the children, in the absence of nurses. He had gone up on deck, finally, and left her to manage them, and had walked back and forth under the starry night, thinking of his uncle, not hating him any more as he once had, feeling only an enervating distaste, and wondering what he would feel called to do, or what, if angered, he might be stirred to do. He found himself turning in his thoughts then, away from those possibilities, and wishing Alyx would join him and walk with him to distract him. But she did not come. She was uneasy and unsure, when he had not come to her in her room in the house of his former master, not thinking of the reasons that could hold him back, unnerved by this reserved stranger in the dress of a gentleman, and very tired. He found her asleep, in the bunk they were to share, in the small cabin. He did not relight the candle, but undressed in the dark, not troubling to search out a nightgown, and got into the bed beside her. She stirred, half-awake, felt his lips silence her cry, and his arms take her, putting her deftly in the way of him. She lay as he put her, breathing quickly as he took his lips briefly from hers, and without a word, not resisting, not yielding, received him. He did not speak when the act was over, but turned away from her onto his back and lay beside her, his side close to hers, warm against it. She was changed, since the birth of the boy. He had noted it when he had been put to her after the birth of the girl; he noted it now again. And why not, he thought. He was no longer the only one to have passed that way; through that narrow opening he had first forced his way through, others, larger than what he had used to enter, had forced their way out.

"Simon of Halford," her small voice said clearly in the dark beside him, "do you always put your seal so at once upon your possessions?"

"Yes, Countess, always," he said.

"To show it is yours, to do with as you like?"

"Yes, Countess."

"I thought I should not like to be married to you," she said in a small voice. "I have always found Earls very peremptory."

The Earl beside her turned to his Countess and kissed her. "You will perhaps like me better another time, Alyx. One must start somewhere, don't you think? It is what we do." He paused, then he said: "Did it hurt you very much, Alyx? Having my babies?"

"Yes," she said. "With the first, I thought I would die; and with the second I knew I was going to. But, you see, I didn't."

"But you do not want me to fill you with any more babies?"

"No," she whispered. "Not very much."

"And yet," he said, "that is just what I am going to do, Alyx, many times. But when we come ashore, and you come to my house and see the lawns where the babies may play, and there are nurses to care for them, you may not mind so very much, after all. It has been a long time, Alyx," he said then, "hasn't it, since we walked along that shore together."

"Yes," she said. "No one would tell me anything about you, Simon. I did not know whether you were alive or dead, until you came in to me again, and then after that, I did not know, and you did not come back, even after the second child was born, and they took it from me. And then, until I saw you, I thought you must be dead."

"When did you know me, Alyx, when they would not let me speak?"

"I do not know," she said. "I was so afraid, and yet so unhappy I hardly cared, and then I knew. Because you knew just how I was, I think."

"Were you put with anyone else after the boy, Alyx?" he asked, half afraid to hear.

"Would you bear it if I said I was?" she asked.

"I should have to," he said. "I could not mind. Were you?"

"No, Simon," she said. "I wasn't. I was bred only with you."

"I am very glad," he said.

"I thought you would be," she said. "It is terrible the way you think of nothing but breeding, as though I were some kind of suitable animal. Myself, I am tired of breeding and being bred."

He began to laugh, shaking, in the confines of the little bunk.

"I do not find it funny," she snapped.

"I doubt not you would," he said, gasping, the laughter shaking him subsiding and rising again and subsiding, like the waves. He laughed until the tears came into his eyes. "Alyx, Alyx," he said, "the law will surely pardon you. To be transported for mounting the horse of one Halford, and to be condemned for the rest of your life to have another Halford mount *you*. Oh, my dear, my dear," he said, "I shall take you to parties, and you shall learn to be young again. Shall you like that? Do you think you will, Alyx? Will it make up to you a little for the babies who hurt you and do not know you and you could not even see? You shall have beautiful dresses that you choose yourself, and a coronet, and little shoes with diamond heels, and everyone will stare at you when you ride in your very own carriage that you shall have to take you wherever you want to go—"

"Not like the other Alyx—" she said.

"Like?" he said for a minute puzzled. "No," he said firmly. "Like yourself. And all the Beaux of the Ton will come mincing up to you and fight just to take your hand, and not one—not one, Alyx—shall ever, ever breed with you."

"Not one but you?"

"No one but me," he said firmly, taking her again into his arms, his fingers this time caressing her gently. "And that Alyx," he whispered, kissing her very gently, "that, Alyx," he whispered in her ear, his hands moving over her, looking for the little buttons to her gown, finding them, and releasing them, and slipping her gown from her, "that you shall just have to get used to."

"No," she whispered.

"Yes," he said.

"No," she whispered, less certainly.

"Yes," he said, pressing his advantage.

"Yes," she said then, holding him to her tightly, as the waves threw them closer together, "Yes."

"That," he said, much later, "will teach you, Countess, not to throw an Earl upon his consequence. I had thought you had learned that with my uncle. A very dangerous thing to do."

"Yes," she said. "I love you, Simon."

"I never thought you did not," he said. "You told me long ago you did, and I believed you. Did you not believe me?"

"I thought you had forgotten."

"No," he said. "I could not. I did not. Not all those three years and more down in the marsh in the cane. I dreamed of you, Alyx. Did you dream of me?"

"Yes," she said. "Not at first. But later. After I thought—" She could not say the words, but held to him closely.

"And then, when I was not dead, and you saw me again, I did not look like what you had dreamed about—"

"No," she said.

"Dreams are for dreamers, Alyx," he whispered, "for the helpless, for the deprived. Life is for us now. Dirty or clean, dressed or undressed, at sea or at home, breeding or speaking, eating or waking, you and I, Alyx, as we are, not speaking dream lines or making dream motions, extensions of ourselves and our wishes, more beautiful and less difficult than we are, dissolving as we reach to touch them, but you, Alyx, where I can touch you, and you can touch me, and we are not afraid to speak, Alyx, or to love. Can you love me so, as I am, difficult, Alyx, and not altogether satisfactory, and very much crowded when we are in this rocky bunk," he added, laughing, as the waves knocked them together. "You cannot dream me about, Alyx, any longer, nor can I you, or dream me away either, if we do not quite suit. But without those dreams," he added soberly, "God knows what I should have done, or what would have been left of me. They reminded me always that you had been with me and that I had known you, and sometimes, Alyx, sometimes you were so real, I thought I *could* touch you. I would reach out my hand, and then of course, there was nothing there. And when I made love to you, Alyx, in dreams, I did sometimes, you know, and spilled my seed on myself and the ground, and was warm and happy until I woke wet and shivering, they reminded me that if you did live, I was responsible to you, and must not let myself go mad, as sometimes I might have liked to do. There was nothing any more I could do for myself, or for you, except not to go mad, and not to let myself forget you."

"Would you have liked to forget me, Simon?" she asked, surprised.

"Yes, my dear," he said. "The pain would have been so much less."

"What did he do to you," she whispered, "when they took me away?"

"Much what my mistress did," he said. "It was less than he might have done, or had promised to do. Let us not think of these things, Alyx. They are quite past."

"You knew, and you risked so much for me," she whispered.

"You had my child, Alyx. I could do no less. I thought you very brave, for you did not care, as I did."

"I was never whipped," she said.

"No, my love, you were a breeding female."

"All that pain," she said, shivering, "for nothing. And that man, with his terrible eyes, waiting and knowing all the time—"

"Not for nothing," he said. "This has come from that. Love," he whispered, "I married you that day."

"They took both my children from me," she whispered. "You told me they would. How did you know they would?"

Simon held her in his arms and did not answer.

"My breasts swelled," she said, "and hurt me so that

I cried, and they put other children to me and made me give them suck."

"Do not think of it, Alyx," he whispered. "It is past now. No one will take your children from you again. They will know you and you will know them. It will not be the same. Do you think you will mind so very much being married to me, after all? No one ever had so beautiful a wedding as we did, Alyx."

"There was no wedding breakfast," she said.

"And no wedding luncheon, and no wedding supper," he said, "and no champagne, no ice, not even any lemonade. A shabby affair, very ill-run, with too many uninvited guests. But the lights were beautiful, and the bride, most beautiful of all. Shall I describe her?"

"No," she said curling deeper into the shelter of his arm. "The bride was a mess, and much too fat. I wonder her husband saw anything in her, for he had lovely clothes, even lace. You did, Simon. You looked so beautiful. Until of course you got wet."

"Was that why you came with me, after all, when I asked you, even tho' you did not want to marry me, because you liked my lace?"

"No," she whispered.

"Tell me why, then."

"No," she said.

"I want to hear. I want you to tell me. Because I am such a very good stud, and can make love to you many times in one night, Alyx, Alyx, disreputable countess and inflamer of men? Did you notice, my love, we had no bridal night, after our marriage?"

"Oh, Simon," she whispered, "I am full of you entirely. Never, never leave me."

"I have to," he whispered. "It is in the nature of things. Nothing stays. But I will come back."

"Oh, Simon," she whispered, "when you are with me, all through me, I am not afraid of anything, not even to be your countess when you did not choose me."

"I did choose you," he protested.

"No," she said sadly, "I just happened."

"So do so many things," he said. "I have told you I love you."

"Why," she whispered. "Why me?"

"I don't know," he said. "I do. Isn't that enough? I want you with me, in my house. I want to take care of you always. I want you to bear all my children. I know when you loved me, and I know why, because when *you* tell me things I remember them. Why did you come with me, Alyx?"

"Because you were whipped for speaking to me," she whispered. "If you wanted me to come enough to be whipped for it, when I knew how much you hated it, because you told me, then I had to come. I wanted you to have what you want, Simon. I will always want you to."

"Is that wise, Alyx?"

"I do not know," she said. "That is how I feel."

"And you married me so I should have what you thought I wanted."

"Yes, Simon," she said.

"Did you not love me at all?"

"Oh, yes, Simon," she whispered, "but that was not why I married you at all."

"Dear brat," he said, "how you put me in my place."

"Do I?" she whispered.

"Yes," he said.

"I do not feel you there."

He laughed, a little shocked. "You snap your little fingers at all our consequence."

"Set me then on your consequence."

"You have quite deflated me," he said, drawing his breath in. "There is no consequence left."

"I like you with or without your consequence," she whispered.

"*Do* you like me, Alyx?"

"Yes," she said. "You are resourceful and brave and very kind and patient and you do not complain. I should like you even if I did not love you."

"Oh, Alyx," he said, "Alyx, my sweet."

"Simon," she said, "why did he let us go, and help us to go? No one told me anything. Did you make him?"

"No," Simon said. "I did not make him. I could not. There was nothing I could do." ("Who uses us to his ends, and not our own," he thought.)

"Why, then?"

"I am not sure," Simon said. "I think he had a change of heart. Alyx, I am going to sleep now. Do you know, this is the first time I have gone to sleep with you when no one will wake me?"

But he was mistaken. His son waked him, crying for his nurse.

"What are we to do with him?" he asked, dismayed.

"I don't know," she said. "I know nothing of children. Should you have brought the nurse?"

"No," Simon said firmly. "He will have my nurse, when we are home." The ship was pitching now, in the high wind, and the baby cried lustily. When Simon or Alyx either tried to pick him up or touch him, he stiffened his limbs as in a rigour and screamed louder, piercingly until they left him alone, and then he began to sob again, pitifully, heartbrokenly, and as his nurse did not come, hopelessly, on and on and on. His sister waked and began to cry with him.

"Perhaps he is sick," Alyx said.

"If he is not, he will make himself sick," Simon said.

"Please do something, Simon," Alyx said, beginning to cry herself.

"My son," said Simon. "My son!"

There was a knock at the door, and Simon climbed out of the bed, forgetting he was naked, and opened the door. The Captain's mate was standing at the door, his grizzled hair puffed out about his head, in his nightshirt. In his hand he held a bottle and a spoon.

"Pap, m'lord," he said. "Perhaps the little boy might like it. I have five myself, grown now. Rum," he said, "and sugar, and some biscuit, and hot water. Babies all like it. Try it, m'lord."

"Would *you?*" Simon said. "He does not seem to *like* me."

The baby had stopped crying and was staring at the grizzled old seaman, enormous in his billowing flannel shirt. Perhaps he was afraid, perhaps the mate reminded him in some way of his nurse. Whatever the reason, he let the mate approach him and nipped at the spoon, and finding it warm and sweet, let the mate feed both him and his sister, their mouths open like little birds. Simon stared, in amazement, forgetting his nakedness, and then he remembered, and hastily put himself back under the sheet.

The mate's lantern cast moving shadows about the room, as the boat rocked, and when the cup of pap was gone, the mate patted the babies gently with his enormous hand, crooning softly a little song that sounded like "Rimini rimini." "You let me go on with them," he said wisely, nodding to Simon, "and you go on with your lady there."

The lantern fell over and blew its candle out, and the mate continued to croon to the children, and Simon fell asleep himself.

Chapter 23

"Simon," his lady said, "you will not kill your uncle?" She had observed his face, and his reserve which on that subject he did not break. The voyage was near its close, after long peaceful months, one day succeeding another on the sea, when the winds did not blow heavily, the rains were brief, and the French did not appear. And nothing came between them and their children they learned to know and love except Simon's own changes of moods.

As the days passed, Simon's preoccupation with his uncle increased. His face was troubled and his nights were disturbed with bad dreams, of the past and of the future. He could not and would not speak to his wife of the strains and difficulties that beset him, not the least of them the discovery as he grew rested, of how strong in him his old habits were and that he could not be near his wife, or he feared, any woman now, for very long without wanting the simplest thing in the simplest way. She saw that he was beginning to avoid her company, without understanding the reason for it, hurt and dismayed and imagining, despite his words, that he was ashamed of her and sorry to be bound to her. For days he would remain aloof and reserved, spending his time with the officers or watching the gentler aspects of the man-of-war, or reading to the crippled priest, or walking with his son or with his daughter separately, showing them the fish and the waves and the ship, and hardly seem to see or notice her. He was unfailingly courteous but he took to coming to bed after she was asleep, putting himself out of the way of repeating the tenderness of their first night, rousing her as he took her in his arms, half-asleep, and without wooing, used her, and slept himself, leaving the bunk early, sometimes before she was herself awake or the children. Then suddenly one day he would be beside her, as she played with the children, the heaviness gone from his face, giving his tenderness and affection openly to the children, and to herself flashes of scenes or anecdotes from his past life in the home he was taking her to, his face boyish, the heavy lines smoothing out as he looked over the railing into the wind blowing his hair and salting his lashes, until she loved him with an aching tenderness she did not know how to show, the least touch of her hand or movement towards his physical or spiritual areas of reserve bringing quickly the mask over his face she had seen first after their release while they were yet at their former master's house. It frightened and chilled and abashed her, and she could not try to remove it when he clearly showed he did not wish her to try. The depths of hurt and fear it covered, either in its reserves or its easy charm, she could not conceive, or his formative years when he was encouraged not to confide. But when he turned to her, and looked at her straightly, his eyes linking them, her own responded without volition to his and his smile, and when he woke at night out of his sleep sweating, unable to shake his dreams off, or cried aloud in his sleep, waking her, she took him to her, comforting and cradling him in her arms, against her breasts, and let him into the safety of her body. Soon after they had come on ship, shy and ill at ease with the Captain and the officers at the table, she had accepted Simon's suggestion, which he made without explanation, she might like to eat with the children, and so little by little the wall of reserve between them grew more difficult to penetrate except by the instrument of his sex, rather than easier, the reserve his, the hurt misunderstanding hers.

She came upon him one afternoon sitting alone looking out to sea as the voyage was nearing its end, and observing his face, she ventured to ask him what he was thinking of.

"Lord, no! child," he said lightly. "And be hanged? In England there are laws."

"In England there are duels."

"I will never duel my uncle," he said flatly. He looked then at her anxious face, and said, his voice carefully light, "You are not to worry yourself about my affairs, Alyx. There are laws on duelling. Besides, I have had enough of such things. I do not mean to have to fly the country, when I have just come home."

"Are they not my affairs too?"

"No," he said, "this is my affair entirely." His face was reserved and stern, and repelling. She was rebuffed, and not reassured, and angered at his coldness.

That night he did not come to their bunk when he
had seen her undressed and ready for bed. He went
instead on deck, and walked its length, among the
cannon, the stars not visible, a patch of damp heavy
fog settled cheerlessly all round the ship, laying a fine
mist on the cannon surfaces and the rails, until he was
cold and shivering. "England," remembered his son,
who was not afraid of him now, and would let him
come near him. He should be, he thought. He was
afraid of himself. He went down to his cabin, and
undressed in the dark, and went to bed. Alyx was
pushed into a small corner of the bunk, her back
turned to him. He thought she must be awake, for
he did not hear her breathing, but she did not move
or turn to him. "Damned stud" he said to himself
savagely—"who cannot get near a woman—" He put
out his hand to her, under the blanket, and found her,
and pushed her nightgown up so his hand could rest
against her. She pulled it down with a quick jerk.

"It is not your affair!" she said, shaking.

He was angered at her too then, and he made it his
affair, quickly and roughly, forcing her, and then he
was sorry. She was shaking with angry sobs.

"I do not think I know you," she gasped. "Someone
should whip you *now*. You are *not* a gentleman. You
have been too long on that place."

"I know I have," he admitted. "Help me, Alyx."

"No," she said. "Go kill your uncle. I hope you do.
I hope they hang you for it. I wish you were dead!"

"Do you, Alyx?" he said, sober now.

"Yes," she gasped. "To do that to me when you
know I love you, and you had only to be kind. What
will you do to those you hate who hate you? I am
afraid of you, Simon. I cannot bear to think I have to
live with you."

"Help me, Alyx," he breathed.

"No!" she said, her voice shaking. "I wanted to. I have seen your face, Simon. All these weeks. And I tried to. You will have to help yourself."

"You are right," he said heavily. "It is my affair. But you are also, Alyx, and when I want you and when I need you, you will have to let me in. That is the law too."

"Oh, God, I wish I had not married you. When will you throw it in my face how you met me and why I was there?"

"I think perhaps I do not know you either," he said. "It does not matter. You will have to do as I say."

"No," she said. "I will not."

"My dear," he said, "do you know what happens to transports who come back?"

"No," she whispered.

"They are hanged, Alyx, or transported again."

"You would not let them, would you?"

He did not answer.

"You have your son," she whispered. "You do not need me now. Any whore with a hole will do for you. And you can hire a nurse."

He turned his back away from her without answering, and lay staring into the dark. After a while she sat up, and stepped over him. He thought she had gone for the usual reason, and he heard her moving about the cabin, but when she did not come back, he dragged himself awake and sat up, and after a while, the cabin seemed empty. A sudden fear struck him, and he took the Captain's tinderbox and lighted his candle, and saw the children were sleeping peacefully in their bed, their mouths parted in sleep, their faces serene and empty. He put on the seaman's cloak the mate had given him, and wrapped it about himself, and went out on deck. The water was foaming and rushing by the ship somewhere in the fog, and he did not see Alyx anywhere. He walked to the edge, and looked over, and knew in that roiling mass that if she had put herself into it he could not find her. He stood at the edge, watching, and she came from behind the cannon where she had been crouching, and stood beside him.

He reached for her hand without a word, and she put it in his. It was cold and shaking, but with the spray and the mist of the fog. He drew her into the shelter of the seaman's cloak, putting it around them both, holding her closer against his nakedness as he had come from the bed.

"Did you mean what you said, Alyx?" he whispered.

"Yes," she said. She put her arms around his neck. "But I meant everything I have said. Not just that."

"Why did you come here, Alyx?" he asked. "And leave our bed? Did you mean to make me follow you?"

"No," she said. "I thought you were asleep."

"I could not find you," he said, his heart beating hard against hers.

"No," she said. "But I saw you. I could find you." She paused. "I did mean to, Simon. But one does not."

"How could you, Alyx?"

"You frightened me so," she said. "I sat on the edge of the ship, on the rail, and I thought it would not matter if I happened to slip. But I did not slip, and I thought of you and of the babies, and I put my hand onto the rail, just before the ship lurched, and I held on tightly, and then when the wave had past, I climbed down back to the cannon and held on to it. And then I saw you, Simon."

"Bear with me, Alyx," he whispered, bending his head and kissing her. Another wave passed, and they lost their footing and fell, against the cannon and its wooden box.

"Alyx," he whispered, feeling her cold and wet beneath him.

Her arms said yes, about his neck, and her lips. The fog was thicker now, and he could not see anything. They felt for each other with their hands, and let their hands speak for them, and then their lips, in the shelter of the cloak, and then they made their peace in the way they knew best.

"You are very difficult, Simon," she murmured.

"Yes, Alyx. I did not say I was not."

"I knew it would be," she said. "I did warn you, Simon, it would be."

"I remember you did."

"I love you, Simon," she said. "Please do not kill your uncle."

He stiffened and was quiet, and then he lost his stiffness.

"I love you, Alyx," he whispered. "He is more likely to kill me."

The next day they entered the Downs, and two days later they disembarked.

His funds were limited. He hired a chaise, and put Alyx and his children into it, and drove to the Dower House on the edge of his estate. It took him two days, but he had not forgotten the way. When he drove into the Dower House, his mother was not at home. The butler was new, and did not know him, or any of the servants. He was informed the Dowager Countess was not at home, and not expected home until the afternoon.

"I will wait," he said. "Where is Sprawlins?"

"Sprawlins is dead," the butler told him, the ice of his manner not lifting.

"Well, where is the groom? Where is Hodge?"

"He is at the Big House," the Butler said. "Her Ladyship's groom is with her Ladyship."

"You must pay the post boys for me," he said. "What is your name?"

"Collins, sir?" the butler said, with some distaste. "I do not know—"

"Pay them, Collins," he said. "My mother will pay you back. Is there no one left?"

"Left, sir?" the Butler said, the mask of his face cracking to show astonishment.

"Left from twelve years ago. Are you all new?"

"There is Cook, sir," the Butler said.

"Good," said Simon. "I will go see Cook. When my mother comes, tell her she may find me in the kitchen."

His mother did find him there, with Alyx, and the babies, having tea. She was not entirely surprised, for the word had quickly spread, as Simon had meant it to, that "Simon" was back, and she had heard it all along the avenue as she returned home through the gates.

She looked at her eldest son, sitting by the brick fireplace in her kitchen, his knees crossed, drinking tea.

"Simon?" she whispered. "Is it you?"

"Yes," he said putting down his tea, and the child he held on his lap. He crossed to her and took her hands and bent and kissed her lips.

"How like your father you look," she whispered. "Simon, they told me you were dead."

"Did you believe them?" he asked. "Who are *they?*"

"Your uncle," she said. "And your servants. Simon," she whispered, "I had to believe them. Your ring was sent to me, and your watch. Why did you not let me know, if you were not dead."

"I could not," he said. "I had no way to tell you."

"I think I am going to have to sit down," she said. "And you will try to tell me now."

"Aren't you glad to see me?" he asked, his lips twisted in a wistful smile.

"I am so cross," she said, "that you are alive, and did not tell me, and did not write me. If your father were here, I think he would want to whip you for it, Simon. How like you, Simon. You made him so very unhappy, Simon, and me, also, Simon."

"I think you will not believe me, mother," he said, sitting at her feet, on the brick hob. "It is too biblical. I was sold into slavery, for my sins and for my estate. I thought it absurd too. But I really was, and very cleverly. I should have died there, but I did not. Do you have my ring still, and my watch?"

"Yes," his mother said slowly, her eyes on his face, "your uncle asked me for them, after they were sent to me, but I said I thought I would keep them. Simon," she said, "if you have anything to say to me about anyone we know, I would not like you to say it to me before my servants. You have been gone a long time, Simon, a very very long time, and your Uncle has been very kind to me."

"I doubt not he has," Simon said.

"How fine you look, Simon," his mother said, her eyes on him. "You put all the men here quite to shame. I cannot believe you are here, drinking tea in my kitchen with Cook, just as you used to do."

"I can hardly myself believe it, ma'am," he said. "I threw myself on her mercy, ma'am, and she rescued my credit with your new butler, who was disposed to put me out."

"You would have been well served, Simon," she said, "if he had, to come without warning as you have and put us all to such a shock."

"I could not write as quickly as I could come," he said. "I had not thought you would be so cross with me. You might be a little more glad to see me?"

"I am glad to see you, Simon. But it has been so long, and we had to learn to go along without you, and now I think you will want to come upsetting everything."

"Yes, mother," he said, his eyes dark. "I will."

"I think your father would not have wished it," she said, unhappily. "Simon, I almost wish if you had to wait so long, whatever your reasons were, you might have waited now a little longer."

"I see, ma'am," he said, rising. "But all the same I am here. You have not asked me who the lady is I have with me? Shall I not introduce you?"

"I have lost my manners," his mother said. "We should have withdrawn long ago. Who is she, my dear?"

"She is my wife, lady mother," Simon said, his eyes dark. "I present to you the Lady Alyx de Vere, and our children, whose names are ours, your grandchildren, ma'am. They are quite shy, and not used to strangers. The gentleman by the fireplace who has not risen is the priest who married us. I will bring you to him another time."

"Simon," his mother said, when they had managed

to withdraw, "you must not be angry with me. You have come so all at once, and so many of you. You must let me kiss you, child, if I may not kiss my grandchildren?" Her frail formal voice quivered, as she bent her face and brushed Alyx's cheeks. "You are a pretty child, I think. I am sure I will grow used to your being my daughter-in-law. But it is so very surprising to me that Simon should be able to have a wife and children and not let me know—anything at all."

"Lady mother," Alyx said, tears in her eyes, holding the older woman's hand. "I did not want to come, truly I did not, for I knew how my mother would have disliked it, but Simon would not have it otherwise. I do beg you to forgive me."

"You will ask no one's forgiveness, Alyx," Simon said harshly. "It is for my mother to ask yours for not welcoming you however you came. You forget, lady mother, that you are living on my land, and subject to my wish except in this your house."

"Simon," his mother said weakly, "I do not think your uncle—"

"He might take my land," Simon snapped, "and use it, and he might seize my person and dispose of it, but he could not change whose son I was, not then and not now. Did you not once think, lady mother, this so kind man might have had a hand in my disappearance?"

"No, never," his mother said, horrified. "I did hear it was the gossip for a while, you know, Simon, what the ondits are, but no one dared say openly such a slander, and I knew from what your servants said it could not be so. Simon," she said, "he has been so very kind to me. How can you say so when he was himself hurt defending you? He has never recovered the use of his hand."

"Has he not?" said Simon. "A small loss, for so large a gain. I hear he has no sons."

"No, Simon."

"Then he should be glad that I have returned," Simon said. "Will you come with me now, lady mother, to see him?"

"I have just come in," his mother said, "and I am very tired. It will be dark soon, Simon, and I think it is too late to make a call."

"And I am not dressed? All the same, we will all go," Simon said. "It is a courtesy you must allow me to this so kind man, not to let him wait on this news which must interest him."

"Simon," she said, "your uncle is not very well. I do not want you to disturb him with—with wild stories that you have dreamed up."

"I suppose," Simon said, his eyes absent, "that you do not still have my father's guns? I suppose my uncle took them?"

"Yes, Simon," she said, "but I will not let you—"

"It is just as well," Simon said. "I thought he might have. Put on your bonnet again now, Mama, and we will stop at all the cottages first. I want everyone to see me with you and see my wife and my daughter and my son. I want everyone to know that I am home."

"Why, Simon?" she whispered.

"So that in the morning, if I should not be here, or my wife or any of us, you will know you did not just dream I came. I do not want you to have delusions too. Hurry, now. The news has perhaps already reached my uncle that I am here, and he will be looking for me."

"Simon," his mother said, "do you mean this?"

"No," he said, "it is merely my delusion, but you will humour me in it."

"You can have no proof," his mother said. "You cannot, Simon! I heard how it was."

He looked at her, and saw she had no conception of what had been done to him, and took pity on her distress, and did not tell her what he knew.

"No," he said, "I have no proof. You do not want a scandal, do you, Lady Mother?"

"No, Simon," she said weakly. "It was all so long ago."

"I will try not to make you one, then, lady mother. But I do want to see my uncle, and I want to see him with my family with me."

His uncle, however, did not know he had arrived. His wife had heard, but his uncle was in bed ill, and she had not told him what the excited servants had told her. She left word they were not to be disturbed.

"I think I may be allowed to enter," Simon said gently to the butler, and the footmen. "This is after all my house. You will inform my lady, as you call her, my uncle's wife, again of my presence and my wish to see her, and that the Dowager Countess is also here, with Simon, her eldest son."

She met him then, in the downstairs smaller parlour.

"This is indeed a surprise," she said, with forced courtesy. "We did not expect—"

"I daresay you did not," he said, gently, "and you need not pretend to be pleased. How could you be? I have after all come to take your house from you, and you do not even know me. I am very sorry for that, madam, and I shall try to put you to no more inconvenience than I must. No," he said, raising his hand, "please, don't say you are glad, and do not thank me. But one thing may please you. You will not have met my wife," drawing Alyx forward. He smiled suddenly, as he saw the expression change on her face.

"Alyx?" the woman said.

Alyx stood uncertainly before her oldest sister, her face frightened and scared.

"Alyx!" said her sister. "How are you here? Does mama *know?*"

"You will not be beastly to me, Maria," she said, recovering her spirit. "I did not intend to take your place away from you, but Simon would have it, and you will just have to accept it, and Mama too."

"I cannot believe it!" her sister said.

"Well," said Simon, "I see that does not please you either, but you will perhaps learn to see the advantages—sister? Now I really want to see my uncle, please," he said. "I had thought he would be here to meet me."

"My husband is in bed, ill," she said. "He does not know—"

"Know I am here? Good. I will announce myself. He is in my father's room? Alyx, introduce your sister to her niece and nephew, and have a nice coze. I shall not be long."

He took the steps two at a time, lightly, his heart pounding hard, and opened his uncle's door that had been his father's. His uncle's candle was lit, and he was in bed, with his nightcap on, reading from a book which Simon could not see. He shut the door with a click behind him, that brought his uncle's attention to him and electrified him with shock.

"Simon, is it you?" he asked, his breath failing him.

"Yes, Uncle," he said. "It is I. I have come back."

"We thought you were dead," his uncle said, gasping for breath, his hand to his throat. He was fighting to recover his presence, choking with fright. "Is it really you?"

"Yes," Simon said, "I see you did, but I am not a ghost. I am very much alive, Uncle Phillip."

He walked over to the bed, noticing the man's face whitening, and put his powerful hands on his uncle's thin shoulders. For a moment, remembering his own thin shoulders when he was seventeen, he toyed with the idea of letting his hands wrap around that thin terrified neck, and frighten his uncle, and then he looked at the stupefied already too frightened eyes of the older man whom he could hurt so easily, and he bent his head instead and kissed his uncle's withered cheek.

"They tell me you have not been well, Uncle Phillip," he said. "I am sorry, I will not keep you. You will have to begin, of course, looking for another house, for I have my own wife and children to care for and I wish to have them settled in their home as soon as may be."

"Did you think I was precipitate, Simon," his uncle said, relief dawning in his eyes, "in moving here?"

"Indeed not, sir," Simon said gently. "There was no reason to think I should ever return, when I did not at once, and no reason to believe I was not dead, as my mother thought, was there? But you see, I did return, and now I want my house. But I will wait on your convenience in so far as I may."

"Dear boy, dear boy," said his uncle, blowing his nose, "always so considerate. Have you met Maria, my dear wife?"

"Yes," Simon said. "My wife is with her now, and my daughter and my son."

"You have a son, Simon, dear boy?" his uncle said.

"Yes, Uncle Phillip," Simon said. "You will understand I want to bring him home as soon as you can make your plans. I see how sudden and unexpected this is, but did you, sir," he asked gently, "never think I might come back?"

"No, dear boy, no," his uncle said, "I never did."

"You should have," Simon said. "It was always possible, as long as you had not seen me dead. And now you see, I am after all alive and I have come back."

"A glorious day," his uncle said feebly, "a day for rejoicing. I am sorry your father could not see it."

"Are you, Uncle Phillip," Simon said. "Do you know, you are the only person who has even pretended to be glad to see me back? You are also the only person who has not asked me why I did not write."

"Well," his uncle said doubtfully, "I daresay we shall all get used to the change. It is a shock, dear boy, you can't deny it. Why didn't you write, dear boy, and let us know how you were?"

"I could not, Uncle Phillip, but I came as soon as I could. My mother is upset, but I see no reason why we should not deal amicably. Do you?"

"No reason at all, Simon, dear boy. No reason at all," his uncle said heartily.

"Well," Simon said, looking at the thin frail man, whose right hand and arm he saw now were withered and deformed, "I wanted you to know I was home. That's all, Uncle Phillip. I thought you would want to know."

"I do, dear boy, I do," his uncle said. "You must tell me all about it, when I am feeling a little more the thing."

"No," Simon said, "I don't think so, Uncle Phillip. There is so much else to do." He looked at the elderly gentleman in his nightcap in his bed, and could not believe himself his uncle had done what he knew he had. "Shall I bring my mother to see you?"

"Yes, dear boy," his uncle said vaguely. "Yes, I think so."

He spoke to the Dowager Countess, met Alyx and did not seem to know her or her name, patted the heads of Simon's son and daughter, absently.

"I think your uncle was very glad to see you, Simon," his mother said reprovingly on their way home. "You should be ashamed."

"About what?" said Simon absently.

"About your uncle."

"Yes," said Simon, absently, "I thought he took it very well." He looked back, and saw a horseman riding towards them at a hard gallop, and felt cold fear strike at his heart. "I cannot hurt him," he thought, "and I shall never be safe." And then he thought, "he cannot shoot me and the boy both. He cannot. He must know it. He is not *mad*." The horseman was alongside the carriage now, and leaning over, called out to him that Halford had had a seizure, and was requesting to see his nephew again, alone by himself.

"It is a trap," Simon thought. "Is he mad after all? Does he think I will come like that into his house?" And then he thought that whatever was to come, it might as well come then.

"Simon," Alyx whispered urgently, as she saw him move to get down. "You *cannot* go. He will kill you. I saw it in his eyes."

"Peace, wife," he said, pushing her back gently. "I have told you this is my affair. But if you are right and I do not come back, you will take care of the boy. He will not harm him; he is too young, and he has himself no sons." He took her face in his hands and saluted her lips lightly. "But I will see you later tonight, I think. Take my mother home now and have a womanly conversation with her, Alyx. I have upset her, and you will know what to say. Tell her whatever you like, as much as you like and as you think best. You there," he said to the groom, "give me your horse, if you want me to come. You can follow me on foot."

He took the reins, and turned the horse around, looking once to see that the groom was following. He saw him conversing still with the carriage, and then the groups separated, and Simon rode back to his house where his uncle was.

His sister-in-law was with his uncle in his uncle's bedroom. She looked up at him in fury and cried, "I told you your uncle was ill! I asked you not to see him tonight. I knew it would upset him, and I begged you not to!"

His uncle was lying stiffly in his bed, breathing with difficulty, his eyes closed, but when he heard his wife's voice, he opened his eyes, and motioned to her to leave them alone. When she had gone and closed the door behind her, Simon stood by the bed and looked down at the sick man fighting for his breath and waited for him to say what he had called him back for. When the spasm passed, his uncle looked up at him appreciatively, his eyes clear of pretence.

"You have spirit," his uncle said. "Do you know what I did?"

"Yes, Uncle Phillip," Simon said.

"I thought you did. I am not sorry. I would do it again if I could."

"I thought you would," Simon said.

"You have spirit, Simon," his uncle said. "I suppose that is why you survived. I did not take it into account. I should have killed you, Simon, but I could not. You were so like your father. Did they tell you I am dying?"

"Yes, Uncle Phillip. Am I to believe it?"

"I think so," he said. "We could not both live now, Simon, could we?"

"I don't know," Simon said frankly.

"Did you have a bad time, Simon?"

"Yes," Simon said. "Very bad, Uncle Phillip. You should not have done it to me. It would have been kinder to have killed me."

"Well," his uncle said, "that must console me, since you have killed me now. But I did not want to hurt you. I tried not to hurt you. I thought it would not hurt you to work. But I did not want you to come back. And after all you have."

"Yes, Uncle Phillip," Simon said. "I have."

"Well," his uncle said, "what can I do for you now, Simon? Anything?"

"Yes," Simon said slowly, "yes, there is, Uncle Phillip."

"What is that, Simon?"

"You could retract an evidence you gave, about a child who rode your horse."

"I do not remember that," his uncle said. "What an odd thing to ask."

Simon left his uncle's bed and went to his desk looking for ink and paper. He sat at the desk for a few minutes, thinking, and then writing, the only sound in the room the rasp of the pen and his uncle's breathing. When he had finished, he sprinkled the paper with sand, blew on it, and came back to his uncle's bed, the pen in his hand.

His uncle was lying with his eyes closed, the flesh drawn back sharply from his nose and the bones of his face, breathing stertorously, the shape of his eyes round and protruding under his thin lids. He opened them, however, at his nephew's approach.

"Well, Simon?" he asked. "What is this absurd paper? Do I sign what I do not wish?"

"It can hardly concern you, Uncle," Simon said. "But if you do wish to do anything for me, you can do this."

"I would rather send you back to Jamaica," his uncle said. "But since I cannot, shall we trade?"

"Trade, Uncle?"

"Do not be hard on my wife," his uncle said. "She does not know what I did."

"I never thought she did," Simon said. "I do not mean to speak any more of what can concern no one now but you, sir, and myself. As I think I told you earlier this evening."

"How angry you did make me, Simon," his uncle said. "Such presumption. I could have killed you then outright as you stood. And how you did frighten me. To come in without a word like an avenging ghost. I thought you were a ghost, Simon."

"I know you did," Simon said, a ghost of amusement in his voice. "It repaid me for much."

"You have killed me, Simon," his uncle said, but without malice. "I hope you are satisfied. Where is this paper? Help me to it."

Simon put his hand behind the thin neck and raised it, so that his uncle might carefully subscribe with his left hand a spidery signature that for all his shaking fingers did not itself waver. " 'Think I may have erred. . . . Wish to amend if the girl may be found—' Poppycock! Simon. Who is the gel? What is she to you?"

"My wife," Simon said. "My son's mother. Your wife's youngest sister." He looked at the dismay on his uncle's face, and folded the paper carefully in half and then in half again, and put it away. "Do not be so dismayed, Uncle. I could have done without your help. But I am glad to have it. It makes it easier." He looked at his uncle curiously. "Did you never once think about me, or wonder how I did, or wish you had not done it, in all those years?"

"No," his uncle said, "not once."

"No," Simon said thoughtfully, "I do not think you did. How strange that you could not." He bent down and gently kissed his uncle's cheek. "I am so sorry for you, Uncle Phillip."

"Don't!" his uncle said, drawing away, wincing at the touch and then at the pain that stabbed him at the movement, and drawing his breath in sharply. "I had what I wanted. I have stewarded your land well for you, Simon, you will have no cause there to complain. You will have it now, I suppose. I never meant you to. Go away, now, Simon, before I become angry again. And ask my wife to come to me, as you go." His features were twisting with pain. "Go," he said, "go on, now, damn you! I do not want to see you, anymore."

Simon went back to the Dower House, shaken by the hatred that had flared up again in his uncle's eyes. He wanted to walk, to forget the feel of his uncle's fingers, and the sight of his twisted broken hand whose use he had lost to prove his innocent right to inherit, what he considered better his. The air was very still, and far away he could hear thunder. It was going to storm, he thought. He felt very tired, and he did not want to think or explain or talk any more. He passed his mother's door, the light on, hesitated, went in, his face drawn, and kissed her goodnight. "I will see you tomorrow," he said. "I wanted you to know I

was home. My uncle called me to retract an error in
evidence he had made about Alyx. He is very ill, I
think, and he wanted that done. It will be all right,
my dear," he said. "You will not be sorry I came
home." He could not bear to stay any longer and
pulled his hands gently but firmly away from hers.
"Where have you put us? In which room?"

The room she indicated was dark. He went in, and
stood at the door, accustoming his eyes, wondering if
Alyx was already asleep, and how she could sleep.
Then he saw she was sitting in a chair by the window, and he went over to her. She was wearing a
loose white gown that he thought must be his
mother's, for he had not seen it.

"I was watching for you, Simon," she said. "It is
lightning now over there, see, beyond the trees. I saw
you come in, and I thought you would have to go
first to your mother."

"I went there," he said, "because I was not going to
stay. Was I long?"

"No," she said. "Not long at all. The children are
not here. They are two rooms over. Your mother
called up someone she said had been your nurse, from
the village. She is very nice, Simon, and she has taken
the little boy to her entirely."

"Has she?" Simon said.

"Your mother and I had a very nice conversation,
Simon, about people we knew that were the same. We
spoke of nothing embarrassing, or difficult."

"How sorry I am," Simon said. "I hoped you would
do that for me. Perhaps it need never be done at all.
Do you like being here? Are you glad we have come
home?"

"No," she said.

"No more than I am," he said. "But we will like it better. You will see. My uncle is dying, Alyx," he said swiftly, not pausing. "I have broken his heart, quite literally, I think, by my return. He does hate me so. Not me, just the fact I exist, that I am here. It was quite horrible, Alyx. But he gave me a paper, I have it here," he said, giving it to her, "retracting his evidence against you. I will have it seen to, or you can have it done yourself. You need not stay with me any longer because you are afraid of me, what I could do, or not do. I do not want you ever to hate me, Alyx," he said, "or want me not to exist. I can bear anything, I think, but that."

"Do you want me to go, Simon?" she asked.

"God knows I do not," he said, "if you do not."

"I do not at all," she said. "And to prove it I will even stay married to you."

He stood by the window, looking out at the trees bending in the rain. "I am so tired of talk," he said, "and explanations."

"So am I too," she said.

"Do you know what I should like?"

"Perhaps," she said. "I know what I should like."

"It does not seem proper in this house."

"I am not myself very proper. Though I have had a lovely bath."

She rose now, from the chair where she was sitting, and stood up beside him.

"I have had such a horrible day, Alyx," he whispered, bending his head to her neck. "And I have not had a bath, Alyx, will you breed with me?"

"Do you ask me?" she said, beginning to laugh.

"Yes," he said.

"Yes," she whispered. "Yes, I will."

The air was still outside. The lightning, wherever it was, had moved on. She went to the bed that was clean, and folded down for the night, and lay down on it in the dark, and waited, and after a little while he came to her, without a word, and entered the room that was his home.

HISTORICAL NOTE

There are two historical footnotes behind this story, that suggested it. In the eighteenth century, the Sixth Earl of Anglesey "is notorious as having procured the kidnapping and bondage in America of his nephew, James Annesley, rightful Lord Altham" (*Letters of Sarah Byng Osborn*).

Then, an account in the *East Anglian Daily Times*, footnoted in Foakes Jackson's *Social Life in England: 1750–1850*: "The case of horse stealing tried in Lancashire in 1791 was a peculiarly hard one. A young lady of good family was condemned to transportation for mounting a stranger's horse, having been dared to do so by a friend. She was only fourteen years of age! She was apparently sent to Australia rather as a passenger than a convict; and married the captain of the ship."

In the eighteenth century Jamaica, Antigua, and St. Kitt's were the places known to be best for selling the Irish and the Scots and the English "refuse," i.e., that paid the highest prices. Their ancient names are still there.

About the Author

Lolah Burford of Fort Worth, Texas, is the author of *Vice Avenged*, *The Vision of Stephen*, *Edward*, *Edward*, and *MacLyon*, all published by Macmillan.

More Big Bestsellers from SIGNET

☐ **SUMMER STATION by Maud Lang.** (#E7489—$1.75)

☐ **THE WATSONS by Jane Austen and John Coates.**
(#J7522—$1.95)

☐ **SANDITON by Jane Austen and Another Lady.**
(#J6945—$1.95)

☐ **THE FIRES OF GLENLOCHY by Constance Heaven.**
(#E7452—$1.75)

☐ **A PLACE OF STONES by Constance Heaven.**
(#W7046—$1.50)

☐ **THE ROCKEFELLERS by Peter Collier and David Horo-witz.**
(#E7451—$2.75)

☐ **THE HAZARDS OF BEING MALE by Herb Goldberg.**
(#E7359—$1.75)

☐ **COME LIVE MY LIFE by Robert H. Rimmer.**
(#J7421—$1.95)

☐ **THE FRENCHMAN by Velda Johnston.**
(#W7519—$1.50)

☐ **KINFLICKS by Lisa Alther.** (#E7390—$2.25)

☐ **RIVER RISING by Jessica North.** (#E7391—$1.75)

☐ **THE HIGH VALLEY by Jessica North.** (#W5929—$1.50)

☐ **LOVER: CONFESSIONS OF A ONE NIGHT STAND by Lawrence Edwards.** (#J7392—$1.95)

☐ **THE KILLING GIFT by Bari Wood.** (#J7350—$1.95)

Still More Big Bestsellers from SIGNET

☐ **WHITE FIRES BURNING** by Catherine Dillon.
(#E7351—$1.75)

☐ **CONSTANTINE CAY** by Catherine Dillon.
(#W6892—$1.50)

☐ **FOREVER AMBER** by Kathleen Winsor.
(#J7360—$1.95)

☐ **SMOULDERING FIRES** by Anya Seton.
(#J7276—$1.95)

☐ **HARVEST OF DESIRE** by Rochelle Larkin.
(#J7277—$1.95)

☐ **EARTHSOUND** by Arthur Herzog.   (#E7255—$1.75)

☐ **THE DEVIL'S OWN** by Christopher Nicole.
(#J7256—$1.95)

☐ **CARIBEE** by Christopher Nicole.   (#E6540—$1.75)

☐ **THE GREEK TREASURE** by Irving Stone.
(#E7211—$2.25)

☐ **THE KITCHEN SINK PAPERS** by Mike McGrady.
(#J7212—$1.95)

☐ **THE GATES OF HELL** by Harrison Salisbury.
(#E7213—$2.25)

☐ **ROSE: MY LIFE IN SERVICE** by Rosina Harrison.
(#J7174—$1.95)

☐ **THE FINAL FIRE** by Dennis Smith.   (#J7141—$1.95)

☐ **SOME KIND OF HERO** by James Kirkwood.
(#J7142—$1.95)

☐ **THE HOMOSEXUAL MATRIX** by C. A. Tripp.
(#E7172—$2.50)